ENOUGH ALREADY

Mary Hargreaves

ORION

First published in Great Britain in 2021 by Orion Fiction
an imprint of The Orion Publishing Group Ltd
Carmelite House, 50 Victoria Embankment
London EC4Y 0DZ

An Hachette UK Company

1 3 5 7 9 10 8 6 4 2

A CIP catalogue record for this book is
available from the British Library.

ISBN (Paperback) 978 1 4091 9467 5
ISBN (eBook) 978 1 4091 9468 2

Typeset by Born Group
Printed and bound in Great Britain by Clays Ltd, Elcograf S.p.A.

www.orionbooks.co.uk

For Zara, my darling bald eagle, and
Ovum Pollock, my muse

1

'OK, Briony. If you just want to hop up on the bed there.'

I'd really rather not, to be totally honest with you.

Is what I *want* to say. But of course I won't; that would be rude and inappropriate. It's not like I've been forced here against my will. I suppose I could pretend to faint or something, but then she'd call for backup and that would mean even *more* attention, directed straight at me and my bright-red face.

Jesus, I can't just *stand* here. I've already taken my pants off and I forgot to wear a dress so I'm just hovering in my puff-sleeved blouse and absolutely nothing else, like some kind of freaky, hairless Mr Tumnus.

Just do it, Briony! Bloody hell. All right, here we go.

The bed's a bit high, so I turn my back, put my hands on it and do a little jump up. My bare arse dislodges the protective paper and hits the plastic mattress with a *slap*. The nurse winces.

This is *horrifying*.

I lift my legs and lie down.

'Great. I'm just going to put some gloves on.' She busies about in a drawer.

I take a deep breath. Here it is. The moment I've been dreading since I got the letter three years ago. This is going to be awful. I'm going to *hate* it. But oh, god, what if I don't? What if I love it? What if I get really turned on and this becomes one of those pivotal, sexual-awakening moments, and I have to start attending underground fetish clubs to get my fix? What if *that* happens? She'd know, too, wouldn't she? She'd be able to tell.

No. I'm sure that's not going to happen. I mustn't get wound up.

The snap of latex makes me jump.

'Right, Briony, you can put your head back.'

I'm craning my neck, peering at her. She's staring at my fanny. She thinks it's weird, I can tell. I've always known there's something wrong with it. I haven't seen any other fannies from that angle. Not in real life, anyway, and everyone knows porn is unrealistic. I can't identify what it *is* that's wrong with it – I just *know*. It's probably wonky, or too big, or too small. Any minute now she's going to call for assistance and get a second opinion. I can imagine her discreetly picking up the phone, glancing over at me, murmuring, 'John? Can you come here a sec? I've never seen anything like this . . .'

I let my head fall back.

'Okie dokie, just let your knees drop to the sides, if you can. That's it.' There's some clattering, the noise of ripping paper, and then a brief silence. 'Right, try to relax now. Your legs are shaking.'

Oh, so they are. They're bouncing up and down. Completely out of my control. Agh, I bet she thinks I'm so *weird*. I concentrate and the shaking reduces by about one per cent.

'OK, this might feel a little bit uncomfortable, but it'll be over in a jiffy.'

I suddenly panic, wondering if I remembered to shave that one, wiry hair that grows three centimetres down the inside of my left thigh. Oh god, it's probably poking her in the hand as we speak, ripping a hole in her glove and rendering this entire process completely unhygienic. I wonder if—

Oh, sweet baby Jesus. OK, no. I needn't have worried about unwillingly enjoying this. She's moving it around, wiggling it and trying to get the angle right. She keeps pushing but it won't go in. I *knew it*. I knew there was something wrong with me!

'You're really going to need to try and relax, Briony. You're very tense. I can't get in.' She clutches my ankle for support, like she's about to get lost in there or something.

'I'm trying,' I croak. I'm really, really scared about the pain. No one has ever 'scraped' my cervix before. It's not normal, is it? Having a stranger roam about inside you like a truffling pig. I want to clamp my legs closed and tell her to fuck off.

'Oooookay,' she says, and oh my lord, it's happening. I'm being penetrated by a sixty-year-old woman. 'This bit might feel a bit funny.'

Funny. Really, Brenda, ya think?

There's a noise and then a strange . . . *stretching* feeling. No pain yet. Ugh, hurry *up.*

Helpfully, I suddenly realise that Brenda can see everything. *Everything.* I am exposed, like a plucked turkey. She can see my bum hole, can't she? It's just there, staring at her. I bet that's not normal, either. She'll probably send me to a specialist. I don't think I've ever seen my own bum hole. I feel suddenly irritated that she's seen it before I have.

'Righto, I'll do the swabbing now.'

I clench involuntarily. I'm going to shatter the speculum at this rate. I squeeze my eyes shut and brace myself.

Oh.

Oh, it doesn't hurt, actually. It feels . . . *weird.* Like a tapping in my tummy.

'All done!' She retreats and the speculum practically catapults towards her. 'Goodness, you were very tense. Was this your first smear test?'

'Yes. Yeah, it was.' I launch myself off the bed and snatch my knickers off the seat, yanking them up my legs as fast as possible.

'You're three years late.' She tuts. 'Do you want to come and sit down, and I'll do a quick blood pressure check.'

I collapse into the seat by her desk.

'Oh. You can put your jeans on first, if you prefer.' She presses her mouth into a line.

Oh my god. I've sat down in just my *knickers*.

'Sure! Yes, no, of course. I was just about to do that.' I stand up and pull my jeans on. My hands are shaking.

'Right,' she says, once I've sat back down. 'We'll have your results in a week or two, and you'll be texted if everything's normal.' She slips the blood pressure cuff onto my arm. Why is she doing my blood pressure *now*? After what she's just done, she thinks she's going to get an accurate reading of my resting rate? 'If anything abnormal shows up, we'll call you and ask you to come in.'

'OK.' I'm not listening. I feel weird, having a conversation with her, after what we've been through together. How can she be so normal with me? I'm sure she'll be heading straight to the break room after this, to tell all her colleagues about my malformed vulva and dodgy anus.

'All right?' She's smiling at me. 'All done. Thanks for coming in. Please don't put this off again next time. It's a potentially life-saving five minutes of your life.'

2

Well, that was totally awful.

I mean, it wasn't exactly as bad as I was expecting it to be. I thought it'd feel like labour or something. Not that I'd know how *that* would feel either, but still. It wasn't excruciating.

I just can't believe I've exposed myself to a woman I've never met before. Surely it goes against basic biological instincts to whap your bits out and let a stranger have free rein. It feels . . . I don't know, *vulnerable.*

Anyway, it's done now, and I should feel light and free because I have literally been stressing over this for weeks and have barely slept at all. It's *done.* I don't have to do that again for another three years, by which point that nurse will hopefully have retired and I will have had a labiaplasty and anal reconstructive surgery. I'll be proud of my new genitals and will probably swan in there and get them out before they even ask.

So, yes. I should feel great.

Except I don't, because I am now absolutely convinced that there is something seriously wrong with me.

I pulled the NHS cervical screening page up as soon as I left the doctor's, and I am sloping down the street reading a list of symptoms that I can completely relate to. My heart is hammering.

OK, I don't have *all* the signs associated with a negative result, per se. But 'pain in the lower back or pelvis' is worryingly accurate. I've got it right now! I stop to cross the road and put a hand on my stomach. Oh my god, this is all my fault. I didn't go to my smear test three years ago and now I'm paying the price.

On another page I find a list of 'advanced' symptoms. My heart has actually stopped at this point.

'Constipation.'

I have had constipation! I had it three weeks ago!

I'm spiralling. I call Sami.

'Hey, Bri, I'm in the middle of someth—'

'Sami, I am dying.' I'm taking shallow breaths and I can't get my words out.

'What? One second . . . wait . . . OK, I'm outside. What is it? Was it another meeting?'

My stomach flips at the word 'meeting'. 'No, I'm serious, apparently I haven't got long left.'

'*What?*' Sami's voice catches. 'What the fuck? I thought you just had your smear test? Oh my god.'

'I did, I have. I just had it. Just now. But I've been having back pain and I had constipation three weeks ago and—'

'Wait, woah, stop. Hold on.' I can hear her passing the phone from one ear to the other. 'Briony. Did a doctor sit you down and diagnose you with an advanced, untreatable disease and discuss your options with you?'

'No, but—'

'Briony,' she says again, and I can hear the warning in her voice. 'Has a professional scientist looked at your cervical cells under a microscope and deduced that you have an incurable illness?'

'No, you're not listening—'

'BRIONY. Is this about your mum? Have you googled your symptoms again?'

'No!' I pause, deciding to ignore her first question. 'Well, technically, I googled a disease and then realised I *had* the symptoms, and—'

'BRIONY!' she roars. She's said my name too many times. That is never good. 'I am going back into work.'

She hangs up.

Oh good, now I've pissed Sami off. This is great. This is just wonderful. I am sick and my best friend hates me and I'm going to die alone. I wonder what Ben will say? Would he stay, if there was something seriously wrong with me? He loves me, so he'd probably come along to an appointment or two, but I couldn't put him through that. I don't want his final memories of me to be—

My phone buzzes with a WhatsApp message.

Sami: *Just checked my calendar. Three weeks ago we ate Taco Bell in the Arndale and both had explosive diarrhoea followed by three days of constipation. Mine ended the Tuesday AM and yours the PM.*

It vibrates again.

Sami: *This Friday, 7PM, Dirty Martini. Followed by Viva, 10PM. LOTS of interesting people. My clothes: white bodycon, nude heels.*

Should I be drinking if I'm this unwell? But then, does it really matter? Surely I should be enjoying myself now, really treasuring the days I have left. You just never know when your time's going to be, do you? I should have known this was coming, though. Why didn't I prepare? I haven't even written a bucket list. Will someone start a GoFundMe page for me? I hope they don't; that would be embarrassing.

Although, Sami is right; we did have that dodgy Taco Bell.

And what does she mean by LOTS of people? Who are they? What will *they* be wearing? My head is swimming.

I've made it to work and a fresh surge of panic sends my heart fluttering into a million chunks again. I stop outside the huge glass door and rustle through my bag, checking everything is there. I'm suddenly worried that I left my purse in the nurse's room and she is going to find one of my embarrassing business cards and pin it on the staff noticeboard under the words *QUESTIONABLE ANATOMY*.

7

But no, they're here. Thank god.

I slink through the revolving doors and clip across the lobby, pretending to be interested in a huge yucca plant to my left to avoid catching any of the security men's eyes. They always try to talk to me.

The lift makes it three floors up before it stops again, and Wiggy gets in.

Oh, *JESUS*.

'*Hoy*, Briony.' He puckers his little lips at me. 'All ready for the big prezzo?'

Wiggy is so posh, it actually can't be real. His full name is *Wigbert*. I am not even joking. This is not a drill. I have no idea why he came up to Manchester, but here he is, ruining my already awful day.

'Yeah, thanks.' I smile politely. No need to be rude.

'Big day, big day.' He rubs his hands together. 'Mmhm, mmm.'

'It is, yes.' I really want to get out of this lift. 'Will you be coming?'

Please don't be coming, please don't be coming, please don't be coming.

'Oh *yas*!' He nods viciously. 'Cheering you on! Mmmm.'

Wiggy has an irritating habit of doing a creepy little hum at the end of almost everything he says. I think it's his ancestors muffling 'what what, sport' through him like something out of *Paranormal Activity*. He's a senior developer, technically one rank below me, and we both competed for the Tech Lead role when it came up. He's had it in for me ever since.

'Great!' I almost shout as the lift finally pings open at my floor. 'See you in there.'

I scuttle off up the corridor and slump onto my desk. Everybody is already here, obviously, because they didn't have a quickie with a speculum this morning. Not that any of them own the equipment that would necessitate a smear test – I'm one of only sixteen women in our 120-person company. At twenty-eight, I'm the youngest Technical Lead, and the only female one there's ever been.

I work at a place called Walkyz: a social networking site for dog owners to meet and exercise their pets together. We match people based on likes, hobbies, horoscopes and even political views, depending on what the user wants to veto. It's not exactly the pinnacle of world-changing start-ups, but it really took off after the *Daily Mail* ran a story about the first Walkyz wedding: a couple that met through the site got themselves, and their dogs, married in a Pictionary-themed ceremony (don't ask). I didn't even know dog-marriages were a thing. They got a certificate and everything. Anyway, I was promoted six months ago, and my new role is to manage a full team of developers, working on implementing new features across the platform.

Part of this role involves attending meetings where the juniors share their ideas for improving the site so I can give feedback on whether they're doable or not. There's one starting in five minutes. The CEO always comes along, as well as anyone else who might be interested, and they're a great way for everyone in the team to feel involved. They've really added to the community feel of the place.

I hate them.

I gaze out of the floor-to-ceiling windows, at the view of the city outside. Can't I just leave?

'Morning, Briony.' Jason, the CEO, looms over me. 'We're getting started; come on through.'

He waits by my side as I get out of my chair. He's looking at me like I've got three heads. Can he see my hands trembling? Is my upper lip sweaty? I *bet* my upper lip is sweaty.

He sets off towards the meeting room and I follow, my knees knocking. This is the most stressful day of my life. I weave around the conference table, bumping my hip on someone's briefcase, and sit in the corner, against the wall, facing the door. I can't *do* this! Why did I ever think I could do this?

Jason stands at the front and addresses the cluster of people in the room. 'Afternoon, everyone.' He spreads his hands out. Not a tremor in sight. The man should be a surgeon. 'Thanks for popping in. I know I speak for all of us when I say how excited we are to hear the new ideas our speaker has to share with us today. Please remember that this is a collaborative session, and anything that doesn't sound like it'll work in practice should be raised by the relevant department.' He claps. My stomach squeezes in on itself. 'So! Let's get to it. Please welcome . . . Carl!'

Carl (small, cute, chubby, twenty) nods at Jason and wobbles towards the front. He's nervous. This makes me feel better. I sink into my seat.

'Hi, everyone,' he rasps and clears his throat. 'Thanks for taking the time to listen to our ideas. Me and a few of the other junior developers have been thinking of some pretty cool ways to erm, like, revolutionise things a bit. We've been innovating lots of new processes and stuff. So, erm . . .'

I'm not listening. I'm not listening and my mouth has lost all moisture because I know I'm going to have to speak at some point and I actually can't bear it. Carl is one of *my* juniors. This will affect *my* team.

OK, no, it's fine. Nobody's looking at me. Nobody cares. Just calm down. Say what you need to say, if you need to say it, and keep it short and sweet. Keep it concise. Start with something like, 'This is *so* brilliant, Carl.' No, wait, that sounds patronising. 'I'm really enjoying our fresh new talent, I have to tell you.' Oh my god, so creepy. No. Maybe I should just jump straight into it? No preamble. But should I keep my voice light? I want to seem encouraging, but authoritative. But not too authoritative, because I'll seem like a shit mentor. It's all about *openness* and *teamwork* here. I should definitely sit up straighter, look Carl in the eye. Maybe I'll just say 'Loving the ideas, Carl.' Or perhaps—

'Any thoughts, Briony?' Jason is peering at me.

So is everyone else.

I flame.

I actually physically become a flame. My heart is suddenly going at 72,000 beats per minute and my hands are shaking and there is sweat pooling under my armpits. I can't breathe properly. Everyone is looking at me.

'Briony?' Jason repeats, but I can't hear him properly through the white noise in my ears.

'Yes,' I manage. I can feel every eye in the room on me like something physical. My voice is wobbling. 'Fantastic.'

'And you think it'd work? From a developer's perspective?' Dave from sales asks, leaning forward.

It suddenly feels like everybody is staring at me. It feels like aeons of time are passing and giving everyone a chance to look at me, really *study* me, and see all my horrible parts. 'Do you think it would work, Carl?' I stammer, desperate to draw the attention away from myself. My teeth are clenching so hard, pain is shooting up my temples. Everyone turns to Carl.

'I think it would work.' Carl nods confidently and gestures to the rest of the team behind him. 'We all think it would work.'

'I don't profess to have the slightest bit of knowledge about the technical side of these things—' Jason laughs '—but the concept is really innovative, guys. If it's doable?'

Everyone turns to me again. I don't know what they're talking about. I need to get out of here. My absolute priority is leaving this room.

'Yes,' I blurt. 'We can do it.'

'Great!' Jason claps again. 'Amazing news. I can't wait to see how this pans out, team, I've got to tell you. Very exciting. Briony, shall we say four weeks to beta version?'

'Yes,' I bleat, again. 'Four weeks.'

The room buzzes with chatter as everyone swarms around Carl and the team, shaking their hands and quizzing them on their inspiration for the project. The project I know nothing about.

My ears are still ringing and I am radiating heat. I need air, before someone asks me questions.

I slide out of my seat and move towards the door. My hand is reaching for the handle when Jason claps me on the shoulder. 'Really exciting stuff, Briony.' He grins. 'Sounds like it'll be quite a challenge. I hope I wasn't pushing it with the four-week deadline?'

'*Blagradum*,' I say. *What?*

There's a beat. Jason peers at me. 'I'm sorry?'

'There's a . . . I . . .' I gasp, struggling to frame the words I'm looking for to explain my predicament. My heart is whooshing in my ears and I can't concentrate.

The silence stretches on for another few seconds as I grasp for something to say. 'Nope,' I whimper, eventually.

'Great.' Jason studies me for a second and then turns back to the huddle, slapping Carl on the back.

I make it out of the door and sweep my bag off my desk, heading towards the lifts. I'm halfway across the office when the doors ping open, and Wiggy steps out.

Argh, *why*. I contemplate pulling my phone out of my bag, but he's spotted me. I feel like a trapped bear.

'Briony!' He's red-faced. 'Did I miss it? Oh, bugger.'

'Don't worry, it wasn't very interesting.' I try to step around him. 'Sorry, excuse me, I've really got to run—'

'*Drat!*' He slaps himself on the forehead. 'No new project, then? Ideas not up to scratch? Mmm.'

I rack my brains for something non-committal to say, something that will make him leave. 'Have you seen the water cooler?'

OK, there is officially something wrong with me. What am I saying? Have I been possessed?

'What?' Wiggy looks around him and points to the corner. 'It's there. Where it always is?'

'Oh. Thank god.' Wiggy looks at me like I'm insane, which I basically am at this point. I feel like I'm watching myself from outside my body. I think I need an exorcism. I am not OK.

'So . . . there actually isn't a project?' He glances at the water cooler again.

'No, no, there is.' I skirt around him. 'Good to see you, Wiggy.'

'Wait!' he yelps as I shoot towards the lifts. 'That's brilliant news! What was it? What's the project? Do you need an extra hand?'

Shit, shit, shit. OK, no, calm down, it's fine. This is an opportunity; I'll tell Wiggy that I don't know what's going on and he can help me fix it. He'd help me, wouldn't he? He's only my number one rival and arch nemesis; he's bound to give me a hand.

'Carl has all the details,' I say, eventually. 'I'm sure we'll be fine, Wiggy, thanks.'

His brow crumples as I finally break away and skirt into an awaiting lift, jabbing my finger on the button. The doors close and I watch as he frowns and then strides towards the meeting room, to speak to Carl about the innovative, dynamic project we'll all be delivering, under my lead, in one month's time.

3

'No, what I'm saying, Bri, is that you should maintain. Don't jump on the deforestation bandwagon. They're there for a reason.' Sami chews on the end of her paper straw and glares at me.

'People say it's unhygienic, though—'

'*Unhygienic?*' she explodes. 'Who told you pubes were unhygienic? A razor company, by any chance? The laser people? Come the fuck on.'

'Well, I can't remember exactly who.' I take a glug of my wine and shrug. 'I can't even remember what colour mine are.'

'They're ginger, Bri. Obviously they're ginger. Christ.' She shakes her head. 'Anyway, neaten them up but *let them be*. What are you going to do if muffs come back into fashion and you're permanently bald as a coot from all that waxing? Did you see Cameron Diaz on Graham Norton? She made a bloody good point. And—' she leans across the table but continues at an extremely audible volume '—you get a really good lather in the shower with a full bush. Your shower gel goes much further. Pure economics.'

She sits back in her seat and smiles at me, satisfied with her argument.

'Mmm.' I nod. I want her to know I hear her, it's just that people are staring. I lower my voice to a whisper. 'The thing is, Ben likes the hairless look. You know, porn star style.'

'I'm sorry, but is your boyfriend a paedophile?' she practically yells, widening her eyes. 'Well? Is he? I bloody hope not. What normal man is sexually attracted to hairless, childlike genitalia?'

Like, literally all of them? I want to say. But I don't.

'He's not a paedophile. He likes it on *women.*'

Sami twirls a coil of dark hair around her index finger. 'How do you know?'

I open my mouth to respond, but I don't have an answer. I just *know.* I've kept myself completely hair-free since we met, and Ben seems to enjoy having sex with me, so obviously it must be that. He must get the horn over smoothness. It's all right for Sami, anyway; she's wild and loud and self-assured. I'm a limp, squishy chicken breast, sadly defrosting under a piece of wilted cling film. I can't assert myself with some kind of hairy protest; it wouldn't be empowering. People would just think I'd let myself go.

'I just hope she didn't see the stray one,' I say, diverting us back to my original topic: the smear test and the wayward pube. I inspected my thighs when I got home from the office and sure enough, there it was. And Sami is right – it was ginger.

She rolls her eyes. 'She won't have given two shits, Briony.'

'I don't suppose it'll matter anyway, once the results come through.'

'Oh my god, Briony, *what* results? You have zero evidence that there's anything wrong with you. ZERO.' She shouts the last word and the couple at the table next to us glance over.

'No, no, you're definitely right,' I agree, not believing a word I'm saying. 'But what if it *is* bad news? I know we both had a dodgy tummy, but what if mine was something else? You had the chicken and I had the beef, and—'

She interrupts me with the loudest sigh anyone has ever heard and throws her hands in the air. 'I give up with you. I officially give up.' Suddenly, she looks over to the door and scrapes her chair back, screaming, 'Julia! Oh my goooooood!'

And she's gone, flapping over to the huddle of people from her work who have just emerged from the street. I stay sitting at the table and throw my wine back, downing it in two big gulps, before signalling to a passing waiter to bring me another.

'Bri, this is Julia. You remember I was telling you about her? She's *hilarious*.' Sami has returned and is brandishing a woman with wild hair and a huge smile. She's wearing a long, floaty dress and Doc Martens, in complete contrast to Sami's white bodycon and nude heels. I suddenly feel stupid in the high-rise jeans and tube top I spent four hours picking out. I'm the only one wearing trousers.

'Briony!' Julia leans down and wraps herself around me. I haven't had a chance to stand up. 'Sami has told me *so* much about you. How are you? What are you drinking? She was telling me about that huge cock-up you had at work. *So* funny. Have you found out what the project is yet? Do you have to order at the bar or is there table service? Bloody hell, isn't it hot? I'm Julia.'

I watch her speaking, my heart picking up pace with every question. I'm putting all my concentration into making my face look interested and attentive, but my eye is starting to twitch. Has she noticed? Her eyes are roaming around my face; they keep landing on my nose. Have I got a bogey? Shit, I think I can feel it. Why didn't Sami *tell* me?

Julia has stopped talking and is peering at me. Oh, god, what did she say? There were so many questions.

'Lovely to meet you. There's table service.' I smile but can't bring myself to make eye contact, so I rub at a smudge on the side of my empty glass instead. I am desperate to go on my phone to give my hands something to do.

'Budge up.' Sami is waving me along the bench, allowing three of her colleagues to squeeze in next to me until I am pressed against the wall. While everyone is distracted, I run a finger around my nostrils. Nothing. Thank god.

Sami sits down opposite me, next to Julia and a man in a bow-tie. 'So, everyone, this is Briony. She's a software engineer and you're all very lucky that she's here this evening, because her boyfriend basically controls her life.'

I feel my face boil. I am so jealous of Sami's ability to be direct and command a room. She always does this with new people: drops a bombshell and then sits back to watch the aftermath. But he *doesn't* control me. That's not fair.

'No, he doesn't,' I say, scowling at her.

'Oh, is it gaslighting?' A woman with poker-straight blonde hair leans forward next to me. 'Does he make you feel crazy?'

'No, not at all—'

'Does he twist arguments, so you feel like you're the one who did something wrong?' Julia chips in. 'Does he repeat what you've said back to you in a really warped way until you're not sure what really happened any more? Does he make you think you've forgotten things? Does he steal your stuff and then pretend you've lost it?'

'No!' I am horrified.

'No.' Sami shakes her head. 'He just says, "jump" and she says, "how high?"'

'Oh.' Bow-tie man slumps back in his seat. 'You're just a doormat, then?'

'I'm not a doormat,' I try, my hands starting to shake. They're all looking at me. I feel like I have PUSHOVER tattooed across my forehead.

'Hm.' Julia frowns. 'Anyway, *did* you find out what the project was?'

'Yes,' I lie, immediately. I want Julia to fuck off.

'Did you?' Sami crumples her eyebrows together. 'I thought you said . . .' She stops and cocks her head to the side. 'Oh. My. God. Is that "How Soon Is Now?" . . . Is it? It is!' she squeals and jumps from the table, grabbing Julia's arm. 'Come on!'

The waiter appears with my glass of wine as Sami and Julia make their way to the small dance floor on the other side of the bar. I look around the table. Four people I don't know, who could, for all I know, be delightful human beings, or my embarrassing best friend and her rudely inquisitive colleague? I neck my wine again, squeeze out of the bench and head over to the bar, ordering another before snaking my way back over to Sami, like I always do.

These are the moments I like the most.

I'm under Sami's bright-orange duvet, the grey of the sky giving the room a dull, faded hue through the curtains. Sami is curled up behind me, her hair in my face. The room smells like washing powder, weed and Britney Spears' Curious – 'Why follow the crowd? Perfume is a lifestyle, not a fashion trend, Bri', she says, whenever I ask why she doesn't upgrade to something a little less . . . sixth form. I snuggle in beside her; I love it when it's just us two. She makes me feel safe and protected.

I'll give myself ten more minutes and then I'll go and make some coffee and toast for us. Then we can spend the morning watching Sami's old Davina McCall exercise DVDs. Or maybe we can get that old 1800s poetry book out, the one Sami's mum gave her to 'broaden her mind' and send lines of it to guys with dickhead bios on Hinge to see who bites. Or Sami might want to ask Maja, her flatmate, if she's got any weed—

'Morning!'

I jump. Sami hasn't moved; she's still breathing heavily next to me. Did I imagine it? Maybe I'm half asleep. I close my eyes for a minute, but I hear a rustling noise and snap them open again.

I catch movement in the corner of my eye and lift my head up, panicked. There's something at the end of the bed! What *is* that?! I watch in horror as a shape rises from the floor at the foot of the mattress; a huge, curly head and a wide, manic smile.

'I said, "morning!"'

Oh my god, it's Julia.

I forgot she stayed over.

Argh, why is she *here*? She's completely ruined the day I had planned.

'Rise and shine, Samuel!' She launches herself onto the bed and lands on top of me and Sami, forcing us apart.

'Ugh, Julia. Chill.' Sami rolls onto her other side and wedges a pillow over her head.

'How fun was last night? That place is so good. I can't believe I've never been there before. Had you been there before, Briony? It's got a sort of Mexican-Scandinavian vibe, don't you reckon? Did you try that wasabi cocktail? I did, it blew my fucking face off. Let's go again next weekend. Are either of you free? Oh my god, did you see that girl with her hands down that guy's pants? How *mental* was that? This bed is really comfy.' Julia sinks down further into the bed and keeps talking, her voice mercifully muffled by the duvet.

Sami looks over at me and rolls her eyes blearily. My mood jumps – I *love* it when we both think someone else is annoying. Me and Sami almost never agree on who's annoying. She gets wound up by people who buy processed cat food and have plastic surgery. I get irked by anyone louder and more interesting than me.

Except Sami, obviously.

'Toast!' Julia gasps, resurfacing from the duvet and looking oxygen-starved. I'd say she probably had about five more minutes under there before she'd have suffocated.

'No, ta.' Sami sits up. 'I want my appetite for brunch.'

Yes! Brunch! I *love* our brunches. I try to catch Sami's eye again to give her a knowing smile, but she's looking down the back of the bedside table for her phone.

'Oh, shit, forgot about that.' Julia stretches her hands above her head and the heat from her armpit smacks me in the face. 'What time do we have to be there?'

Wait, what? We're going out? When was this organised? I wasn't *that* drunk.

'I think they said eleven.' Sami finds her phone and stabs the home button. 'Ugh, it's already half ten.'

'Bagsy first in the shower!' Julia rolls over on top of me, almost breaking my arm, and springs off the bed. She grabs a used towel off the floor and trots out of the room.

'My god.' I roll over and lie face-to-face with Sami. 'Is she always like that?'

'Yeah, pretty much.' Sami laughs. 'She's funny, isn't she?'

No, I think. What happened to our mutual irritation?

'Really funny,' I say, nodding. 'Who's coming to brunch?'

'Oh.' Sami sits up and starts fiddling around with her hair clasp, which has slipped out during the night. 'Hair's ruined now. That's great.'

She gets up and pads over to the dresser, opening a tub of moisturiser and slathering it all over her elbows. 'I'll shower later, Julia will be ages. It's a work brunch, Bri. We're brain-storming the next campaign.'

'On a Saturday?' I frown. I don't want to sound needy, but surely everyone will be hungover? Can't they do it on Monday, then me and Sami can have one of our mopey mornings?

'Yup. Never stops. Anyway, you're welcome to stay here for a bit. Maja isn't back from Sweden until tomorrow.' She starts trying on different dresses, inspecting herself in the mirror.

'Oh, right.' I'm not even invited, then. Great. I bet they discussed this last night and contemplated asking me to come when I was in the bathroom or something. Someone probably vetoed it because I'm so boring and trembly. That's why I didn't hear about it. One of them probably said, 'Don't mention this to Briony, or she'll want to come too, and she'll completely sap the dynamic, creative vibe we've spent billions of pounds curating.'

There's been a strange shift in the dynamic between me and Sami over the last few years. As children, we were in each other's pockets. As teenagers, Sami started to expand her social circle. Now, as adults nearing thirty, the gap feels like it's widening even more, and I feel the gaping hole her increased absence is leaving. She's drifting, like she can't be bothered with me any more, and I'm holding on for dear life.

'Worst shower pressure ever, Samuel.' Julia bursts back into the room in a towel. Why does she keep having to say 'Samuel'? 'I'm bloody freezing.'

As if to contradict the point, Julia drops her towel and lopes, bollock-naked, over to the air mattress, ferreting about for her clothes and launching into a detailed story about her friend's goldfish, who can apparently smell a gas leak from three streets away. According to Julia, she's hoping to breed them and sell them to the armed forces for £80 a pop.

'Right, let's go.' Sami interrupts and grabs her bag from the floor. 'You staying here, Bri?'

'No,' I say, suddenly, not wanting to be on my own. I jump out of bed and change quickly into last night's clothes. 'I'll get the bus.'

Ten minutes later I am standing, shivering, at the bus stop, a fine mist of rain drenching through my denim jacket. I wave as Julia and Sami disappear into the warmth of the café across the road. I feel so *shit*. I'm mildly hungover and certain that I upset somebody last night. I bet it's not even a work brunch – it's probably just Julia and Sami and they needed an excuse to get rid of me after all the horrible things I don't remember saying.

When the bus finally arrives, I skulk towards the back and lean my head against the window, staring blankly through the steamy glass. I feel a weird cramp in my tummy, and my heart jolts. It's been four days since my smear, and I haven't heard anything. They're probably running special tests, double-checking, because the results were so abnormal. Or maybe my cells aren't cervical at all, and I don't even *have* a cervix, and they're sending my sample over to America because it's so rare and under-researched. I'll have to have a metal one inserted, or maybe even a pig cervix transplant. I'll have to give birth with a pig cervix. Oh my god.

21

By the time I reach home I've worked myself into a frenzy, and I let myself into the house with shaking hands. What if this is one of the last times that I put my key in this lock? I dump my bag and jacket in the porch and go into the living room, where Ben is sprawled on the sofa. What if this is one of the last times I walk into a room and see him like this, my heart swelling at the sight of him?

I stand in the doorway for a second and drink in the scene. Our stuff: the fireplace, the mantlepiece, the solid oak floors that sold this house to us the moment we saw them. I think back to where I lived before: a flat share with a girl called Ronnie, who was a students' union rep and used to have communal baths with her colleagues in our shared bathroom after nights out. Ben used to come over twice a week, and we'd cook dinner with the TV on full volume to drown out the excitable splashing. Once, Ronnie had six sambucas on an empty stomach and told me she'd been using my toothbrush to clean her fingernails for over a month.

It was the trauma that ensued that prompted Ben to suggest moving in together, and then two years later we were getting a mortgage. A place where our toiletries would be safe. It seemed like a trick at first, like it was too good to be true. The entire time we were house-hunting right through to signing the paperwork, I waited for a bomb to drop. But we've been here nearly three years now, and he's still lounging on the sofa, waiting for me.

'Hey!' He hears the floorboards creak and turns around, catching sight of my face. 'What's wrong?'

'I don't feel well.' I throw myself on top of him and he cuddles me.

'Aw, baby. You want some soup?'

'Yes, please.'

He kisses me on the head and wanders through to the kitchen. 'How was last night?' he calls.

'Good!' I shout back.

'Sami didn't make you feel like shit again?'

'No, she was great.'

I snuggle back into the sofa and try to let myself relax. I have a hangover, but it's mild; that kind of almost-nice shitty feeling, where you're just a bit wiped and can indulge in lying prone and feeling a bit sad. I imagine an entire afternoon snuggled up here with Ben, watching some old re-runs of *Friends* and dozing as he strokes my hair. But that won't happen – it hasn't happened in a while. He's got too much work to do at the moment.

After a couple of minutes, he treads back into the room with a bowl of steaming tomato soup and a crusty roll.

'Let's get the train to Formby later? Go for a walk?'

I glance out of the window, where the rain is pouring down. I need to clutch this moment – it's so rare for him to have an afternoon off. 'OK, that sounds good.'

He puts the bowl on the coffee table and drags it towards me so I can reach. 'Make any progress on the big project yesterday?'

'Loads.' I take a spoonful. It's gorgeous.

Ben rubs my hair and I feel guilty for lying. I should tell him. I should have told him days ago, when I first pretended I knew what the project was and got myself into this mess.

Because the truth is, I haven't been to the office since. The truth is, I've been pretending to work from home under the ruse of a stomach bug. The truth is, I haven't got a fucking clue what I'm doing.

4

It's Monday morning and I am sitting at the dining table, leafing through the magazine that came with Sunday's paper and trying to find the section on this week's soaps. I flick past an article about Katie Price and stop, turning the pages back and peering at the photos. My god, she's got an incredible stomach. Especially considering how many kids she's had. Who's she with at the moment? I start scanning the article for details but I hear Ben's footsteps coming down the stairs and slap the magazine closed, pulling the paper on top of it.

'Morning, love.' He bends down and kisses me. 'You got a coffee?'

'Morning. Yeah, thanks.'

He flicks the kettle on and starts scooping Nescafé into his travel mug. 'What you reading?'

'Erm—' I skim-read the subheading ' —they're upping the NHS budget.'

I have no idea if that even sounded right. Is it even *called* the NHS budget? Or is it called like, the health budget, or something? The kettle is boiling loudly and Ben doesn't seem to be listening too carefully.

'They're what?' He finishes making his drink and leans over my shoulder. 'Ah, yeah. We'll see if *he* sticks to his word.'

'God, yeah. Never going to happen,' I agree. I have no idea what I'm talking about.

'You know they were talking about a snap election yesterday?' Ben's brow furrows. 'Can you believe it? What kind of message is that sending? Public confidence in this government is at an all-time low.'

'Totally. It's an absolute joke, isn't it?'

'I mean, I know how I'd bloody vote.' He puts his hands on his hips.

'Oh, god, same.' I nod aggressively, knitting my eyebrows together in outrage.

'Really?' He looks surprised. 'Would it be that cut-and-dry for you, too?'

'Are you kidding? Of course!' I'm starting to panic a bit now.

'Who d'you reckon would win it though?'

Damn. Pick one. 'Oh, Conservatives. Obviously.' I start folding the paper away.

'Really? Would you vote for them?'

There's silence as I try to figure out the correct answer. Does Ben want me to say yes, or no? I don't know what I'm supposed to think. Are Labour anti-Semitic? Or was that the Lib Dems? Do we still hate the Conservatives because they're too posh? I just don't *know*. Ben talks about all of this stuff but he slates individuals and I have no idea which party they belong to. I just can't get into it. Shit, shit, shit. He's staring at me.

'LOOK!' I jump up from the table. 'Let's not ruin a perfectly lovely Monday morning with politics, shall we?' I wrap my arms around his waist.

He melts into me. 'You're so right,' he mumbles into my hair. 'Busy day?'

'Oh, yeah. Yep. As always!' I laugh and pull away, fussing about with the breakfast dishes.

'Right, I'd better run.' He kisses me hard. 'Have an amazing day, beautiful.'

'You too,' I call as he disappears up the hallway. 'I'll miss you!'

I hear the front door shut and then wait for the slam of the car boot and the purr of his engine as he reverses off the drive. I cock my head until it's completely silent on our street, and then wrench my blouse over my head, undo the zip at the back of my skirt and let them both fall to the floor. I pad into the living room and wrap myself in a blanket, flicking the TV on and loading the *Emmerdale* omnibus on catch-up.

Cain Dingle is having *another* barney with Moira when my phone starts buzzing through the floor upstairs. I want to ignore it, but what if it's the doctor? What if I have to come in *right this second* for treatment? I jump up from the sofa and run, half-naked, up to the bedroom, accepting the call just before it rings out.

'Hello?' I'm out of breath and lying spreadeagled on the rug on the bedroom floor.

'Briony? It's Jason.'

'Oh, hi Jason.' Damn. I forgot to tell him I wasn't coming in again.

'Listen, I know you've not been feeling great, but things are pretty hectic over here with the new project. I think the team could do with you being in the office, if you're well enough?'

Shit. I really don't want to. I really want to find out what happens to Charity at the pub and pretend my real life doesn't exist. I suddenly realise that Jason is probably imagining me tucked up in bed with empty packets of Buscopan and hot soup, while in reality I'm lying half-naked on a sheepskin rug. I glance at the window instinctively, in case he's standing on a ladder with a video camera, ready to catch me out.

I've let the silence hang for too long; I'm just going to tell him I'm not up to it. But . . . if I stay at home now, at the start of the project, and let it run itself into the ground, there won't be a lot I can do about it further down the line. Plus, I've spent four days doing this now, and I've mainly passed the time in a state of constant anxiety at the prospect of Ben coming home early and catching me lounging around braless on a weekday.

I tell him I'm coming in and then head back downstairs, putting my clothes back on and checking my reflection in the mirror before leaving the house. The bus takes half the time it usually does without the rush-hour traffic, and I make it to my building by 10 o'clock.

As I take the lift up to my floor, I start to think I've made a mistake. I could have come up with an excuse if Ben had quizzed me. What if I'm called in for another meeting? What if Jason takes me to one side and tells me he's had my YouView box hacked into and has seen how much *Coronation Street* I've been watching when I should have been working? What if he asks me to wee in a cup to prove I was ill? Can you *imagine?* He'd probably find something, though – one of my many hidden diseases would come to light.

I get out of the lift and make my way over to my desk, where I am greeted by total fucking chaos. Carl looks like he's about to pass out; he's standing in the middle of our section, gesticulating wildly, his face puce. Half the team are talking back to him, the other half tapping determinedly at their keyboards. I try to slink over and slide into my desk, but Carl clocks me.

'Briony!' The rest of the team swivel towards me. 'Oh, thank god. Is your Slack broken? You've not been answering any of our messages.'

No, Carl, it isn't broken, but Kat Slater's heart is, and isn't that more important?

Everyone is looking at me. 'No, no, I'm sorry. I had my notifications turned off by accident,' I lie.

'We can't get past the first bit of infrastructure, nothing's working.' Carl looks like he's going to cry. Now would be the time for me to admit that I haven't got a clue what he's talking about.

But what will they think of me then? They'll know I've done nothing for almost a week. They'll know I wasn't listening during the meeting. What kind of manager *does* that?

'Send me everything you have,' I say, a stroke of genius striking. If he sends me all his work, I should be able to figure out what we're doing.

Carl rushes over to his computer and furiously bashes the keyboard until a file appears in my inbox.

Right. Come on, Briony. I open the file and scan through it quickly. It's all just spaghetti code – thousands of lines of long methods – I can't even tell what they're trying to do. I roam around looking for some comments, some hint at what the end goal is. Nothing.

'Carl?' I peer over my screen. 'Is this everything?'

He jumps up and rushes over to my desk. 'Yes. Yeah. I'm sorry. We've been trying really hard.'

Oh, god. I've completely fucked this up. 'It's OK. It's not your fault. I'm sorry I wasn't contactable. Is there a text doc?'

'No.' Carl shakes his head and a piece of my soul dies. 'We planned it all out on the whiteboard. The concept is basically everything we said at the meeting.'

'Hm. Maybe you could write it out? It might help us get a clearer idea of what we're aiming for?' I just want him to TELL ME WHAT TO DO.

'I've got my notes from the speech, but they're handwritten scribbles, really. I think – sorry, I don't want to be contradictory – I think maybe it would be better if you could just tell us what direction to go in? We really haven't got much time.'

Bloody hell. I stare at the computer, willing it to give me the answer.

'It might be worth starting with the geotagging stuff? Then we can go from there?' Carl nibbles on his fingernail.

Part of me wants to stand up and scream, *what geotagging stuff?!* But people are staring, so I don't.

'Sure. I'll make a start and we can talk after lunch.'

OK, come on, I can do this. Geotagging. Geotagging what? We already match users based on location – are we improving the accuracy? That doesn't exactly sound like a ground-breaking idea. I saw how excited Jason was after the meeting; it must be something bigger than that. *Think, think, think.* Argh, it's useless. I don't have the first clue; it really could be anything.

I look out of the window. I wonder what everyone would do if I just lay on the floor and cried. That would be embarrassing. Everyone would hear about it. Maybe I could just slide off my chair and curl up under the desk. Load *Emmerdale* up on my phone and drape my coat over the gap so no one could see me? Would that work?

No. No, I can't do that. Someone would find me and I'd be labelled as the weird desk hermit.

'Briony?'

I spin around on my chair to find Jason, smiling down at me.

'Hi!' I leap to my feet. 'I was just – trying to – there's a lot to get through, and we're . . . we're making progress. Yes. We're making progress.'

'Right. Well, good.' He scratches his nose, looking bewildered. 'Erm. I was – god, I've completely forgotten what I was going to say now.'

We stand in silence, my heart whooshing in my ears. Is he stalling? He's going to ask me questions he knows I can't answer. I am penning my letter of resignation in my head.

'Oh!' He clicks his fingers. 'I've sent you a meeting invite – just wanted to make sure you got it. I know your Slack's been playing up. Tomorrow morning, to discuss how the project is coming along.'

'No problem.' I feel sick. 'Yes. Brilliant.'

Jason nods and walks back to his office.

I can't believe this. I can't believe I've just agreed to orally present a report of *nothingness* in less than twenty-four hours. What have I done? What am I going to *do*? There's a wedge of terror in my throat.

'We won't have anything to report by then!' Carl gasps, helpfully, as soon as Jason is out of earshot.

'We'll be fine.' I sit back at my desk. 'I'll sort it.'

I'm trying to convince everyone that I have some kind of control over this entire thing. I'm trying to convince myself even more.

How am I supposed to salvage this? I am acutely aware that I should have spoken to Carl one-on-one last Wednesday, the day after the presentation. I should have asked him to explain to me exactly what his vision was, without the pressure of an audience. Why didn't I do that? Why did I hide at home and leave everyone in the shit? I can't admit to it now – it'd be obvious I'd been blagging and skiving for almost a week. We're all going to be fired and it's all my fault.

I feel a jolt of pain across my stomach again. It's higher up this time. Whatever it is has spread.

'We're going for lunch. Are you coming, Briony?' Freddie and the rest of the team are standing, looking at me. I've been staring into the distance.

'No, no, I'll keep going here. You guys head off.'

I watch as they leave, and then gaze over to the empty cluster of desks in front of me.

Suddenly, an idea forms.

Carl's scribbles.

I wait until they're all in the lift, and then walk slowly around our section, checking that nobody is watching. I get to Carl's desk and shuffle some papers about. If anyone asks, I'll say I'm looking for a paperclip. I glance over the documents – all utility bills and tenancy contracts for his new apartment.

I'm going to have to dig deeper.

I crouch down and open his top drawer. Empty.

I try the second one. Nothing.

I open the third and see a scrap of paper, scrunched up at the back. I snatch it out.

'Briony?'

'Shit!' I jump and lose my balance, grabbing onto the desk to stop myself from falling over. Wiggy is standing above me, frowning.

'What are you doing in Carl's drawers? Mmm.'

'I was looking for a paperclip.' I keep the piece of paper in my hand. I'm not sure how much he saw. Does he know it isn't mine? 'He always has some.'

'Does he?'

'Yeah.' I cough and stand up, making my way back over to my desk. I put the ball of paper on the side nonchalantly, trying to hide how much my hands are shaking.

Wiggy's eyes travel down from my face to the desk. 'What's that?' He reaches forward and my heart stops.

He picks up a paperclip.

'Oh!' I smack my forehead. '*There* it is.' I take it from him and slide it onto a few random scraps of paper.

'There are loads here.' He grabs a handful from the penholder next to my screen. He narrows his eyes at me. 'You've got tonnes.'

'I've got to head out, Wiggy.' I take the ball of paper and shove it in my handbag. 'Catch up soon.'

'Wait, do you need help with the project?' Wiggy's eyes are wide again as he follows me towards the lift. 'I'd love to have a look at what you've done so far?'

'I'll let you know if we need an extra pair of hands.' I stab the button and the doors open. 'See you tomorrow!'

The lift doors close and Wiggy disappears as I descend slowly to the ground floor. I rush out across the lobby and through the main entrance, half-running down the street until I'm at the bus stop. I don't have time to think about what Jason will say about me leaving again. I need to get out of that office, away from the shame. I need to read this piece of paper. Nobody will care once I've got my head around this and made it the best it can be.

As soon as I'm home I kick off my shoes and run up to the bedroom, throwing myself on the bed and pulling the ball of paper out of my handbag. I squeeze my eyes shut, hold my breath, and smooth it out in front of me, already calming down now that I am home, on my own turf. Once I've seen Carl's presentation notes, I'll work all night to get something ready for tomorrow. I won't sleep – I'll put everything I've got into it. I'll make up for all the stress I'm causing.

I open my eyes.

Welcome to Walkyz

Congratulations on being appointed a new member of the Walkyz team. As a Junior Software Developer, we know you're going to be an invaluable asset to our company. This guide will help you get the most out of your time in your new role, so please keep it to hand during your first few months . . .

No. No. This can't be it. I flip it over. More Walkyz induction rules. No, no, no! I feel tears pricking behind my eyes. What am I going to *do*? I need to go back into the office. I can't, though – what would I do there? Sit and keep pretending to work until someone asks me a question I can't answer? I'll be caught out in thirty seconds.

I screw the paper back up again, moaning. I bet Wiggy has told everyone I was snooping in Carl's desk, too. I bet they think I've run away with something of his. They're probably all discussing me now; Carl will be rifling through his rental documents, wondering whether I've stolen his bank statement. Jason will probably call a company-wide meeting and get a search party going for me. They might even report me to the police. Then I'll end up in prison for time theft, and my cellmate will be a girl who pulls her own teeth out and smears poo on the walls. Ben will never visit me because he's scared of prisons, and I'll die alone when someone beats me to death with a bag of oranges.

Wiggy will definitely take my job. That's what he's after, I know it is. He's always lurking around me, looking for an opportunity to do something better than me and usurp me. He was really pissed off when I got the position over him. Even if I don't get incarcerated, he'll keep wheedling away until I'm demoted and he can step in my place and command the troops.

He'd deserve it, too.

A sharp pain shoots across my temple. I clutch my head. Oh, great, now something's going on with my brain. I'll collapse and nobody will find me for hours and then I'll be stuck in hospital for months, and Ben will leave me and Sami will employ Julia as her new best friend and forget I ever existed. I don't even have a good legacy – the final story of my normal life won't be my promotion to Tech Lead, but my thieving and abandoning. I've pissed away everything I've worked so hard for.

My phone buzzes with a text. I bet it's Jason, telling me not to bother coming in tomorrow because I don't have a job any more.

Dad: *How r u fdarling?? No timre to come n see ur old manb?*

I wince. I try not to untangle the typos – I don't want to see what's underneath. My head screams with pain. I put my phone on silent, turn off the light, close the curtains and climb into bed.

I've ruined everything.

5

I wake up at 2.45 a.m., Ben snoring softly next to me. I've slept for over twelve hours.

I get out of bed and pad down to the kitchen, scooping two heaped teaspoons of Nescafé into my mug and flicking the kettle on.

And then I remember I have an update meeting at nine o'clock.

My heart starts smacking around in my chest before I've even had my first sip of coffee.

OK, no, come on, it's going to be fine. What's the worst that can happen? I pretend to know what I'm talking about and then get caught out in front of everybody in the room? Or I tell Jason that I don't know what I'm doing because I didn't listen in the meeting and have been avoiding everyone ever since, and he gets annoyed with me? I'm not going to *die,* am I? No. No, I might be slightly embarrassed, but I will survive.

I take my coffee into the front room and load up last night's *Coronation Street.* I'm fine. I'm actually totally fine. I might lose my job, but so what? It's only taken me six years of my life to get where I am. That's *nothing.* That's like, a drop in the history of humanity. What about Harry Hill? He was a doctor for ages and then became a comedian. I bet he doesn't sulk about losing his medical career. I mean, yes, sure, I don't actually want to be a comedian, and I am rather happy in Software Engineering, but that's not the point. It's the *principle*. Life might knock us down, but we will come back fighting.

I try to concentrate on what Ken Barlow is saying. Something about an undercover drug smuggling operation he's become aware of. See! It's not like I've done anything illegal, is it? I'm not trafficking cocaine around Media City or anything. I've fucked up a little bit, and don't we all do that? Look how well David Platt bounced back from all that stuff with his mum. Nobody even mentions it any more.

I down my coffee in one boiling hot gulp.

Yes, everything is going to be absolutely fine. I've caused this mess, and I will deal with the consequences. I will apologise to Carl and the rest of the team, and work day and night to bring their brilliant mystery idea into fruition. I will smash this. I just need to be confident.

I catch up on all my missed soaps until 6 a.m. rolls around, and then call Sami to tell her about my new attitude. She loves stuff like this.

'Briony,' she sighs, once I've finished talking, 'that is literally the worst idea I've ever heard.'

'What?' My teeth start clenching. 'How is it the worst idea? I'm owning it. I'm being a boss bitch.'

'Being a boss bitch would have been listening in the first place, Bri. Or like, I don't know, talking to someone as soon as you realised you'd messed up. Or just asking for clarification when you missed something. You can't just walk in there now, a week later, and say "I fucked up". You'll be laughed out of the building.'

'I don't – I don't *mind* being laughed out of the building,' I stammer. I'm starting to think I'll really, really mind being laughed out of the building. 'It's my fault. They'll respect me more if I admit it straight out.'

'It's not straight out though, is it? They'd have respected you a week ago.' I hear her turn the shower on.

'No, no, you're definitely right. Definitely.' I've ripped my nail down to the quick in the last thirty seconds. 'Anyway, got to go and get ready. Thanks for the chat. Sorry for waking you up. See you soon!'

I hang up. There's a sharp stabbing in my left temple.

OK, keep going. Come on, get upstairs and get changed. You're prepared for this. You're going to take the consequences on the chin. *Own it, Briony.*

I take the stairs two at a time and stealthily feel around in my drawers for my clothes, before taking them into the bathroom and scrubbing myself raw. Everything is totally fine! People go through situations like this all the time, don't they? Some people even *kill* other people, and then go on to have families and houses with nice sofas and decorative rugs. This will all be a memory one day, something I laugh about when I'm ninety and my back's given out. *Oh, remember how worried I was about that work project when I was twenty-eight? Remember when I thought I was dying of an incurable disease? LOL.* And my grandchildren will look at me and sigh, and say, 'Nan, no one says "LOL" any more.'

Once I'm ready, I grab my bag and leave. It's only seven o'clock, but I need to catch Jason before the others arrive.

I'm three stops away from work when my phone rings.

It's Dad. I stare at it for a second, weighing up my options. I don't want to speak to him, but I could do with the distraction, and it's the morning; it should be safe.

'Hi, Dad.'

'Hello, love! How are you?' He sounds croaky and forced.

'Fine, yeah. I'm OK. How are you?' I resist the urge to give in and match his chirpy tone. He always does this; he'll reel me in and then something will snap and I'll be on the back foot, with no idea what I did wrong.

'All the better for hearing your voice! When are you coming to see me? I've got fish fingers in the freezer. Some nice toastie bread, too. If you bring some tartare sauce we can have fish finger butties. Your favourite, do you remember?'

I try to steady my breathing, the guilt pushing against what I know to be true. 'Yeah, I remember.'

'Every Saturday, wasn't it? Watching Dick and Dom after swimming.' He sounds tearful.

'Yeah, it was.' I pause. I can't do it; I can't just give him nothing. 'It was nice.'

'Well, come over, then! Whenever you like. How about this weekend?'

The proximity of his request makes panic rise in my chest. 'Look, Dad, I'm nearly at work. I've got to go. I'll call you, OK?' I hang up before he can reply, and the tears come immediately, oozing down my cheeks.

I can't think about this now. It's not a priority. I have to get into work and speak to Jason before everyone else gets in.

I wipe my nose and dab the corners of my eyes with my fingers. I take a long, noisy sniff and walk into the building, striding across the empty lobby and straight into a waiting lift. I can do this, I can do this, I can do this. I'm just going to get in there and tell him what's happened. There will be no excuses, no pity parties – I've brought this all on myself and I deserve everything I get.

As soon as the lift doors open I march across the room, heading straight for Jason's office. His door is closed, so I knock, but there's no reply. Maybe he's in the kitchen getting coffee. But there's no light coming from under the door – it doesn't look like he's been in since yesterday. I knock again, just in case.

'You're here early.' A voice behind me.

I turn around. It's Carl. He looks awful; his hair is all over the place, his eyes are sunken and his face is grey. He doesn't look like he's been home.

'Carl, have you slept?' I walk over to him.

'No, I've been trying to fix this. I'm trying to put something together.'

Oh my god, this is all my fault. He's trying to implement a brand-new system all by himself. As a *junior.* I've driven him to insanity.

No, this is all OK - I'm going to fix this! I can't undo the past, but I can do the right thing now. I am ready to take my punishment and transform this disaster into a charming, badass story for the imaginary grandchildren I'll never have because I will be dead within the year anyway.

I sit down next to him. 'Go home, Carl. Seriously. You need to sleep.'

'I can't!' he shrieks. 'We've got the update meeting in an hour!'

'I know,' I say calmly, even though I'm certain the meeting isn't going to happen. 'I can deal with that. I'm serious. Go home.'

'How can you deal with it?' He turns to look at me for the first time, his eyes bloodshot. 'You haven't *been* here. You don't know where the fuck we're up to.'

I sit back heavily. I feel like I've been slapped.

Carl runs his hand down his face. 'Jesus, Briony, I'm sorry. That was completely inappropriate. I shouldn't have - I'm just so stressed, I'm - god, I'm sorry.'

'Don't worry.' I stand up and move round to my desk, not looking at him. 'I'm going to do some work now.'

I feel sick. My resolve that everything is going to be fine is fading fast. I need to sort this out, right now. Where is Jason? Why isn't he *here?*

Carl stays quiet as I catch up on my emails, and people start filtering into the office. Every time the lift door opens I look up, but it isn't Jason. The minutes inch by in the corner of my screen until the entire team is sat around our section, glancing at me every so often, waiting for me to tell them how we're going to play this. I keep my head down.

At 08:55, Carl and Freddie head into the meeting room and start moving the chairs around and setting up the projector.

Everyone else files in, and at 08:59, Carl pokes his head around the door.

'Are you coming in?'

'Yep. Yes. One sec, I just need to speak to Jason before we start.'

'He's running late. One of his kids is poorly.'

'All right.' *SHIT*. 'I'll just wait out here for him.'

'He said to make a start without him, though? They need the room back at nine thirty.'

Fucking hell, fucking hell, fucking hell.

I get up with all the enthusiasm of a woman being led to her death. Which is basically what I am. Sami is right – I'm going to be laughed out of the building. This is not, and will never be, a funny story. I'm going to be humiliated in front of every single person in this office.

I walk inside, my knees knocking, and Carl closes the door.

There are so many more people in here than there were last time. Carl has saved me a seat at the front, facing everybody. I sit down and stare at my hands.

'OK, so, I think I should probably defer to Briony, our Tech Lead, for this.' Carl looks at me. He's dropped me in it, and rightly so; I bloody deserve it.

I look up at all the faces in the room, hopefully expectant. I open my mouth to speak.

Suddenly, the door swings open and Jason appears, breathless and sweating.

'Morning, everybody! So sorry for the hold-up. Annabelle had the squits. Bloody nursery.' He runs his hand through his hair and stands next to me. 'Have we started?'

Out of nowhere, I spot Wiggy, sitting at the back of the room. He's got a notepad balanced on his knee. I can feel my pulse in my neck.

'Briony was just about to give the update,' Carl says, when I don't answer.

'Brilliant. I don't know about the rest of you, but I'm really excited about this.' Jason claps his hands. 'Over to you, Briony.'

There's a hum in the air, like radio static. I can see everybody's pupils, honed in on me.

'Briony?' I can hear Jason's voice, but it feels distant. My hands are trembling in my lap. A fierce, stinging heat is spreading from my chest through to my face. Sweat drips down my back.

'We haven't—' I start, but my words come out thick. I think I'm dying. My heart is beating so hard I can feel my ribs vibrating. My fingers and toes are tingling with pins and needles, and my scalp is prickling. I suddenly can't get my breath at all; my chest feels like it's collapsed and my airways are tiny, thin tubes.

'I think—' I stand up. I need to get out. I need to be outside. 'I, erm—' My voice is shaking so much I can't get my words out. My breathing is shallow and there are black spots dancing around the edges of my vision.

'Are you OK?' Jason puts his hand on my shoulder.

'I don't feel well,' I manage, and move for the door, my legs just about sustaining me. I reach for the handle but my hands are trembling so violently I can't get near it, and when I do, my palms are slick with sweat and it takes me three tries to wrench it down. I can feel the room's eyes boring into my back and my stomach leaps further into my throat.

I fling the door open and flee across the open office space, wheezing against the pressure in my chest. Behind me, I distantly hear Jason saying, 'Right, let's reschedule this for tomorrow . . .'

I head for the lifts but I can hear footsteps, someone calling, 'Are you all right?'

I swing in the opposite direction and throw myself into the ladies' bathroom, hurtling into a cubicle and locking the door behind me.

It is completely silent.

I sit down heavily on the lid of the toilet and rest my hands in my lap, watching them jerking and twitching and listening to the roar of my pulse in my ears. I try to slow my breathing

– in and out, in and out – but I'm hyperventilating, my heart skittering with the lack of oxygen. I put my head between my legs and stare at the underside of the toilet, my eyes wide and blurry.

Slowly, slowly, everything starts to flatten, and as the panic subsides, a colossal wave of tears pushes its way up from my throat and out of my eyes.

I sob noisily on the toilet. What is *wrong* with me? This has never happened before. I have never felt this bad before. Is this a symptom of something? Is this death? Will I be like this forever?

I can't go back into that meeting room. I don't think I can ever come back here at all. I can never go anywhere ever again. There is suddenly something unfixable in me; I can't calm down.

I am a monster. Carl slaved over this. He was stressed and hadn't slept and had this absolutely *brilliant* idea that he was willing to work really hard on. They were all looking up to me, hoping I'd encourage and support their plans and help them to implement them. I've damaged far more than my own reputation.

I need to go home. I get off the toilet and unlock the door, washing my hands in the sink through habit rather than necessity. I am suddenly completely exhausted. My hands have steadied and my heart rate has slowed, and I feel weary and rattled and miserable.

I pull the bathroom door open a crack and peer out, checking the coast is clear before making a beeline for the lifts.

'Briony?'

I stab the lift button. They're all on the ground floor. I turn around. It's Jason.

'You OK?' He moves towards me. 'You look terrible.'

'I don't feel right,' I say. I don't know why I didn't say *I'm poorly* or *I feel sick*. It just came out. I don't feel *right*.

'I can see that.' He cocks his head sympathetically. 'You don't find these meetings easy, do you?'

My stomach somersaults again at the word 'meetings'.

'I'm fine with the meetings,' I manage.

'Please tell me if I'm speaking out of turn—' he bites his lip '—but the company runs workshops for things like this. Helping with social anxiety.'

'I don't have social anxiety,' I say automatically. I *don't*.

'No. Of course not. I'm sorry.' He pauses. 'It's just . . .'

He doesn't say anything further. Here's my chance. I need to tell him I don't know what I'm doing. I need to nip this in the bud right now. The lift pings open behind me. The logical part of my brain has switched itself off and I need, more than anything, to be outside. I make to turn around and he stops me, his hand on my arm.

'Sorry. What I meant was . . . there's support if you need it.'

'Thanks, I'm fine.' I step into the lift but he presses the button and keeps the doors open. 'I'm *fine*, Jason. I just feel sick.'

He stares at me for a second, and then releases the button.

'Briony,' he calls softly after me as the doors slide closed, 'I know a panic attack when I see one.'

6

Before I'd even made it home, it had appeared in my inbox.

Calendar Invite: RESCHEDULED: Project Update Meeting – Tomorrow, 09:00.

I hadn't thought my body had the physical capability to produce any more adrenaline, but I was wrong. I spent the entire evening feeling like I was going to vomit. Ben made spaghetti, which I picked at, and then we watched a documentary about ostriches, during which I stared at the edge of the TV screen and destroyed my cuticles. At one point Ben said, 'Oh my god, look, it's hatching!', and I nearly jumped out of my skin.

He kept asking if anything was wrong, and I grinned manically and said I was still feeling funny and just wanted to read on my own for a while. I waited in the kitchen until he came in to say goodnight, and then tiptoed into the living room. I sat there all night, going over and over and over what happened in the meeting, and wondering again and again what I could do to solve it. I veered from rationalising it all to wanting to die from the shame – I tried six times to write my letter of resignation but each time I screwed it up and threw it in the bin.

And then, just as the sun was coming up, I made a plan.

*

I'm walking to the bus stop now. I haven't slept for nearly thirty hours. I'm far too early, but the idea of pacing the living room for a second longer makes me want to rip my face off. There's a church hall at the end of my street, and a flyer in a plastic wallet has come loose from the railings. I stop, tying it back on to kill some time, and then keep going.

I keep questioning whether I'm doing the right thing. I'm not sure I'm thinking straight. There's a possibility I could be dreaming all of this, or – the thought hits me like a hammer – hallucinating. What if I'm not actually on the bus? Am I going mad?

I stare out of the window unseeingly. Surely, there must be something else I can try. What I'm about to do can't be my only option.

I run through the endless choices and scenarios in my head for the billionth time. Again, I circle back to this one. It's the only way.

I step off the bus and into the glare of the early morning sun. I cross St. Peter's Square and walk into Caffè Nero, ordering a large Americano and finding an empty table by the window. Now that I'm doing this, I feel calmer. I've backed myself into a corner.

At eight o'clock, he walks in. He spots me immediately and decides against the long queue, heading straight for my table and sitting opposite me.

'Hi,' I say.

'Morning.' Wiggy looks smart and well rested. Obviously. Why wouldn't he be?

'Sorry for dragging you out so early.'

'Not a problem at all. Mmm.' He nods, licking his lips. 'Are you OK? You didn't seem OK yesterday.'

'Oh, yep, fine.' I smile convincingly. 'Totally fine.'

He looks unsure. 'So . . .'

'So—' I sit up straight '—I wanted to run something by you. See how you felt.'

'Go on?' He stares at my coffee longingly.

I take a deep breath. I'm going to do it. It's career suicide, but I don't have a choice. 'How would you feel about running the new project?'

'What?' Wiggy raises his eyebrows. 'What do you mean? Co-management?'

'No. No, I mean . . . do you want it? Do you want to take it off my hands?'

He frowns and stares at the table for a second, before meeting my gaze head-on. 'Why?'

'I've got . . . I've got something going on. Other things. I'm snowed under.' I hadn't thought about how I'd explain this. I didn't think he'd care. What could I possibly be snowed under with? My inability to behave like a functioning human being?

'Right. Well, I'd love to, obviously. But I'd have to switch teams. We can't have two Tech Leads, and—'

'Don't worry about that,' I say impatiently, taking a gulp of my drink. 'Do you want it or not?'

He looks at me for a second. 'I mean, sure. It'd be great experience. It's a lot, I'm not sure how well I'll do, but it'd be a nice challenge, I suppose . . .'

'It would.' I nod.

'Could you brief me on everything so far?' He's animated now, reaching into his bag. 'Actually, I won't waste your time – I'll hear about it in the meeting.'

'No, I'm not doing the meeting.'

'Oh. OK, so shall we—'

'If you want this, we'll go and see Jason now and sort it. Carl can tell you everything.'

'Carl? OK, but . . .' Wiggy looks dazed. 'Sorry, I'm trying to wrap my head around this. I wasn't expecting it. Are you going somewhere?'

'No. Well, I don't think so.' I don't know what I'm doing, to be honest. 'If you want it, it's yours. That's all.'

'I do.' Wiggy nods. I want to cry.

That's that, then.

Mercifully, Jason is in his office this time.

'Good morning?' He looks surprised as Wiggy and I walk in together.

'Hi, Jason.' I shut the door behind us. 'Do you have a minute?'

'Sure.' He gestures to the seats opposite him. 'How are you feeling? Better?'

Oh yes, miles better, thank you; I do believe I've made a full recovery from my imaginary illness now. I'm not sure when I last slept, and I'm about to throw myself under a bus here, but everything's on the up. I've even been meditating, really honing in on the tiniest fuck-ups of my existence – it's been very cathartic. I imagine I'll think about this exchange for the rest of my life, which I'm led to believe is a very healthy and mature coping strategy. So yes, all fine and dandy, really, thank you for asking.

'I'm fine, thank you,' I say, sitting down. I'm just going to have to come out and say it. 'Erm, I wanted to put something to you. Well, *we* wanted to put something to you. I've got a lot going on here at the moment, and I thought it might be better if Wiggy took over the new project. I can switch over to Wiggy's team and he can have a go at being Tech Lead for a bit. For the experience.'

Jason looks at me. He knows I don't have a lot going on, especially as I just offered to switch teams. He's silent for a second.

'And you're happy with this, Wiggy?'

'I'd love the opportunity.' Wiggy is practically salivating. I'm giving him everything he's ever wanted. 'I think I've got the skills and the experience, I was a high contender for the role when Briony was promoted, and—'

Jason holds up his hand. 'I have no doubt you're up to the task.' He chews his lip. 'Would you mind giving Briony and me a second?'

'Sure.' Wiggy jumps up from his chair and scoots out of the door, closing it softly behind him.

'I really think he'll be great—' I start.

'I know he'll do it well, Briony.' Jason cocks his head. 'I'm just wondering what *you'll* do.'

'Well, I'll help Wiggy's team in his absence, and—'

'Wiggy's team already has a Tech Lead.' Jason raises his eyebrows. 'You'd take a demotion because you've got . . . *a lot on?*' He does air quotes.

'I think it'd be good to get back into coding for a few weeks. I mean, it's useful to stay in the loop.'

Jason is peering at me worriedly. I suddenly realise I don't have any make-up on.

He sits back in his chair.

'Wiggy can take over the project,' he says.

Relief and defeat flood through me. 'Great.'

'*But—*' he leans forward again, his elbows on the desk '—I'm signing you off on sick. One month of mental health leave.'

There's a beat as I try to register this. 'What?'

'You're not coping, Briony. The promotion has taken its toll on you; there's a lot more responsibility. The meetings aren't your forte, and they're a huge part of being a Tech Lead. You've got the knowledge and the enthusiasm to do this job well, but right now you're not at the top of your game.'

'But I am! I can do it! I'm—'

'Look. You either stay on and see this through, or you take the month off. It's up to you.' He sighs. 'I strongly recommend the latter.'

I stare at him. He can't be serious. Is he letting me go? Is this the penultimate blow? Will I be coming back at all?

I know things have been different since I was promoted six months ago. I *know* that. The day I got the news that I'd be Tech Lead was one of the happiest days of my life, but it also felt like a switch was flicked. The bubbling feelings of inadequacy and shame I'd carried around for as long as I could

47

remember overflowed; I felt like I was at the top, but in no way was I in control.

Isn't this what I've been expecting ever since? I knew I was inadequate. I knew Wiggy was after my job. And now I've handed it over to him, along with my own noose, just like that.

'Four weeks today,' Jason says softly, somehow seeing through me and knowing that as much as I love my job, my fear is far, far greater.

I stand up. I feel numb.

'OK.' I nod. 'OK.'

I open the door and head back out into the office, walking slowly to the lift this time. Running home suddenly doesn't feel like the priority any more.

'Well, it's sorted now, at least,' I say, watching Sami lick the edges of her rolling paper.

'Yeah but . . . I mean, *fuck,* Bri. You handled that *really* badly.' She taps the end of the joint on the coffee table and puts it in her mouth, mumbling, 'This Wiggles literally has your job now. You know you're not coming back from that, don't you?'

'Wiggy. And I know.' I sigh. Now that all the panic has been taken away, I feel empty. 'They can't sack me though, so I'll just wait a month and then work my way back up again.'

Sami flicks the lighter and takes a deep drag, holding her breath for a second before replying thickly, 'This mental health thingy will be on your record forever. You'll have to switch companies and start afresh.'

She holds the joint out to me but I shake my head. 'I've got to drive later,' I lie. I want to, because Sami loves it when we get high together, but it'll tip me over the edge.

'Boring.' She picks up the remote and flicks through the channels aimlessly, her eyes starting to soften. 'What's Ben said?'

'I'm telling him tonight.' I don't know if I really *am* going to tell him. Telling him why I'm not working would mean telling him *everything*, and that would be mortifying. I'll figure it out later.

'How is *Ben*, anyway?' She pronounces his name like she's talking about Donald Trump.

'Fine,' I nod. 'I think. I don't know.'

'What? Why?' Sami sits up and I immediately regret saying anything. She hates Ben because she thinks he makes me do boring things like hiking and talking about politics. He hates her because he thinks she makes me do reckless things like staying out until 6 a.m. and smoking weed. Neither of them make me do anything – I like both contrasting facets of my life, thank you very much.

Not that I've ever said that to either of them. I don't want Sami to think I'm a doormat, and I don't want Ben to think I'm shallow. Best to just let them both detest each other without my input.

'He's . . . quieter. Not as focused on me.' I shake my head. 'That sounds really bratty, but he's usually so attentive. I don't know. He's a bit distant.'

Last night aside, Ben has been working a lot the past few weeks. Staying in the study, leaving me to watch TV and go to bed alone. He seems distracted. Less interested in spending time with me.

'Fucking hell, you don't think he's cheating on you, do you?' Sami is halfway through the joint now and her words are slow and precise.

'No!' I hadn't even considered it. Now I have and it will haunt me until the day I die. Wonderful. 'Maybe something's going on at work.'

'Hmm.' Sami lets her head fall back onto the sofa. 'I was reading an article the other day about this girl. Her boyfriend was really weird with her for ages and when she finally confronted him he said it was because he was bored.' She lifts her head and looks at me meaningfully. '*Sexually.*'

'Oh.' Sweet baby Jesus. I'm boring in every other way and now I'm sexually boring too. This is just the icing on the fucking cake.

'That's men for you, Bri. They make you fall in love with them and then decide your tits aren't big enough, or small enough, or that actually they used to like your tits and now they want a different variation. Or that you've put on a bit of weight, or got too skinny, or that they used to like it mad and kinky but now want to be all sensual and deep, or that missionary is boring and they want to tie you up and whip you with a feather.'

My head is spinning. 'How can you whip someone with a feather?'

'I don't *know*, Briony. Ask them.' She checks her phone. 'Julia's coming over.'

'Oh, right.' I stand up. 'I'd best be getting back anyway.'

'No, stay! Stay and smoke with us!' She's trying to be enthusiastic about the idea but she's way past vigorous movements and raising her voice at this point.

'I've got to pick Ben up from the station.' I haven't, but I'd rather do literally anything than get the Spanish Inquisition from Julia right now.

'Owwww,' Sami says, but her eyes stay fixed on the TV. I wait a second, but she seems to have forgotten I'm here at all.

'See you later,' I say.

'Hmm? Oh. See you later.'

I walk out into the corridor before I hear her call over her shoulder, 'I'm sure he's not bonking anyone, Bri. You're being paranoid again.'

Ben is frying haddock in garlic butter when I get home. The smell of it makes me want to gag. Why does fish smell so delicious when you're starving, but repulsive when your life is falling apart?

'Hey.' I wrap my arms around his waist and he drops a kiss on my head.

'Hey, you. Hungry?'

'Ravenous,' I lie. *Say it, Briony, say it, just say it.* 'So, a weird thing happened at work today.'

50

Casual. Relaxed. No big deal. These are the key words of my 'BREAKING: Your Girlfriend Is Crackers' news bulletin.

'Oh?' He reaches down into the oven and shakes a tray of potatoes.

'Yeah. Really weird.' I swallow. My mouth is dry. 'Completely unexpected.'

Ben flips the tea-towel over his shoulder and turns around, leaning against the hob. 'Well, go on!' He laughs.

'You won't believe it!' I wipe the back of my head with my hand. I'm sweating. Why am I making such a big deal out of this? It's not like he's going to break up with me just because I've been signed off work. He's not a bad person. He'll try to support me; I'm sure he will. But for how long? How long until his perfect image of me unravels? Or what if he uses this as an excuse? What if missionary-doggystyle-cowgirl once a week is boring him to tears and he jumps on the chance to run away and blame my instability? Oh, god. No, it's fine. It's totally fine. If he's enough of a dickhead to leave me because I'm sexually tame and completely unhinged then that's his problem. I must be true to myself. I am going to own my life and he can take it or leave it.

I take a deep breath.

'The ceiling fell in and we all have to work from home for a month.'

It just comes out. I swear, I didn't know I was going to say it.

'Jesus! Are you OK?' Ben comes over and inspects me.

'Yeah, I'm fine. Everyone's fine. It was during lunch.' Gosh, this ceiling had impeccable timing.

'Well, thank god for that!' He looks at me for a second and then turns back to the fish. 'That's good news really, though. You love working from home.'

Jesus, he's so optimistic.

'True!' I say as enthusiastically as I can. Does he know I'm lying? Why *did* I lie? I sit down at the table as he plates up and brings the food over. 'This looks amazing, you're the best.'

51

He smiles but doesn't say anything, blowing on a piece of fish.

'I guess I can do all the cooking now.' I smile. 'I'll be around all the time.'

He pulls a face and laughs. 'Fine, but no egg surprise.'

Ugh, the egg surprise. It was our third date and I'd invited him round for a meal and some inevitable, long-awaited shagging. I was a total wreck so naturally I spent forty-eight hours preening and checking my ankle hair and completely forgot to think of a menu or buy any ingredients. I figured I'd try to be one of those off-the-cuff girls who shoves things from her cupboard into a pan and comes up with something delicious that instils itself as 'our meal' for the rest of the relationship. In the end I fried some olives and then blended them with tinned tuna and served it stuffed inside a boiled egg. It looked like something Jamie Oliver would have made if he had been able to use a hob in the seventies. It tasted like a fart.

I ate it because I didn't want to be the girl who doesn't eat her own dinner party food, and Ben later revealed that he ate it out of politeness and threw up inside his own mouth three times. In the end, I got the worst dicky tummy of my life and had to make an excuse so he'd leave before I exploded.

We didn't end up having sex until the fifth date. We were both still too raw on the fourth.

'No egg surprise.' I nod. I'm happy that we're having this shared memory moment together. It means he hasn't forgotten about us. Who knew that just a year later we'd be moving into our first house together? My endorphins still flare at the memory, even though I know it's unhealthy and says nothing for my self-esteem: the validation of being picked to share a life with. 'Shall we watch *House of Cards* later?'

Ben loves *House of Cards*. I love watching it with him because it makes him all energised and excited, but I don't really get it. Why did Kevin Spacey have to push that girl under a train? It was only a *job*, for Christ's sake. I just gave mine up for the sake of avoiding a meeting.

'Ah, I'd love to—' Ben rams his last forkful into his mouth and takes his plate over to the sink '—but I've got loads to do for this London thing tomorrow.'

He won't meet my eye. Something is going on. Is it because I look tired? I bet my eye bags are awful today. I've got a huge spot on my chin as well. He probably feels a bit sick when he looks at me; that's why he ate his food so fast. He's probably going to spend all evening in the study watching old episodes of *Have I Got News For You* and pausing it every time he hears my footsteps. A shooting pain passes across my stomach.

'No worries.' I stand up and put the three potatoes I haven't eaten back into the pan. 'I'll clean up here, you go ahead.'

He kisses me on the cheek. 'Love you.'

'Love you too,' I say, but he's already gone.

7

I'm still not sleeping properly. I've been going to bed before Ben and managing to drop off, but keep waking up in the early hours of the morning with him snoring next to me and visions of Wiggy, Jason and Carl dancing around my head.

I almost can't see straight, I'm so tired. I'm walking to the hairdressers and my stomach is in bits. I pass the church hall at the end of my street, and see that the flyer has come loose again. I don't have time to fix it; my appointment is in five minutes. God, I *hate* the hairdressers. I hate the polished and edgy people, the endless mirrors, having to stare at yourself while looking like a newborn vole for two hours. I considered training as a hairdresser when I was eighteen, just so I could do my own layers and never have to step foot in a salon again. But then I realised I'd have to *work* at a salon, and it'd basically be my worst nightmare, day-in, day-out.

I can see Barbara's Bangs (a really troubling name in many ways, but Barbara has dementia now and her successors haven't had the heart to change it) looming in the distance. I might just go home. Or maybe I'll rebook for next month, when things are better. I pull the ends of my hair up to my eyes. It's already been a year – I have to do this. Plus, I want Ben to think I'm making an effort, not just sitting around and neglecting myself.

I push open the door and every head in the salon whips around. A woman in foils nearly paralyses herself with the force of it. I immediately feel hot.

'Hi?' The woman behind reception peers at me. She's definitely judging my hair. She thinks it's horrifically under-conditioned; I can see it in her eyes. She's right, of course.

'Hello, hi.' I approach the desk and flip my fringe over my face. 'I've got an appointment at midday?'

'What's your name?' She's chewing gum and she thinks she's better than me. She *is* better than me; her highlights are superb.

'Briony.' I cough. 'Cox.'

'If you just want to take a seat over there, Shelley will be with you in a sec.' She motions towards a cracked leather sofa, which I sink into gratefully. 'Can I get you a drink?'

'No, thanks,' I say automatically.

I am *really* thirsty. I watch a woman on the other side of the salon lift a glass of orange juice to her lips and take a long sip. Jesus Christ. It's really hot in here. I might faint.

'Briony?' The woman I assume is Shelley walks towards me, holding out a cape.

'Thanks, Shelley.' I put my arms in forwards, almost hugging her.

'Oh, it's like a coat, actually. You put it on this way.' She steps back awkwardly as I flap about, trying to pull my arms back out again. 'And I'm Pippa. I'll do your backwash and Shelley will do your cut once she's done with her other client.'

Oh my god, I want the floor to open up and swallow me and then just shoot me into another dimension because I am so *stupid*.

I follow Pippa to the backwash and lean my neck against the rim. I've heard about people having strokes with these things. The edge of the basin can damage your artery and cause a chunk to shoot off into your brain or something. I try and hold my head up to stop the compression, but Pippa is quite vigorous in her scrubbing technique and it gets wedged down even further.

Well, at least if I die now, I won't have to have my hair cut ever again.

After an excruciating amount of time, Pippa finally finishes scraping my scalp with her three-inch acrylics and wraps my hair in a towel, leading me over to a seat by the window. People are walking past, doing their shopping, and keep glancing in at me and my vole face. I did my make-up just before I came out, but somehow it has caked around my eyebrows and my mascara is clumpy. I grab my phone and flick through Instagram.

'Hiya. What are we doing today, then?' Shelley (this *has* to be Shelley, but I'm taking no chances) has appeared and removed my towel, and is now raking her fingers through my hair. 'God, when did you last have this cut?'

'Erm. A year or so ago?' I flush and reluctantly put my phone on the little shelf in front of me. I want to ask for a glass of water but I can't bring myself to. Shelley is too busy judging my follicles anyway; I bet she thinks I'm some kind of hobo.

'Hm. Are we taking a lot off?' She holds some strands out. 'It needs a lot off, if you want it to look healthy.'

I have a picture on my phone of what I'm after, but I feel like Shelley will think I'm ridiculous for wanting hair like Alexa Chung when I am so obviously *not* Alexa Chung.

Ben likes choppy bobs. His ex-girlfriend – a quirky, dungaree-wearing type – had one.

'Like, a choppy bob length, maybe?' I manage.

'OK. Fringe? Short layers? How long?'

'Um. What do you think?' I'm sure Shelley knows loads about face shapes and hairstyles. She'll definitely be better equipped to choose a cut than I am.

'It's up to you, love. I'd go choppy, layered, high-neck, full-fringe. But it's up to you.'

I didn't really catch what she just said, because I was concentrating on making my face look interested again. 'Sounds great.'

She whips the scissors out and starts hacking chunks of hair off left, right and centre. I actually don't care at this point – I'm tempted to ask her to shave it just so I can leave faster.

'So, you got the day off?' Shelley asks, crouching down to cut the back. 'Uncross your legs for me.'

'Yeah,' I say. 'Well, I'm working from home.'

I don't know why I keep lying. Why don't I just say, *no, actually, I've been signed off on mental health leave because something recently broke inside me and I can't figure out what it is. Isn't it obvious?*

OK. Maybe there's a reason I don't say that.

'Lucky for some!' Shelley and her scissors have moved alarmingly high up, and there are some very, very long strands of ginger hair nestled in my lap. 'Not like I could ever work from home.'

I think about suggesting mobile hairdressing, then technically she could work from *someone's* home, but then I realise she'll obviously already have thought of this, and I'd just look stupid. By the time I've processed it all in my head, there's been at least a four-second gap, and it's too late. We lapse into silence.

Shelley moves round to the front of my chair and starts snipping at my fringe, which is a relief because it gives me a break from staring at my own face.

'All right, are we blow-drying it big and bouncy?' Shelley asks, stepping away to retrieve the hairdryer.

I catch sight of myself. I have almost no hair left.

'Yes, please,' I croak.

Shelley sets about blasting my head and balancing huge, round brushes all over my scalp.

'Ha co fa?' she shouts.

'Sorry?' I can't hear her.

'Co fa?'

What the fuck is she saying to me? She's literally directing a stream of roasting hot air at my ear and trying to talk to me at the same time.

'Pardon?' I try and laugh. 'Sorry, it's really loud!'

'HA CO FA?' she yells.

'Yes.' I smile. Just smile. Smile and it'll be fine.

Shelley frowns. I pick at my cuticles, my chest prickling. What did she *say*? Ha co fa? I run over it in my head. Have? Far?

Oh my god. *Have you come far?*

Yes. I just responded *yes*.

I hate myself.

Eventually, Shelley removes the brushes and sprays me all over with something called *Pumpkin Spice Slick*, before giving me a two-second glance into a tiny mirror and allowing me to vaguely take note of the fact that I look a bit like Deirdre Barlow before whisking me out of my cape and ushering me over to the tills.

'Sixty-eight pounds, please.' The woman with the incredible highlights holds the card reader out to me.

On the website it said it was forty pounds. It *definitely* did. Oh, well. I can't be rude. I enter my pin.

'Bye, then. Thank you.' I call over my shoulder and hurtle towards the door, ramming my shoulder into the glass to open it.

It doesn't move.

'It's pull,' someone drawls behind me. There are sniggers.

I yank the door open and rush out onto the street, gulping the cold, scalp-less air. I scuttle past the window, where everyone is staring at me, and then slow down as I pass Greggs, turning to check my reflection in the glass.

I look *exactly* like Deirdre Barlow.

I speed up again, dragging my fingers through my hair and praying for rain to come and squash the volume Shelley has instilled upon my head. I grab the lot and manage to pull it up on top of my head, securing a bobble around it and creating a one-centimetre ponytail. Looking *and* smelling like a pumpkin. Maybe people will think I'm in fancy dress.

As I pass the church, I see that the flyer has now come almost completely loose. I lift it up and pin it back onto the railings, tying the string around tight. I step back and read it, trying to decipher the brightly coloured, hand-written scrawl.

Social Anxiety Support Group

Do you suffer from social anxiety? Would you like to find solace in a group of similar people, in an open and welcoming space?

Take the first step towards coming out of your shell and join us on Tuesdays at 5 p.m.

Discretionary £1 entry. Coffee, tea and biscuits provided.

NO NEED TO SPEAK OR JOIN IN – YOUR PACE IS THE ONLY PACE.

Hm. Well, I've done my bit. I've fixed the sign. Now all the socially anxious people of Greater Manchester have the opportunity to walk past and be inspired to take charge. Good for them.

I meander home, slotting my key in the door and wondering what I'm going to do for the rest of the day. I've exhausted all of my soaps, and listened to the new Milky Chance album three times. I'm getting a bit sick of it, which I never thought I'd say.

It's still six hours until Ben is home, and tomorrow morning he goes to London again for a week. His work is taking him down there more and more often, and I just keep rattling around at home feeling useless and panicky and wondering if I'd be sat in some glass office in the capital if I had bigger balls.

I step into the hallway and am greeted by the smell of a house that has had a grotty, purposeless woman living in it for days on end. I go around and open all the windows before sitting at the kitchen table and staring at the clock.

Five hours and fifty minutes. Maybe I'll make something nice for tea. A lovely little send-off for Ben. I wonder if he'll miss me? Sami's voice flashes into my mind: *Her boyfriend was really weird with her for ages and when she finally confronted him he said it was because he was bored. Sexually.*

Ben hasn't been *that* weird. Maybe I was exaggerating. This project is really big, and he's putting everything he's got into it. It's probably because I've got nothing on, it seems like he's just busy, busy, busy. It's just comparison, that's all.

Although . . . what if there's no big project in London? What if he's got some gorgeous, gigantic-boobed mistress down there? Or she's up here, and they're going for a mini-break? What if every night he's sitting in his study, sending her dick pics and saying he can't wait to whip her with a feather?

My stomach gripes with pain. I've got to make him love me again. I've got to spice things up and make him see that I can be feisty, too. I can be kinky and spontaneous and wild. I'm not a boring, aimless wreck sitting at home while he works his arse off.

I need to do it soon, because whatever these pains are, they're getting worse, and I still haven't heard back from the doctor. It's probably only a matter of months now before my brain explodes or a tumour makes its way into my lung. I can practically feel it there already. I need to be adventurous while I still can.

I send a quick text to Sami, tug my hair from its bobble, grab my bag, and leave the house again.

8

I walk to the bus stop, my heart still hammering, and decide to google some advice for reigniting a stale relationship. I search: *spice things up*.

Mumsnet seems to be a very popular source for this kind of advice. It makes sense, really; stressed-out mothers looking for a way to keep the fire alive in the bedroom. This is good! Ben and I don't even have children who could burst in at any moment and wee all over the floor, so we've got a head start already.

There are quite a few threads on here about cooking, which is not what I'm after, but I do find an alarming amount of open conversation about sex toys, positions and inattentive husbands. I gather, from a quick browse and my existing knowledge of women in films, that the failsafe method of seduction is taking control through the medium of surprise.

Surprise and lingerie.

I must purchase an incomprehensibly expensive piece of string, secure it to the rude parts of my body, and then lie spreadeagled on the bed (or wait at the front door in a trench coat) when Ben comes home. And *then*, because I am (according to Mumsnet) sexually coy and unwilling to ask for what I want, I must dominate and commandeer the entire process.

I feel sick.

I fire off a text to Sami: *You nearly there?*

I go back to Mumsnet, and manage to get so deep into one particular thread that I don't notice the bus entering the city centre. I hop off and head towards Lacy & Grey, the up-market ladies' intimate wear shop. I am not exactly in my comfort zone in places like this; Sami has dragged me into Ann Summers a few times and forced me to buy a vibrator (which, actually, I really do have to thank her for) in an effort to make me 'express myself', but I don't find this kind of shopping experience particularly enjoyable. All the PVC and silicone is a bit . . . much.

Sami is standing outside as I approach, a smile on her face.

'I see we have a convert.' She winks at me.

'Makes a change, doesn't it?'

'So, what are we after?' She walks inside as though she owns the place. 'I've heard the new LELO bullet is mind-blowing. Like, it actually makes your brain explode. The *Daily Mail* said one girl got admitted to hospital and she *still* went back for more.'

A few customers turn around as we enter and my face flushes. I feel a sudden rush of hatred for myself; I'm a twenty-first-century woman, for Christ's sake. I should be able to chat about vibrators while walking around a sex toy shop. We're hardly discussing butt plugs in the middle of John Lewis, are we?

'No, nothing like that.' I try to keep my voice casual, as though we're chatting about which sandwich to get for lunch. 'I'm trying to . . . spice things up. You know, after what you said about Ben. And the sex stuff. The boring sex thing.'

'Oh, that.' Sami nods. 'Good idea. What about this?' She pulls a red leather catsuit off a hanger and holds it against me. It squeaks as it moves, and people turn around again. 'This would make your boobs look incredible.'

'No, no—' I try to prise the slippery material out of her hands '—that's ridiculous.'

'Excuse me?' Sami pulls the material taut against my front and turns to a woman next to her. 'Isn't this the most shaggable person you've ever seen?'

The woman blinks. 'Erm, well, I suppose—'

'See! You can tell from the look in her eyes.' Sami grins. 'Get it.'

'Let's keep looking?' I move away, my face as red as the catsuit. 'It's not very practical, is it? I mean, in terms of taking it off?'

Sami nods. 'You're right. Yes, let's go for something more skimpy.'

She starts riffling through the racks, pulling out £150 knickers and £200 bras. I slink over to the sale section, spotting some pieces more in my price range. My phone buzzes as I'm holding a long piece of green lace, trying to figure out what it is.

Dad: *Are u in town? Think I just saw u. Meet 4 a drink?*

My heart leaps into my throat. I spin around on the spot, but I can't see him through the windows. Where is he? He must have seen Sami and I outside, or perhaps he saw me walking from the bus stop? I don't want to see him. There are no clues in his text about what his mood is like today.

'What about this?' Sami calls loudly across the shop, brandishing a bodice with holes where the nipples should be.

'Let's go downstairs.' I grab her arm and drag her towards the back of the shop, where there is a sign declaring that only those over eighteen should proceed. So the nipple-less bras and crotchless knickers are fine for children, are they?

'What are you doing? There are no *clothes* down here, Bri.' Sami staggers after me, stumbling down the steps.

We emerge at the bottom into a room full of unwearable items, lubes lining every wall and wobbling sex toys suckered onto a large, round table in the centre. There are about five other customers down here, inspecting the displays.

Sami looks at me out of the corner of her eye. 'Oh, I *see*.' She takes a step into the room. 'We're looking for something like *that*, are we?'

I leave her to wander and check my phone, my pulse still jumping in my throat. There's no signal down here; no way for him to contact me. I absent-mindedly look around the lube section, my mind running over my escape route. A line of hand-pump bottles are lined up in front of each flavour, and I deposit some water-based, cola-scented lubricant onto the tip of my finger and take a sniff.

He wouldn't come in here, surely. But what if he loiters outside, waiting for me? When he's at his worst, we're in private; it's a long time since I've seen him among the masses. It's not like I never see him, but when I do, I have time to prepare myself and up my defences.

I push the plunger on the next bottle along, but my hand slips and a stream of cherry-scented oil shoots out onto my palm. 'Shit.' I put my phone in my pocket and try to rub it in with my other hand before wiping it on my pants.

'What size is he?' Sami calls over, and a woman looks up from inspecting sachets of body paint.

'What do you mean?' I try to drag my head back to where we are and what we're doing, but I'm on high alert every time I hear footsteps on the stairs behind me.

'Small, medium, large, extra-large?' She holds up an array of packages. 'Knowing Ben and his raging inferiority complex, I'd say he's a small, but you know better than I do.'

I reach the collection she's standing in front of and flush. Cock rings. 'Shut *up*, Sami,' I hiss, 'people can hear you.'

'So? We're all down here doing the same thing, aren't we?'

'Yes, but don't . . . *talk* about him like that.' There's a fire in my belly. I'm annoyed with her.

'Jeez, tetchy. Someone's got a bit of a complex themselves, it seems.' She rolls her eyes. 'So are we going medium, then?'

'No, we're going nothing.' I turn around angrily and walk straight into a table of dildos, sending the ones that aren't suctioned down flying across the room. A large, purple one rolls across the carpet and bumps against a middle-aged lady's shoe.

'Oh.' She looks down.

'I'm so sorry,' I gasp, skirting around the table. I bend down to pick it up, but my hands are still oily with cherry lube and it slips straight back onto the floor, bouncing off the toe of her orthopaedic pumps. 'I'll just . . .' I try to grab it again and again, and each time it slithers out of my grasp, boinging across the carpet.

'Here, let me help you.' She bends down as I make another grab for the dildo, and it flies out of my hand and smacks her in the chest.

'Oh my god, I am *so* sorry,' I whimper, my voice shaking. My panic is rising by the second.

'Oh dear, Briony, are you attacking strangers with rubber dicks again?' Sami appears from behind me and deftly takes hold of the dildo, plonking it down unceremoniously onto the table. 'Sorry, she does this.' Sami frowns sympathetically at the woman and twirls her finger around her temple, indicating that I am a hopeless, dildo-launching fruit loop.

'No problem.' The woman rubs her chest.

'I don't,' I murmur. 'I have never done that before, really, I swear.'

'Have you picked something?' Sami grabs my elbow and drags me back over to the cock rings. 'I think the turbo charge might be a bit much if you're new to it, but—'

'No, let's go.' I've had enough, the stress is exhausting me. He must be gone by now.

'But you haven't chosen anything.' Sami scuttles after me as I climb the stairs, back up into the brightness of the shop.

'I'll have this.' I pull a pink stringy thing off the sale rack, choosing purely by price, and take it over to the till, glancing out of the window at Market Street bustling past. There's no sign of him.

'You haven't even tried it on!' Sami protests as I tap my card against the reader. I know she offended me down there, and made fun of me, but I also know she thinks I'm boring. I know she thinks I've completely overreacted to all of this; that I can't just loosen up and have fun. I know I'll go over everything I said and did a million times later, convinced she doesn't want anything more to do with me.

'I'm being spontaneous!' I try, flashing her a smile.

Sami raises an eyebrow as I take the bag from the counter. 'Bri, you're never spontaneous.'

'Well, maybe I am now.' I try to say it in a casual way, as though I really am laissez-faire and relaxed about this, but it comes out tense and stifled.

'I have to get back to work.' Sami checks her watch and leans in for a brief hug. 'Let me know how it goes!' She winks and saunters off, disappearing into the crowds.

I take a quick glance around me and then set off for the small alleyway down the side of Boots that will take me to the bus stop. I walk quickly, dodging the crowds and the charity collectors, and before I know it I'm on the other side of the street.

I'm going to make it. I skirt around another man in an Oxfam T-shirt and go to veer left up the alley, but, suddenly, I feel eyes on the back of my neck.

He's here. I can feel it.

I stop where I am, ignoring the people around me, my heart hammering.

I turn around slowly, and there he is, across the street. Waving.

My dad.

'I've got to run, Dad.' I pull away from his hug and hide my kinky carrier bag behind my legs.

'Aw, no, love. Come and have a coffee with me.' He smiles and he looks so hopeful I want to cry. He's nice today. For now, at least. I feel like the biggest bitch on the planet.

'I can't. I've got a meeting in five minutes.' I stick to cold and distant out of habit, and his face crumples.

'Oh. All right, then.' He removes his hand from where it's been clasped around my arm. 'Will I see you for tea this week?'

'Erm, probably not . . .' I back away, already turning my face from him. 'I'm really up to my eyeballs in it. Maybe next week, OK? I'll call you.'

I walk and he doesn't follow me. As I get to the end of the street I turn around. He's still standing there, looking small and sad and completely, utterly alone.

66

9

Ben is due home in an hour. I've got a chicken that I'm going to put in the oven just before he gets here. It's stage one of my Make Ben Miss Me plan, which goes as follows:

1) Put chicken and cauliflower cheese in oven.
2) Lie in wait for Ben, dressed in new all-in-one piece (allow time for figuring out where arms/legs/head go).
3) Relish look of desire on Ben's face as he enters bedroom and DO NOT PANIC and back out the moment he walks through the door.
4) Have best sex of life (for maximum of forty-five minutes or chicken will burn).
5) Eat chicken and cauliflower cheese.

I send the plan to Sami and she comes straight back with a long line of laughing emojis: *Mmmm, the smell of cauliflower cheese – a known aphrodisiac.*

I google this. It isn't. She messages again: *Just bonk him, Bri, it's not that hard. Did you get cuffs?*

I panic. Should I have got handcuffs? Would it be weird of me to ask Sami to lend me hers? Yes. Yes, that would definitely be weird.

After a long shower and, with fifteen minutes to go, I head

into the bedroom and pull the lingerie out of its unsubtle pink carrier bag. The woman in the shop took it off the hanger, so I can no longer see which way round it's supposed to go, or, in fact, which way up. I turn it over in my hands a few times until I think I've located the neck hole, and then attempt to step into it.

On the first two tries I get my legs in the wrong holes, and I fall spectacularly into the wall like a naked, drunk toddler. I eventually manage to pull it up to my waist and over my shoulders, scraping most of my moisturiser off and leaving vivid, red scratches up my legs. I turn to face the mirror.

I look like a joint of beef. The lace has managed to almost completely garrotte me and force every single inch of my flab (even bits I didn't know I had) into full view. My belly-button is about an inch right of where it should be, winking like a wizened eyeball through the fishnet hole of the fabric, and one of my boobs is squished up near my shoulder. I am certain I will not get out of this again without the assistance of the fire brigade. The crotch is so small, though, that Ben probably won't even need to take it off, so that's a blessing. Then again, it makes my fanny look so repulsive there's a high chance he won't even come near me.

The exertion required to simply dress myself has made me hot and flustered, and my new haircut sticks limply to my forehead. I turn away from the mirror and go back into the kitchen, where I turn the oven on and slide the chicken onto the shelf, followed by the tray of cauliflower. I wonder whether I look like something from a glamour magazine: the half-naked woman provocatively sliding a roasting tin of pungent vegetables into an oven. Then I catch a glimpse of myself in the window and grimace. If Ben comes home and sees me like this, he might mistake me for the butcher's cut and shove me in the oven too.

Tea sorted, I go back and lie down on the bed, holding a full-length mirror over myself with difficulty. Gravity is definitely on my side from this angle – my stomach has flattened and the cheese-wire tension has moved to my back. I'll just have to not move, which fits well with my usual tactic of lying there and hoping that I'm making the right noises.

Right on cue, I hear Ben's key turn in the door. My heart jumps and I throw the mirror across the floor quickly, wincing as it smacks against the wall.

'Briony? You OK?' I can hear him taking his shoes off. I reposition myself into a 'seductive' position, head to one side, legs slightly bent. It's incredibly uncomfortable.

I hear his footsteps trail through the kitchen, to the lounge and then up the stairs. I feel sick. He treads quickly to the bedroom, turns the handle, and opens the door.

His eyes flit around the room before he notices me on the bed. His jaw drops.

'Oh, god, sorry.' He covers his eyes. 'Were you – are you—'

What? What is he saying? Why is he covering his eyes?

He starts backing out of the room.

'Ben!' I say, panicked. Is he so repulsed by my outfit that he can't even look? Is the crotch situation that critical? I think I'm actually going to vomit. My eyes are throbbing. 'Don't you like it?'

He brings his hands down from his face and looks at me properly. 'Is – are you – wait, is this for me?'

'Yes! Who did you *think* it was for?' I am still holding my suggestive position.

'I thought you were . . . I thought you were masturbating.'

I want to die.

'What?! No. No! Do people generally dress up to masturbate?'

He looks at me more closely and giggles. 'Why are you lying like that? You look like you're part of a crime scene. Your neck's at a really weird angle.' He laughs loudly.

For god's sake. I'm not trying to make him laugh, I'm trying to make him *miss me*. 'Stop laughing.' I feel the heat of embarrassment tiding up my chest and into my face.

'Ben,' I say, and he stops. This is completely humiliating. I pull myself up onto my elbows and look at him. A piece of

Mumsnet advice comes into my head: *Use a deep, sultry tone. They go mad for it.*

'Ben,' I say again, my voice an octave lower.

No, abandon that idea; I sound like I smoke fifty a day.

I cough. 'Come here.'

He swallows and walks over to the bed, his eyes trained to the wall above my head. He waits until he's lying down next to me before looking me in the eyes.

'Hi.' He smiles.

'Why won't you look at me?'

'I am! I am looking at you!' he says hurriedly. I turn away and he sighs. 'It's just *weird*, you know? Seeing you like that. I'm not used to it.'

'Why is it weird? You've seen a woman in lingerie before, haven't you?'

'No! Well, yes, obviously, but it's different. It's . . . you.'

This is such a turn-on, this reduction of my role in life to that of a matronly, sexless blob. So it's true – he *does* think I've let myself go. That's it. He hasn't commented on my new hair, which means he hates it, and the Deirdre Barlow look is obviously adding to the idea that I am officially middle-aged and completely undesirable. I'm like a lamb shank in a wig.

I risk a glance over at him. He's looking at my legs. This is a good sign, surely? I want to curl up into a ball and cry. But I can't abort this plan, not after all the humiliation I've already caused myself. I might as well completely abandon my dignity whilst I'm at it. It's all-or-nothing time.

In one quick movement, I push Ben onto his back and straddle him, smacking my elbow on the bedside table as I go. Tingling shoots up my funny bone but I quickly transform my grimace of pain into a brooding pout. Ben stares up at me, wide-eyed.

'Are you OK—'

'Shhhh.' I jab my finger against his lips and miss, scratching the inside of his nostril with my nail. 'Sorry! Sorry, sorry . . . lover.'

Ben snorts and I duck my head to hide the boiling, raging heat of self-consciousness on my face. This isn't *fun!* I am not horny, I am not having a good time. I want, more than anything ever, to put on my biggest, ugliest jumper and lie down by the radiator.

I persist, trailing a line of kisses down Ben's chest. In an impulsive, bold and entirely miscalculated move, I start circling his belly-button with my tongue.

'What the fu—' Ben squeals. 'What are you doing?'

'I'm seducing you.' I whip my hair over my shoulder and push my chest out, praying he isn't paying attention to the flab bulges under my armpits. Tracing my finger around his waistband, I undo his button and slide down the zip.

'Bri, wait—'

'Shh, don't speak.' I wink at him but my eyelid gets stuck and I have to blink rapidly to get it open again.

I slide my hand into the waistband of his boxers and slowly reach downwards, trying to force myself to feel empowered, trying to kid myself that I am enjoying myself and that this is what I want and how it's supposed to be. I reach down further.

'Bri.' Ben sounds serious now.

My hand finally makes contact.

Soft.

Small and soft, like a newborn slug.

I raise my eyes to meet his. He looks back at me, wincing.

'I'm sorry. I'm really sorry, Bri. I just . . .' He blinks, and closes his mouth.

'It's fine.' I stand up quickly and scratch my leg on the side of the bed. I fling the wardrobe open and grab my jumper and trackies, bundling them up in my arms and skidding out of the door and into the bathroom, hitting my shoulder in my rush to get out of the room.

'Briony.' Ben makes a feeble attempt to call me from the bed.

I thud down onto the toilet seat and sink my face into the clean clothes. I breathe in the familiar smell of my detergent, of the comfort of something that cannot hurt or embarrass or reject me. Tears build in my eyes and I choke back a wail of disgust and despair. Am I this unattractive? I am tied to one man, exclusively linked to him for anything sexual, and he can't even bring himself to touch me. Can't even get excited at the prospect of me. Can't even look at me.

'Briony.' Ben raps on the door. 'Bri, come out.'

I swallow hard. This is all my fault. Why did I have to interfere? Of *course* he isn't attracted to me; who would be? And now, when he's down in London bonking his mistress, he'll remember me looking like a Ziploc bag of soup and shudder. I stand and look in the mirror at my body under the stark bathroom lighting and appraise it. Embarrassing. All of it, every inch, just totally fucking embarrassing. I bet he'd have preferred me boho-style: boy shorts and a bralette, like I'd just stepped off the beach. Why didn't I *think* of that? Why did I get my hair cut like a sixties soap star? My head suddenly sings with pain. I peel the underwear off and shrug on my clothes.

I lean against the sink, take a few deep breaths and splash my face with cold water. I unlock the door.

'Bri.' Ben is immediately on me, his arms around me. 'I'm so sorry. I don't know why it did that.'

'It's fine, it happens.'

'It does.' He nods. 'I think it was the pressure, you know?'

'Yeah, I'm sorry.' I scoot from under him and downstairs into the kitchen, where I throw the lingerie in the bin.

'You looked great.'

'Thanks.' I open the oven. 'The chicken will be ready in half an hour.'

Ben looks at me for a second, arms hanging by his side. Eventually he flops down onto the sofa and pulls his phone out, tapping away.

Great. Wonderful. That's his attempt at reconciliation complete then, is it? I should be doing more. Maybe I should be comforting him? Does it upset men when this happens to

72

them? I glance over at Ben, who is staring intently at something on his phone. Obviously not. But he must know that this has upset *me*? How embarrassed I must be?

It's not his problem, I think, as I drop new potatoes into a pan of water. I can't change what's just happened, I can only try something new. And I don't want to push him away even further by starting an argument.

Maybe I should wait until the next time it happens organically, and then try out some new stuff. It's the pressure; he's right. There's no point in ruining a nice evening together, especially when he's leaving tomorrow. I *so* don't want him to leave me. In general, but also just for a week. I turn the hob on and scoot up next to Ben on the sofa. He quickly locks his phone and gives me his full attention.

'I'm sorry,' he says again, swiping his hand through his hair. 'I'm so stressed.'

God, I'm *selfish*. He's got so much on and I'm trying to force myself on him like some needy hanger-on.

'No, I'm sorry.' I nuzzle my head into his neck. He puts his arm around me and the tension in my chest loosens a little. 'I know this project is taking it out of you.'

'It really is.' He stares at the wall and I study him. What's he thinking about? The project, or us, or whether I know he's lying? *Is* he lying? What proof do I have? His late nights in the study could be evidence of either.

The oven timer pings and I get back up, sliding the food out and checking the potatoes. Once it's ready, I plate up and we sit down.

'Thanks for this.' Ben smiles. 'I could get used to you working from home permanently.'

'I hope it's nice. I don't know if the chicken was in a couple of minutes too long; tell me if you think it's too dry. Is the cauliflower cooked? I didn't know how to check—'

'It's *delicious*.' He reaches for me across the table. 'All of it.' He strokes my hand with his thumb and looks at me intently. My heart flips. 'Are you OK?'

'Yes, of course!' I laugh and pull my hand from his, spearing a potato. 'It happens; you can't always be in the mood exactly when I am.'

'No, I don't mean that.' He's still staring at me. 'I mean in general. Are you all right? Not being able to go into the office must be hard.'

I smile. 'No! Not at all. I love working from home, you know that.'

'I know—' he frowns – 'but don't you miss the human inter-action a bit?'

I don't know how to respond to this. How do I tell him that I don't, at all? I don't miss the feeling of being watched, or the knowledge that I'm fucking things up in front of everybody. I don't miss worrying about my outfits and coming up with inventive excuses to skip meetings. I feel safe here, at home. But Ben is so sociable. People love him, and he loves people. I used to watch him, when we went out more often, in awe of the way he spoke to people and gained their trust, making them laugh or coaxing them into deep conversations when they had something they needed to get off their chest. I used to stare at his hands moving smoothly through the air as he spoke, his eyes warm and open as he listened, no matter how boring the person was. And always, without hesitation, he'd know when I needed him, and turn to give me that big smile and a slight lift of his eyebrow, reminding me that while everyone loved him, he was mine, really. I've never seen him look at anyone else that way.

He's always known I'm a little quieter than him, but I didn't used to be this bad. I used to listen too, and join in sometimes, if I'd had a drink. He thinks I'm fun and personable at heart. I can't shatter that illusion by confessing that I'm happier alone than surrounded by my dynamic, inspirational colleagues.

'Oh, yeah, that bit is really hard—' I nod '—but it's only a month.'

He frowns again, but goes back to his food. He can tell I'm not being honest. He's starting to see who I really am; he's drifting away from me. He deserves better than this. Why can't I be more like Ben? Why can't I own a room and feel relaxed in front of strangers? If he knew how nervous I got about such silly things he'd be out of the door in a shot.

I have to be proactive. I need to be the one to save this relationship and convince Ben that I'm not an uninteresting, motivation-less bore. I want him to miss me; I want him to come back from London feeling like the only thing he needs is a night with his fun, gregarious girlfriend. I want him to want to have sex with me. I want him to be *proud* of me. It's up to me to make that happen.

My sex mission for the evening might have failed, but maybe the next step is to work on being better with people. That way Ben might start to recognise the girl he thinks I am when he looks at me; then he might actually want to shag me. He might want to spend time with me.

It's time to admit that there's a problem; that things are getting worse. I've got to start from the bottom and work on my confidence. I can't take Jason up on his offer of work support, not now that I'm on leave. It'll take me months to get an appointment with someone through my GP, and I don't know how much longer Ben is going to stick around.

I need something quick and convenient; something that will transform me into the Briony I've always wanted to be.

'Hair's nice, by the way.' Ben grins. 'Didn't feel like the right time to say so, before. You look . . . edgy.'

I smile and put my cutlery down. I can be edgy. I can be anything I want.

I know exactly what I need to do.

10

I've been pacing up and down the street for fifteen minutes. The woman from number thirty-two keeps giving me strange looks through the curtain.

The social anxiety support group session starts in twenty minutes. I forced myself to get ready early so I wouldn't back out with excuses of having no time, and then just couldn't bear sitting in the house any longer. I keep trying to convince myself to turn around and go back home, but I need to stick this out. I decide to call Sami.

'Well?' she says as soon as she picks up. 'Did he go mad for it?'

It takes me a second to realise what she's talking about. 'Oh. Yeah, yeah, it was lovely.'

'*Lovely?*' she scoffs. 'Who calls wild, kinky sex *lovely?*'

I laugh. 'You know what I mean. It was . . . exhilarating.'

Why can't I stop lying?

'Jesus, you and your adjectives. I bet he loved it, though. He's probably glad you got signed off work if this is what you turn to.'

'Yeah. Yeah, I mean, he doesn't know I've been signed off, actually. I feel really shitty about it,' I confess. I don't know why I tell her. Ostensibly to change the subject, but really I just want someone to complain to, I suppose. Sami always seems to have the answer.

'What? What does he think you're doing all day?' I can hear her turning on the tap in the kitchen, Maja speaking in Swedish in the background.

'He thinks the ceiling fell in and I'm working from home.' I suddenly feel like I want to cry. I feel so guilty.

'Oh, Bri.' Sami sighs. 'You get yourself into some right states. Don't get upset, come on. Just tell him.'

'I can't.' I sniff. 'He's working in London all week and he'll just think I'm insane. I hate myself.'

I hear her opening a cupboard. 'I don't know why you're so *scared* of him. It's not normal.'

'I'm not scared. I just don't want him to think I'm a liar,' I object.

'Well, you know what I think. I think you can do better than someone who makes you feel like a shit person all the time,' she mutters. 'Anyway, no time for being sad. You need a distraction. Come out with us tonight.'

I stare at the church hall and the people starting to filter in. I open my mouth to tell Sami that I can't, I'm doing this instead, but I stop myself. She'll think it's ridiculous.

'I'm not sure. Maybe. I'll call you later, I've got to run.' I smooth my hand over the flyer, still stuck fast to the railing.

'Where to? Where are you?'

'I'll tell you later. Got to go. Bye!' I hang up and swing the gate open, forcing myself to keep moving forward and making my way up the path.

This is, literally, my worst nightmare.

The church hall is musty and carpeted, and a circle of ten velveteen chairs has been arranged in the centre of the room. I am sat on one of these chairs, staring at my lap and listening to my own heartbeat, as people slowly make their way over to join me with cups of coffee.

I want to leave. If I look up, I'll be face-to-face with at least six strangers, probably all wondering what I'm doing here and why I'm behaving so weirdly. I bet all of these people have been coming here for years. They're probably almost cured by now.

I am distinctly aware of myself occupying space. I can't let my arms relax; I feel like the obvious focal point of the room. It's like I'm radiating waves of energy, alerting everyone to my presence.

My phone buzzes and I yank it out of my pocket, relieved by the distraction.

Wiggy: Just wanted to update you – project going v well, quite the challenge!

I seethe. God, he's so smug. He's actually rubbing it in my face now. *Oh, hoy, Briony. I'm doing really, really well at the job you weren't good enough for. Also, it's awfully difficult but I'm absolutely smashing it. Jason, in his infinite wisdom, is already sensing that I should have got this promotion over you. MMMM.*

I look up from my phone and see a woman on the other side of the circle frowning at me. I realise my face is scrunched up in anger. Oh, Jesus. I'm making an awful first impression. I mustn't think about Wiggy now. I can't think about work at all.

But what am I *doing* here? I shoot a few glances around me. There are about eight people in the room, including me, and none of them look like the kind of people with social anxiety. Everyone seems totally fine. I probably don't even have social anxiety – I'm sure Jason was wrong. I've probably got some ultra-intense, general nervousness that no group or counselling or medication can ever fix. My head sears with pain. I should just go, this is a waste of time and I'm bound to embarrass myself. I'm probably taking up a seat that someone who really needs it could use—

'Hhhhhelloooo, everyone.' A woman with short, grey hair breathes, entering the circle and taking a seat directly opposite me. She's wearing a brown tweed waistcoat over a multi-coloured blouse, with beige slacks and sensible black shoes. Her voice is so quiet I can barely hear her. 'Thank you so much for coming.'

There are a few murmurs from around the room.

'I see we have some newcomers today.' She scans our faces. My heart pounds. 'But don't worry – I won't be singling anybody out. The ethos of our group is that the attention is on nobody, until they need it to be.'

I relax a little. Now that the concept of speaking has been removed, I feel like I can listen. I can't imagine ever needing the attention on me.

'I'm Fran, and I'm the group facilitator. I'm available whenever you need me, between five and seven p.m. on Tuesdays. Now, does anybody want to say anything?' She opens her arms to the circle.

To my left, a middle-aged man in a flat cap and a tartan shirt coughs.

'Yes, Stuart?' Fran nods.

'Well, I—'

'Nobody look!' Fran yelps, and I jump. 'Eyes averted, remember the rules. Myself excluded, we don't look at anyone who's speaking.'

Jesus Christ. It might have been worth mentioning that at the start, surely? A heads-up would have been nice. I look at the floor, my face beetroot.

'Erm, I just wanted to say . . .' Stuart starts, his voice deep but unsure. 'I – I hugged the postman yesterday.'

Everyone starts clapping. I join in. What the fuck?

'Excellent, Stuart.' Fran is leaning back on her chair, staring at the ceiling. 'That is such good progress. Well done.'

There's a silence as everyone continues to stare at inanimate objects. I flit my eyes around the room. What are we supposed to be doing now? Why is Stuart hugging the postman?

'Now—' Fran gestures with her hands and everyone turns to look at her again '—if you were here last week you'll remember I said that we had a couple of new tasks. Number one is *asserting ourselves.* We are going to practice this in role-play today, and the second task will be your homework.'

My hands start trembling. I don't want to do role-play. I can feel the people around me fidgeting.

'Now, Sarah, do you want to go and get the plate of biscuits, please?' Fran gestures to a girl to her right, who stands up and shakily retrieves a plate of bourbons, custard creams and digestives.

'Great. Now, Sarah is going to offer each of you a biscuit. She is going to say, "Jane, please take a digestive", and Jane, if you were answering, you would say, "no thank you, Sarah, I'll have a bourbon", or whatever biscuit you would prefer.' Fran nods at us all. What fresh hell is this? Is she joking? I look around the room for signs of cameras. This has to be a prank; it just has to be.

Sarah makes her way around the room, nervously offering each person a digestive and being rejected every time. This can't be great for Sarah's confidence, surely. I scan the walls until I spot the poster for this group – in the top left-hand corner is written 'NHS'. My god, the government *funds* this? Maybe Ben would change his mind about cutting the health budget if he knew where the money was really going.

Sarah looms in front of me. I start to sweat. Everyone is looking at me. I thought we weren't supposed to look at people when they were speaking? I am so confused. I suddenly wonder whether the spot on my chin needs popping. Are people staring at it?

'I'm sorry, I don't know your name . . .' Sarah looks terrified.

'Briony,' I rasp, my throat dry.

'Briony, please take a digestive.'

I really do want a digestive. The only remaining bourbon is broken, and the custard creams look a bit off.

'Thank you.' I take a digestive from the plate.

'Assertion!' Fran squeals. 'Don't say yes to things you don't want!'

'I do want a digestive, though . . .' I start, but people are frowning at me. 'No thank you, Sarah, I'll have a custard cream.' I put the digestive back.

Sarah moves on. My mouth is so dry. That was quite awful, and now there's a mouldy custard cream starting to sweat in my palm.

We carry on like this for a good long while, Sarah being relieved by a man called John, who offers us all orange juice that we have to reject in favour of blackcurrant. By the time we're done, I am holding the custard cream, a glass of juice, a cup of tea and a pink napkin, when I wanted the blue.

'Brilliant. You all did *wonderfully*,' Fran whispers when everyone has sat down again. 'I am so proud of you all.'

She looks like she's welling up and I cringe, staring at my feet.

'We're nearly out of time, so let me tell you about task number two: your homework. I want you to write about an experience in which you felt socially anxious. But don't write it from your own perspective; I want you to give a detailed account of the thoughts of everybody you encountered. What did they think of you when they saw you? How did they appraise you? Write it all out and bring it along next week. You'll hand them in to me and I'll read a couple out anonymously.'

I won't be coming next week. There's no way I'm putting myself through this again.

'Goodbye!' Fran wails, and leaps up from her chair. I jump again. 'Have a positive week.'

Everyone scarpers, pulling their bags from the floor. A few people make a beeline for Fran who, according to what she said earlier, is sticking around for another hour to provide support. I head over to the bin to dispose of my custard cream, desperate to get out of the door.

'Did you really want a digestive?' a quiet voice says behind me.

I turn around. It's Sarah. She's about my age, with bright-blue eyes staring permanently downwards. 'Yeah, I did.' I smile. 'Sorry, I don't think I really got it.'

Sarah scratches her nose and glances up at me before averting her gaze. 'Nobody gets it.'

'Do you do that every week?' I feel OK, talking to Sarah. I'm not too bad one-on-one as it is, and her nervousness is making me feel weirdly confident. Like when you've had eight shots of tequila and can't see straight but your friend is way worse and you become impossibly sober and mature at a moment's notice.

'No, it varies, really. We've never done that one before.' She bites her lip. 'It's all that kind of thing, though.'

'Hm.' I am desperate to ask a question, but I don't want to be rude. I decide to do it anyway. 'Are we all supposed to be hugging postmen?'

Sarah throws her head back and laughs, and then reddens and covers her mouth with her hand. 'Sorry. No, no, that's just Stuart. He has trouble speaking to people he doesn't know, so Fran suggested he tried physical contact first.'

'What?' I am bewildered. 'That's not *normal*, though.'

'I know.' Sarah shakes her head and catches my eye again. 'It's *really* not normal.'

'I thought – I expected it to be . . . different.' I struggle to find the words.

'Me too, when I started.'

'Is . . . I mean, is it all legitimate?' I gesture around the room. 'Like, are these scientific techniques? Is she a psychologist, or something?'

Sarah shrugs. 'I've never thought to ask.'

I pause. 'Does anyone find it . . . helpful?'

She shrugs. 'I don't know. It's better than doing nothing, though, isn't it?'

11

'BRIONY!'

I crane my neck over the sea of people and spot Sami, dancing aggressively in the corner and waving her arms about, screaming my name. Next to her is Julia, and a bloke I've never seen before.

Once I'd said goodbye to Sarah, and thank you to Fran (although god knows why; if anything I feel even more shaky than I did before), I walked back home and the house suddenly felt so empty I couldn't bear it. I changed my clothes and came back out again.

I battle my way through the crowd and over to Sami, who crushes me into a hug.

'Oh, god, I *missed* you.' She keeps her arms around me, rocking me from side to side. 'I'm so glad you came.'

My heart swells. It's so long since Sami has been like this with me. When we met, at primary school, we were joined at the hip. We went to secondary school together and didn't bother with anybody else; we had more inside jokes and emotional support and lunch-swapping moments than the rest of the people in our class combined. Then we turned thirteen and Sami became this fiery ball of independence, branching out into the more popular circles, and I feel like I've been trying to tug her back to me ever since. I never grew out of us, but it's always felt like she has. Sometimes I think she keeps me around out of pity or nostalgia, but then there are moments like these and I wonder if it was all in my head.

'I missed you too!' I hug her back, hard. I spot Julia over her shoulder, swaying and dancing, her head thrown back and giant teeth on show. Jesus, she looks fucked. She rolls her neck and her eyes meet mine, pupils huge and glistening.

I pull away from Sami. 'Has Julia taken something?'

Sami looks at me and I notice that her eyes are glassy too. 'Hm?' She reaches out a hand and cups my chin. 'My little Briony. You're such a lovely friend.'

Oh, god. She doesn't miss me; she's just high. *Stupid* Briony.

'Do you want some?' The guy they're with has come over to us, and is holding a twisted ball of cigarette paper in his hand. 'It's good.'

'No.' I take a step back instinctively. 'No, thank you.'

'Briony is . . . sensible.' Sami grins at me. 'Lovely and sensible. Everyone needs a Briony. They keep you grounded.'

She takes the ball from the man and pockets it. She shuffles from one foot to the other rhythmically, licking her lips. 'Where have you been, anyway? Did you go and see your dad?'

'No, I—' I'm about to tell her, but something stops me. She's not in the right frame of mind. I don't want to be the sober person at the party, harping on about my mental health while everyone else is off their tits. It's a contradiction. 'I did a big shop. At Lidl.' I can't think of a better story, but right now I think I could tell Sami I'd been on a steam train with Brian Blessed and she'd believe me.

'Woooo, the big shop!' Sami grabs Julia. 'Julia, Briony did a big shop. Aren't big shops just *lovely?*'

Julia nods viciously. 'You're so pretty, Briony, with your funny orange hair.'

'Yes! Where is all your hair?' Sami grabs my shoulders and spins me round. 'Where has it *gone?*'

This seems to be too much for them both, and they collapse into fits of giggles, shrieking, 'Where *is* it?'

I feel hot and claustrophobic. I want to tie my hair up but I can't without looking like a pumpkin. My face pulses. 'Just going to grab a drink,' I say, and rush over to the bar, ordering two shots of tequila and a triple gin. I neck the tequila and then turn to look at the group, sipping the gin and waiting for the alcohol to hit my brain before I re-join them. All the booze in the world will never get me to their level, but I just need the edge taking off.

I watch the drug guy take another bomb, and Fran's voice echoes in my mind. *Assert yourself!* And I did, didn't I? I said no. I said no to Class A drugs. It's a start.

I suck the rest of my gin down greedily, and then order another. The warmth is already flowing through me; I can feel my inhibitions lifting from my skin like a physical relief. I walk back over to the group and let the drug dealer spin me, round and round in circles, watching the faces flit past: Sami, Julia, Sami, Julia, Sami, Julia.

I can be fun, too.

Maybe being fun is overrated. My head is pounding and my mouth is so dry I can't taste anything.

I'm lying on Sami's bedroom floor, staring at Julia's crusty feet poking through the foot of the bed above me. I've been delegated, obviously, because I'm boring and alcohol is not the cool person's party elixir. I don't recall getting home; the last thing I remember is standing on a table, and Sami pulling at my arm, hissing, 'We're coming down. We need to go, everyone's coming down.'

Sami's phone alarm suddenly erupts into the silence, and I squeeze my hands over my ears. Sami groans and turns it off, nudging Julia.

'Julia,' she croaks, 'come on, we have to go to work.'

My heart stops for a second, before I remember that I don't have a job to go to.

'Oh, Jesus.' Julia sits up. 'I want to die. I really, truly want to die.'

'Me too.' I call up from the floor. 'I feel like shit.'

'You didn't even take anything, Bri.' Sami snaps. 'I'd kill for a hangover.'

'Is Maja in?' Julia swings her legs gingerly over the side of the bed. How does she know who Maja is? How often does she come here?

'Probably. She leaves at eight; go see if you can catch her.' Sami crawls to the end of the bed as Julia leaves the room, peering through the slats at me. She looks awful. 'Good night, huh?'

It wasn't, really. The entire evening I felt like a child during a horror movie, screwing my eyes up so I didn't have to see what was going on. 'Yeah, so much fun.'

'You should try it one day.' Sami rolls over onto her back. 'You don't know what you're missing.'

I study the top of her head, her wiry, black curls springing out towards me. It doesn't look that fun now, from where I'm sitting. But god, that sounds so judgmental and boring. Have I wasted my twenties, not getting accustomed to ecstasy and acid and all the other scary things I told myself only sad people do to feel better about themselves? But actually, everyone I know is doing it, and they all seem to feel better about themselves than I do. And what's so different about alcohol?

I don't want to think about alcohol.

Anyway, there's me, yet again, on the sidelines, being sensible. If I'm not careful, Sami will really start to realise what a bore-bag I am, and will finally cut me off.

Julia slinks back into the room. 'Got some.'

She sits on the edge of the bed and starts rolling a joint.

'Oh, thank god.' Sami watches Julia as she finishes rolling and lights up, and then holds her hand out for a drag, blowing plumes of smoke into the room. 'That'll take the edge off it a bit.'

She passes it back to Julia without offering me any and their eyes meet. They burst out laughing. Sami starts telling

Julia about something funny she did last night. I can feel that shrinking feeling coming over me, like I'm ceasing to exist but also completely, glaringly obvious, tucked up on the floor like an annoying stain.

'Er, hello?' I sit up. 'Thanks for offering me some.'

Sami stops talking and stares at me. 'You're serious?'

I nod and Julia hands me the joint. 'Yes, Briony!'

What am I doing? I don't want to do this. It's not the first time I've smoked weed – I didn't grow up in a vacuum – but I know what it does to me. I lift the joint to my lips and take a long drag. This is fine! I'm part of this now! We're all going to have fun and laugh about all the stupid things we did last night, and then everyone will forget what an anti-drugs square I am. I hold my breath for a moment before letting it go and taking another.

'Steady on, pal.' Julia plucks the joint from my fingers. 'We're in far more dire need than you are.'

We're quiet as it's passed round, and I feel the heaviness hit my eyes like a truck. That's enough now. I should be OK if I stop here. I've proved my point.

'You all right, Bri?' Sami is looking at me.

'Mmm, yep.' I nod. Did I nod? If I did, I did it really, really slowly.

Julia keeps glancing at me. Did she see how slowly I nodded? Does she think I'm weird?

'Sami, are you free this weekend? I was wondering if you wanted to . . .' I can't remember what I was saying. Where was I going with that sentence? How did it start? A dart of panic shoots through my chest. I'm losing my mind. I'm losing my mind and they can both tell.

'Wanted to what?' Sami is pulling a dress over her head and frowning at me.

What is she talking about? How long has she been looking at me? It feels like years. Did she ask me something?

The silence suddenly feels oppressive. Julia's mouth is turning up at the corners. She's laughing at me. But why? What did

I do? I've done something ridiculous and I can't get focus on what it was.

'Let's go, come on,' Sami says to Julia.

Go where? What are we doing? Oh, work. They're going to work. But where am I going to go? I can't get up from the floor; I'm stuck.

'Up you get.' Julia grabs my hand and yanks me to my feet, but I rise so slowly that I feel terrified. Why can't I move properly? I can see them both staring at me but I keep forgetting what I'm doing.

Sami and Julia pick up their bags and walk out of the bedroom door, and I use all my energy to scan the space around my makeshift bed, hours passing as I place all my things into my handbag. I'm wearing last night's clothes.

And then, suddenly, I've forgotten whether I'm wearing anything at all. My heart jolts and I look down. Tights, skirt, top. OK, calm down. Just calm down.

It feels like three days later that we emerge onto the street. I look at the bus stop across the road. I need to go there. I need to get myself across the road to the bus stop. But there are cars, and I don't trust myself.

'Let's walk her over,' I hear Julia mutter. 'She's baked.'

All the air seems to leave my body. I'm completely out of control and they're laughing at me. I turn around but they're not smiling, and the thought leaves my brain as soon as it came, completely irretrievable. The panic remains, though, as they take my arms and move me, slowly, across the road.

'You going to be OK?' Sami peers at me. Is there something wrong with my face? I want this to stop now. I can't get a grasp of myself or where I am or what I'm doing. I ache with trying.

'Yes, yes,' I say, and it feels like so much time has passed since she asked the question. I can't even remember what it was.

'All right, text me when you get back safely.' Sami gives me a squeeze and I want to hold onto her for stability. I don't trust myself.

Suddenly, they're walking away, and a bus is coming and I know I have to wave my arm to call it. Is it the right number, though? What number do I usually get from Sami's? I slowly, slowly, raise my hand and it stops.

I use every ounce of energy to step onto the bus and tell the driver my address. He scowls at me.

'This isn't a taxi.'

Adrenaline rushes through me. What have I said? Oh my god, what am I doing? Where am I going? He's staring at me. I can't breathe.

He's printed a ticket anyway, and he waves it through the window impatiently. I reach out and take it, and then move, slowly, to the back of the bus.

I need to call Ben. I can't sit with my thoughts; I keep losing track of time and I'm scared.

I check my phone. Sixteen missed calls from Ben last night. I can't call him back now; he'll hear now much of a mess I am. He'll be really angry that I got so drunk, and beyond livid that I smoked weed. I've ruined everything. He's going to break up with me. I'll have no job and no boyfriend.

I stare out of the window. Every five seconds I forget where I'm going, and have to focus everything I have on remembering and staying on course. The anxiety in my chest is paralysing.

I think of Sami and Julia sitting in their office, putting their minds to good use. I miss it. I suddenly miss it so, so much. I miss the clarity. I miss having a problem and working all day to untangle it, spotting a bug buried in a line of code and ironing it out, watching the smoothness of the process once it was perfected. I was *good* at it.

I forget where I am again, panic, and then remember. I want to go back to work. I want the stability and sense of purpose. The idea of a meeting now, though, seems even more daunting than before. The last time is like a blueprint in my mind; every single group discussion appears like a physical threat, my heart skittering and hands shaking.

I spot the church hall and realise I've missed my stop. I reach my finger out and press the button, hyper-aware of the feeling of my skin against the plastic, the 'ding' as it registers.

The bus slows and I walk down the aisle, holding each pole so tightly my knuckles blanche. I forget to thank the driver and he yells, 'You're welcome!' as the doors slide closed. My breath feels tight again. I'm completely out of control. I don't think I can cross the street.

There's a break in the traffic and I run blindly across the road, skidding to the other side in a blare of angry horns. I'm not safe out here. Why won't this feeling disappear? Why the *fuck* was I stupid enough to smoke that joint?

I make it into the house but instead of relief I feel total dread. I'm alone here and nobody can help me. I pull a bottle of orange juice from the fridge and throw it back, drinking every last drop.

I need music. Something calming. I go into the living room and put on Classic FM, sitting on the sofa and curling my legs up under me. The music hits my ears but it's creepy, ominous. Something bad is going to happen. Someone is watching me.

I screw my eyes up and pull the blanket from the sofa over me. I feel so heavy, like I've been tranquilised unwillingly and the adrenaline of trying to stay awake for something important is battling against the forces trying to drag me under.

But what do I have to stay awake for?

12

It's six days later and I think the weed has done something permanent to my brain chemistry.

I'm sure that's not how it works, but I can't stop flaring up with panic, wondering if I'm losing my mind again. The pain in my stomach is so severe, and when it relents my head takes over with blinding jabs across my temples.

I still haven't had any news from the doctor's. Part of me is terrified and the other is angry; if there's something wrong with me and I'm going to die, I'd rather just know. Then I can stop moping about the house planning my own funeral (all-black dress code, mourning veils mandatory, at least one person flinging themselves on top of my coffin), and relax, knowing that my worst fears have been confirmed and there's fuck all I can do about it.

Ben has just messaged to say he will be back three days later than expected. He's called me every night, telling me the project is going well, but always ends the conversation to go and keep working or get an early night after a long day. I told him I fell asleep early the night I was out at Sami's, and left my phone on silent. Every time we speak I picture him sitting at a desk in a hotel room, a stunning woman lying behind him, ushering him to finish the call so he can come back to bed.

I bet she's funny and loud. I bet she organises nights out and stays up until 6 a.m. sitting on a roof somewhere, picking at a chip naan and talking about the state of the economy. She probably wakes up early and goes for jogs around the park, and has done a soul-searching backpacking trip up Machu Picchu. I bet she leaves her hair to flow down her back and barely wears any make-up, and strolls around in Lucy & Yak dungarees without a bra.

I'm making my eighth coffee of the day. I've slipped into a sort of routine: wake up, make a brew, watch *Emmerdale*, make a brew, watch *Coronation Street*, make a brew, watch *EastEnders*, make a brew, watch *Hollyoaks*, and on and on and on. I swing between eating everything in sight out of boredom, to eating absolutely nothing because I can't get food past the ball of terror in my throat.

I wonder whether Ben misses me. What does he think I'm doing? He probably pictures me sitting at the kitchen table, tapping away at my keyboard and saving the world, one line of code at a time. I bet he thinks I'm listening to Foo Fighters (who I don't particularly like but always put on because he loves them) and taking pauses to stare dreamily into the distance.

He has this idea of me: sweet, thoughtful and reserved, but sure of myself. Confident when it's necessary. Obviously, it's all a total lie, and I can feel the entire relationship crumbling around me as my real self slowly emerges.

I met Ben four years ago. I'd just finished my Software Developer training and was overwhelmed at the end of my first week at my new job. I went to Manchester Art Gallery after work and just walked around for hours, standing in front of the paintings and trying to be someone who uses artwork as meditation. Ben's office had rented the big exhibition room for the evening, and waiters were handing round glasses of Prosecco beyond a velvet rope. I was wandering in the Pre-Raphaelite room when he hopped over and joined me, glass in hand.

'You've been walking around for ages.' This was the first thing he ever said to me.

'Me?' I glanced around, but we were on our own.

'Yeah.' He looked up at the painting we were standing in front of. 'You like art?'

I nodded. 'Yeah.' It seemed weird; the atmosphere was soft and intimate with a tinge of the forbidden – like being in school after hours. I felt seen, like I was part of some kind of social experiment and his friends were going to jump out and laugh at me for engaging hopefully in conversation.

'I don't get it.' He peered at the plate under the painting. 'It's just a miserable-looking woman under a tree.'

'Well, obviously you won't get it if you look at it like that.' I raised an eyebrow at him. I was *flirting*. Things weren't too bad back then; I was looser, more in control. All of my shit was easier to hide. It's like the more I've gained, the more neurotic I've become.

'How should I be looking at it, then?' He stared at me, for far longer than he'd looked at the painting. His eyes roamed over my face and landed on my eyes, and I felt like a living, breathing exhibition. It felt like he was soaking me in. 'Show me.'

He stole a bottle of Prosecco and we walked out into the darkness, swigging and talking. I thought he was magical; an untouchable force beyond my reach. He thought I was arty and mysterious.

Later, he told me about his ex-girlfriend. They'd been together for five years when they'd amicably decided it wasn't working and that they'd outgrown each other. Most people would rejoice at the prospect of a man who doesn't slag off his ex or hold any girlfriend-related baggage, but I saw it as a way to see what had come before me and try to live up to it.

From looking at her Facebook page, Matilda was edgy. She had short, choppy hair, wore crazy outfits picked out from the charity shops in the Northern Quarter and always had bright-red lips. She was on-brand, and the brand was herself. I wanted to be better than that. I wanted to be a different type of woman; the one that Ben had found in the art gallery that evening. I didn't want him to outgrow me.

And I've spent every day ever since trying to prove that I am worth his time.

My phone starts ringing on the coffee table. It's Wiggy. Ugh, god, *go away.* He's desperate to tell me how well the project is going. Can't he just piss off and enjoy his promotion without rubbing my face in it?

I let it ring out, and two minutes later, a voicemail pings through.

'Hoy, Briony. It's Wiggy. Just calling to see if you'd be up for meeting to discuss the project? It's going well, and we've been given another month to deadline. It was a lot to do in four weeks; I don't know why you agreed to it! Mmm. I spoke to Jason and he's fine with an extension. I'd love to pick your brains, if you're feeling up to it? Give me a call back when you can.'

Oh, *great.* Wiggy gets an extension because Wiggy goes to Jason and *asks* for an extension. That entire voicemail is basically just him telling me everything I did wrong: didn't ask for clarification; didn't ask for an extension; didn't listen in the meeting in the first place and offer a reasonable timeframe for the project.

I delete the voicemail.

I miss it, I miss it, I miss it. But what's the point in coding if I'm going to lose my job anyway? I'm certain there's no position open for me to return to. It's two weeks until I'm due back, and the project now has another five left on it, so what would I even do when I returned?

But I can't keep sitting around here like someone who's given up. At some point, unless I start a Deirdre-Barlow-themed OnlyFans, I will actually have to start working for my money again. I stand up from the sofa and pull my laptop out of the bookcase, wiping off the thin layer of dust that has formed since I last touched it. I take a pen and paper and sit at the kitchen table, sketching out a new idea, something fun and creative with no pressure behind it. I'm going to pass my time doing what I love – even if nobody's going to pay me for it.

Twenty-four hours later, I have the foundations of something I like. I worked until bedtime, slept for six hours and then kept going. I feel energised; I remember all the parts I loved about this before I got promoted and the responsibilities started piling on.

I check the time. The social anxiety support group meets again in an hour. I wasn't planning on going, but if Jason really is going to sack me, I'll have to look for another job at some point, and that will involve interviews and human interaction. Plus, I keep remembering Sarah's words from last week: *It's better than doing nothing, though, isn't it?*

I rip a blank page out of my notebook and scribble down my homework, cringing as I imagine Fran reading it out to the group. She won't though – it's too boring. I'm sure Stuart has some far more interesting postman updates. Maybe he's kissed him by now?

At ten to five, I change out of my three-day-old pyjamas and head out onto the street. I call Sami on my way again.

'Hey, where have you been?' she says when she answers.

'Oh, just busy,' I breeze. 'How are you?'

'Busy doing what? Is Ben back? Why haven't you called me?' She sounds annoyed and I feel a strange mix of emotions. I'm glad that she's noticed I've withdrawn – it means that she pays attention to me. But also, I'm worried that she's angry with me and isn't going to put up with me being distant much longer.

'Just working on a new project. I'll tell you about it soon.' I haven't spoken to Sami since just after the weed debacle. I felt too delicate; she'd have sensed my regret and thought I was boring for taking it all so seriously.

'A work project? Aren't you on leave?' she tuts. 'Fuck. I think a bird's just shat on me. Anyway, are you about? I can come over if Ben isn't there?'

'Oh, he's in, actually,' I lie, not wanting her to know where I really am, 'but maybe another night?'

'Hmm, it's a hard swerve from me if he's going to be hanging around judging my life decisions,' she huffs. 'Come to mine? Oh, god, I've got to go, it *has* shat on me. Call you later.'

She clicks off and I stare at my phone for a second. Maybe I should go to Sami's instead? I don't want her to think I'm neglecting her. I look at the church hall and see Sarah hurrying through the door, head bowed.

I carry on through the gate.

There's a new person here today, sitting nonchalantly in the circle and sipping on a cup of tea while Fran spends the first twenty minutes of the lesson reading our homework in silence.

I wonder if this is an exercise in itself? How to cope with discomfort and tolerate awkwardness? Eventually, she sighs and puts the papers on her lap.

'Hello. Welcome. Welcome, especially, to our newcomers.' Fran stands up and starts walking around the circle. 'In my hands I have some very enlightening accounts of life with social anxiety. I have chosen my favourite two, and we are going to read them out and discuss as a group.'

Fran shuffles her papers and I feel a dampness oozing in my armpits. God, please don't pick mine. Please, *please,* just don't.

'OK, the first. And remember, this is anonymous.' She pulls her glasses to the end of her nose and starts to read. 'On Sunday I went to the garden centre. Everyone was staring at me. I think they all thought I looked like I didn't belong there. As I was picking out a rosemary bush, someone behind me shouted, "Jane!" and I—' Fran stops and looks up. 'Oops, sorry, Jane. You really shouldn't have used your name in this if you didn't want to be identified. Anyway, someone behind me shouted, "Jane!" and I felt like they were mocking me. I felt like I was back at school again. I didn't find out who it was because I dropped the bush and ran back to my car and went home.'

Fran stops and studies us all over her glasses. Jane is staring at her lap, her face beetroot. I want to cry for her.

'What does everybody think about this?' Fran wafts the piece of paper in the air.

Everyone shuffles nervously.

'Erm,' Sarah starts, staring at the floor, 'I found it relatable.'

'Relatable.' Fran nods. 'Good.'

'I think it was really sad.' The new person pipes up, still leaning casually on the back of their chair. I study them. Long, blonde hair down to their waist and huge, beautiful eyes, lined with the most perfect wings I've ever seen. But the voice is deep and gravelly.

'Nobody look!' Fran shrieks, and I put my head down. 'What's your name?'

'Jordan.' They reply. 'I just think it's really sad that she didn't get the chance to see who it was. It could have been a good friend or something. They might have made her feel better.'

'That's a *really* good point, Jordan,' Fran effuses. 'Now I ask the wider group, do you agree with Jordan's comment? Do you think he – I mean, she – is right?'

'It's *he*.' Jordan sighs. 'You could just ask.'

What is Jordan doing here? He has zero qualms saying anything to anybody.

'I, erm, I think Jane should have practiced putting herself in her fear and stuck it out.' A weedy man to my right glares at Jane, who looks like she wants the ground to swallow her up.

'OK, good!' Fran claps her hands together. 'She should have stuck it out and *put herself in her fear*. We've talked about flooding, haven't we? When sometimes we have to expose ourselves to our greatest fear in its worst form to see that there is no real danger. Exposure would have been the key there, Jane. Have a go next time.

'Number two, everybody pay attention.' Fran moves on, leaving Jane, I'm sure, feeling ten times worse than when she walked in here. 'A woman walks into the hairdresser's. The girl behind reception recoils, thinking how unkempt and hideous this new customer is. She watches as the woman sits on the leather sofa, her hands shaking and her eyes darting around the room. She thinks the woman must be unhinged. The assistant comes over and tries to help the woman into the cape, but the woman tries to hug her, and she feels violated and like she should perhaps call the police because the woman is evidently not right in the head. The woman ends up with a hair cut like an ageing soap star, and then runs into a pull-door on her way out. Everyone discusses her at length after she leaves.'

I want to die. My heart is pumping at such a rate I feel like my face must be flashing: red, white, red, white. I am drenched in sweat. Mine was *nothing* like Jane's. It was ridiculous and from completely the wrong perspective. I mean, this isn't a creative writing class, but I have royally fucked this up. Everyone definitely knows it was mine. They must think I'm *so* weird.

'So, what do we think?' Fran asks.

'I think it's bollocks,' Jordan offers.

'Language!' Fran throws her hand to her chest and looks up at the ceiling. 'In the house of the Lord, of all places.'

'It's a church *hall*, not a church. And bollocks isn't one of the top five, we should be fine.' Jordan waves his hand dismissively. 'Anyway, I think it's bullshit. Nobody thought those things; they were probably more bothered about what they were having for their lunch.'

Fran clears her throat. 'Jordan. You are new to this group, so perhaps you don't know how it works. We aren't here to discuss the accuracy of this person's account. We are here to offer suggestions as to how it could have been handled better.'

'I think whoever it is handled it fine. It's just not true that people were thinking that.' Jordan shrugs.

Stuart coughs. 'I think they could have noticed that the door was a pull, not a push.'

'Fantastic, Stuart,' Fran beams, 'paying attention to our surroundings. Excellent.'

'*Anyone* could have done that, though.' Jordan throws his hands up in the air. 'I did it last week. Shouldn't they be focusing on not catastrophising every single thought someone else has about them?'

'OK, thank you, Jordan. I think that's all we've got time for, actually.' Fran has gone pink. 'Now, we're going to try something new. Apparently, to run a group like this, support needs to be offered outside of sessions. Unfortunately, I have a very busy schedule, as you all know. My baking, for example, takes up several hours a week. So, just like Alcoholics Anonymous, you are all going to get a *partner*. And your partners will be your support system outside of this group.'

Fran walks around the circle, pointing to people on opposite sides of the room to each other and matching them up. Oh, no. I don't want a partner. I don't want to come next week and I'll feel even more shitty about it if I'm leaving someone support-less. What kind of help could I offer, anyway? Guidance on how to conspicuously stare at your hairdresser's tits? Top tips for caving in to peer pressure and giving yourself a marijuana-induced panic attack?

'Briony, you can go with Jordan.' Fran beams. 'He certainly had things to say about your homework, so I'm sure you'll find lots to talk about.'

Everyone stares at me. Fran claps her hand over her mouth. 'Oh, it's fine,' she whispers, 'nobody heard!'

Great. Fucking brilliant. Everyone knows about my hairdresser crisis and now I've been paired with someone supremely confident and therefore totally unrelatable, who is definitely going to judge me for being so weak and make me even more nervous. A white-hot pain flares in my stomach.

'Hi!' Jordan strides over on six-inch platforms and holds out his hand. 'Nice to meet you. Is it Briony?'

'Yes,' I squeak.

'Cool. Shall we swap numbers, then? Here, give me your phone.' He whips my phone out of my hand and taps away before handing it back. 'One-bell me.'

I do as he says and his phone vibrates in his pocket. 'Perfect! See you.'

And he's gone, striding out of the door, flicking his hair over his shoulder without a backwards glance.

13

I'm sitting outside the church hall with Sarah, who is having a panic attack.

'You're all right. I promise, you're all right.' I rub her back, trying to remind her that she exists and isn't floating in a hellish cloud outside of her own body.

'Oh my god, oh my god, oh my god.' She shudders, her head between her legs. Eventually, she surfaces, trembling. 'Fuck, that was a bad one.'

'Looked nasty.' I grimace. 'You OK? Should I go and get you a biscuit?'

'No, thanks.' She shakes her head and looks away. 'God. I can't believe she paired me with him. She did it on purpose, I know she did.'

It turns out that Fran paired Sarah with the judgmental, scowling guy who told Jane she should have 'put herself in her fear'. His name is Geoff and apparently he ruins someone's day every single week. Last time, after I left, he told Sarah her 'obscene' fringe was probably the reason people didn't like her. It hasn't done wonders for her self-esteem.

'Balls to him. Just don't reply to his messages,' I offer. 'Text me instead, I'll do dual support.'

'You don't have time for that.' Sarah runs a shaky hand through her hair.

'I do! Seriously, I've got nothing going on. Nowt. Plus, I don't reckon Jordan will be hanging around much; he seemed to find the entire thing pretty ridiculous.'

'OK. If you don't mind.' She pulls her phone out and hands it to me, her fingers still buzzing with adrenaline and not up to typing.

I put my number in her phone and one-bell myself, before standing up.

'Are you sure you don't need anything?' I feel like I should invite her to mine for a cup of tea, but I'm nervous about her being in my home and seeing how I've been living. It smells like a teenage boy's bedroom in there.

'No, honestly, I'm fine. I have to meet my mum in half an hour, so I'd better be off.' She glances up at me again through her hair. 'Thanks again. Text me if you need anything, too, OK?'

She wobbles off down the street and as I watch her I feel a wave of tears gathering behind my eyes. It's so *unfair* that we have to put up with this shit. I'm really, really tired of it.

As soon as I'm home, I call Ben.

'Hey!' He answers on the first ring. 'I was just about to call you. How are you? What have you been up to?'

Why is he so chipper? He sounds almost manic. Is he happier down there than he is up here with me? Was he in the middle of bonking her when I called? No, no. He wouldn't have answered, surely.

'I'm fine, yeah, how are you?'

'Amazing. Bri, I've got the best news.' I can hear his grin through the phone. 'The project was a huge success. They're promoting me.'

Oh my god. This is everything Ben has wanted and worked for for *years*. I can't put a downer on things by being moody over his hypothetical affair.

'Ben! That's brilliant!' I cheer. 'What does this mean? You don't have to relocate, do you?' I suddenly panic, imagining him saying he has to move down to London and giving me an ultimatum. What would I do? I have no reason to stay here, but I've got nobody down there. Although it's not like I interact much as it is. Maybe I could live out my days in a cute loft apartment and buy a few cats. I could start painting, and then, when we make enough money, I could move out into the suburbs and Ben could use the central flat for nights with his mistress.

'No! Jesus, no.' He laughs, breaking my thought process. 'No, no, I'll be staying in Manchester. *We'll* be staying in Manchester. I'll just have a lot more on my plate. It'll be like the past few weeks, but full-time. The pay-rise is eye-watering, though.'

This is great news, obviously. Wonderful news for us, our finances, everything. But our relationship? If he's holed up in his study every evening, where does that leave us?

'I'm so, so happy for you.' I want to cry, because I really am. He deserves this more than anyone has ever deserved anything, even if he is humping someone prettier than me on a nightly basis. 'We have to celebrate.'

'Yes! Tomorrow night. I *miss* you. I miss you so fucking much.'

I well up. 'I miss you too. It's so hard without you here.'

'I know, baby,' he soothes. 'Don't cry. Look, what if I come back up earlier tomorrow? I can work on the train and then skive for the afternoon. We can have loads of time together, if you can get it off?'

My heart soars. 'Yes! Yes, of course I can.'

'I'll see you tomorrow, then,' he says. 'Now, I'm going to go to my room and sleep for, like, a million hours.'

'You deserve it!' I say enthusiastically, trying to imagine that everything is fine and I am really relaxed and happy about the entire thing.

I end the call and push the thoughts aside. This is great, isn't it? He's happy, he misses me, he's coming home. That's more than enough. I should be grateful to have someone like Ben. Why do I have to be so negative all the time?

102

I pick up my phone again and start making notes, planning a celebratory homecoming to remind him of everything we have.

'Bri!' Ben rushes up the platform towards me, his bag slipping off his shoulder. 'I didn't expect you to come and meet me off the train!'

He picks me up and spins me round, peppering kisses all over my head. I suddenly worry that the people trying to get past us think we're really irritating. I don't know why I came, really. OK, fine, I do: I wanted to see if anyone else got off the train with him. If they did, they've disappeared into the crowd. Maybe he saw me from the window and told her to scarper? Or, more likely, she lives somewhere prettier, like Cheshire or something, and has gone back to pet her twenty ponies and do some expert Pilates.

'Congratulations,' I whisper into his hair, breathing in his familiar smell. No women's perfume, just him.

He puts me down and studies me. 'You OK?'

'I am now you're back.' I take his hand and we walk back to the car. 'I've got an exciting night planned for us.'

I'm suddenly nervous, wondering if he's going to pie me off for an evening in his study. I feel my cheeks colour. Wouldn't that be mortifying?

'Really?' He slams the car door and leans over to me, grabbing my face in his hands. 'You're the *best*. The actual best.'

My stomach flutters with happiness. He really did miss me! He's so excited. But is it just because of the promotion? Is he just riding on the wave of his good news?

We get home and Ben dumps his things, changing into a T-shirt and his favourite jeans. I quickly put on a quirky dress in the bathroom and swipe some red lipstick across my lips.

'Wow,' Ben says, when I emerge. He looks confused for a second.

'What? Does it not look right?' I've tried really hard to make myself seem off-the-wall and fun. I probably look like a Cabbage Patch Kid.

'No! No, you just looked like someone else for a second.' He shakes his head. 'You're gorgeous. Come on, tell me where we're going.'

Matilda. He thinks I look like his ex-girlfriend. Was that what I was going for? I feel stupid.

I take his arm and pull him downstairs, depositing him at the kitchen table. With my back to him, I open the fridge and wipe my lips across the back of my hand. I pull out a bottle of Prosecco and pop it, cheering, 'Yay! Congrats!' I pour a hefty measure into two champagne flutes and sit on his lap. 'You deserve everything.'

Ben clinks his glass against mine. 'Thank you. You're so lovely.'

He looks distracted. Is this boring, Prosecco in the kitchen? Probably. I should have lit some candles and played some jazz. Maybe got a banner or a flash mob or something. I neck half my glass. 'We're going somewhere even better soon, I promise!'

'Can't wait!' He grins at me.

We drink quickly and I quiz him about his new role; what does it mean? What will it involve? What's the money like? He talks animatedly, waving his glass in the air. I feel so proud of him, but the contrast with my own work situation gives me a heavy feeling in my stomach.

'Come on, then.' I put the empty glasses in the sink and shrug on my coat, and we step outside, making our way up the street.

'Tell me where we're going!' Ben laughs.

'Guess!' I glance up at him. 'We had Prosecco . . . and now we're going . . .'

He should get this. Prosecco is what we did the night we met, and our first official date was at Randall & Aubin, the seafood restaurant.

'Hmm . . . somewhere Italian?' He looks at me hopefully.

For fuck's sake. Would he prefer Italian? Why isn't he getting it? Ugh, *obviously* he doesn't remember. He has other things going on in his life and I just have this. Maybe I should change the booking. See if Pizza Hut have a table.

'You'll see,' I say eventually, and we clamber onto the bus and head into town.

As soon as I press the stop button on Bridge Street, he twigs.

'Randall and Aubin!' he gasps. 'Our first date!'

He *does* remember! I need to cut him some slack; he's been very stressed.

Once inside, we settle into a booth in the corner, and immediately order a bottle of white wine and moules frites. The Prosecco I had earlier has swum straight to my head, and I feel looser. Of course he isn't cheating on me! He's had a work project and I've blown it all out of proportion. Look how great I am, organising all these lovely things. I'm like a normal, adult human being.

We chat and mop up the garlicky sauce with thick slabs of white bread, dunking our chips into mayonnaise. Ben accidentally flicks a mussel shell onto the table next to us and I laugh my head off.

'Shh!' he giggles. 'You're so loud!'

I *am* loud. I am wild and crazy and just so *fun*.

'How's your week been?' he asks, once he's retrieved the shell.

'Good!' I lie. The words slip out easily now they're lubricated with wine. 'Very productive. Saw Sami, too.'

Ben's face darkens a little. 'Was she nice to you?'

'Of course! She's always nice to me.'

'She isn't, Bri.' He shakes his head and the mood drops.

'She is!' I laugh, desperate to keep the good energy flowing. 'You just don't know her properly. She's really great, honestly. Just very feisty and independent. She speaks her mind!'

'You're always miserable after you see her.' Ben reaches for my hand. 'Is there . . . I mean, would it be worth trying to meet some new people? What about friends from work?'

We've had this conversation before. 'They're all men, Ben. And they're not my kind of people.'

'How do you know if you've never socialised with them?'

I twist a mussel shell in my fingers, opening and closing it until the hinge loosens and it snaps in two. 'It's not about how many friends you have, it's about the quality of those friendships.'

'Exactly.' He looks at me intensely for a moment. 'Anyway, let's not talk about it. Shall we go?'

We pay and the waiter compliments my outfit, telling me I look like Twiggy in my swing dress. Ben snakes his arm around my waist and breathes in my ear, 'Lucky me, eh?'

And just like that, we're on the same level again; totally in sync and gelled to each other the entire bus ride home. As soon as we get through the door he's pulling my dress off, murmuring, 'You're beautiful. You're so beautiful.'

I need him. I've never needed anything like I need him right now. His breath is hot on my neck as he picks me up and carries me over to the sofa, putting me down and gazing at me, soaking me in. When he looks at me like this, it's like all my bad parts don't exist; I'm the most beautiful woman in the world.

'God, I love you,' he gasps, and pulls me towards him, moulding us together like we've never been apart.

14

I'm in absolute heaven.

The sun is streaming through a crack in the curtains, illuminating a stripe across my belly as I lie, spreadeagled across the bed. Last night was incredible. Ben and I haven't connected like that in so long. It was like we'd found each other again. I felt like the best version of myself: chatty, funny and bright, and I could sense him needing me and missing me and really *seeing* me, the perfect version of me he has in his head.

Everything is going to be fine now. I'm certain of it. If Ben and I are solid, everything else will slot into place. I'll go back to work soon and he'll never need to know what happened, and if I carry on feeling this good I can stop going to those weird support group sessions and just get on with my life.

I'm going to send Ben a nice good morning text to motivate him for his first day in his new position. I might say, 'Last night was amazing – I miss you already.' No, too cliché. I want it to be something romantic though, so that if the girl he's sleeping with is there she'll see it and – Jesus, *stop it!* Why am I still thinking these things? I shake my head. And why am I *over*-thinking a text to my boyfriend of four years, for god's sake? I need to get a grip.

I decide on a simple, 'Good luck!' with loads of heart emojis, but as I unlock my phone to send it I notice a text from my dad that came in last night.

Dad: *u forgotten I exist?*

I throw my phone face down on the bed, my good mood evaporating. Guilt and nerves slosh around in my stomach. Where do they come from, these feelings? I imagine the inside of my body like a big, empty tank with pipes leading into it. Sometimes, a shitty little troll wanders over to the 'anxiety' pipe and turns the nozzle full-whack, without any warning. And, in my body, anxiety is corrosive, dissolving all the happy substances like satisfaction, contentment and security.

No. No, I have to hold on to this good feeling. I will not be governed by this . . . *nervousness* any more. I get out of bed and pad to the bathroom before making my way downstairs. Ben has hung my dress on the bannister, and my insides twist again. What was I thinking, wearing that? And that *lipstick?* It's embarrassing, it really is.

I make a coffee and sit at the kitchen table, flipping open my laptop. I'm going to keep working on my project. It makes me feel motivated and it's a good distraction – time doesn't seem to exist when I'm coding. It's like architecture; creating something from nothing with only the tips of your fingers.

I've been working for three hours when my phone buzzes with a WhatsApp message.

Jordan: *Hola! Don't need support, just bored. Do you need support? Can I provide it? Probably not. I just found myself wondering whether frogs have fingerprints. Like I said – BORED.*

I let out a little laugh and slap my hand over my mouth. I can't remember the last time I laughed spontaneously. How ballsy of him to text me something so random when we've barely said two words to each other. I lock my phone. I know I can't write anything even remotely interesting back, and if I try being funny it'll just come off as needy.

I glance at the clock. I've got a long afternoon ahead of me. Maybe I should see if Sami's free for some lunch. I don't want Ben to come home and find me twitchy after a day indoors. I want to have stories to tell him over dinner. I want a *life*.

I send a quick message to Sami and she replies immediately, telling me she's working through lunch.

I suddenly realise how few people I have around me. Ben was right; when he and Sami are busy, who can I turn to, really? Certainly not my dad. I've isolated myself entirely – I am almost completely alone. And while the two central people in my life are running about living full and complex lives, I am wandering around my own mind, debating every tiny detail of my existence.

I flip my phone over in my hands. I can't keep depending on two human beings for my every need. Especially not two who hate each other, have other shit going on and who will probably leave me if they realise how bonkers and desperate I am. I need a neutral zone, someone who doesn't know me and who, if they abandoned me, wouldn't leave a gaping hole in my heart that I'd never recover from.

Me: *Hey! Bored out of my brains here, too. Work not fun? Not sure whether I need support or not – could be a good day, haven't figured it out yet.*

Me: *P.S. Frogs don't have fingerprints, just googled it.*

He replies immediately.

Jordan: *Eugh, thank god for that. The thought of it was freaking me out a bit. Imagine how fingerprint-y the rainforest would be. A total CSI nightmare.*

Jordan: *Hypothetically, though, if they DID have finger-prints . . . what do you reckon they'd look like?*

Jordan: *Ignore that, I've freaked myself out again. I reckon it's a good day – come to town!*

I stare at the last message. Jesus, that's a bit much, isn't it? He doesn't even *know* me. I can't just go to town and meet a complete stranger. What if he drags me into an alleyway and murders me? More importantly, I don't know what I'd wear, or what we'd be doing, and I can't ask because I'll look needy and weird. Or will I? He knows I'm a bit of a fruit loop, and we go to the same support group, so surely he understands?

Me: *Ha, I don't know what to wear? Where do you want to go? Also, their fingerprints would look like tadpoles. It's basic science.*

Again, he replies at breakneck speed.

Jordan: *Don't ask me for style advice. Wear whatever makes you feel AMAZING. And fuck knows, who cares? We can roam.*

Jordan: *Shut up about the fingerprints or I'll vom.*

Oh my god. I don't know what to do. I should just text back and say that something has come up, or I have a doctor's appointment or something.

I look at the clock in the kitchen. Seven hours until Ben gets home. I can't sit here for that long – I really will go mad.

Me: *OK. I'll be there in half an hour. Where shall we meet?*

15

Jordan wants to meet at Afflecks.

Affleck's Palace is a gigantic, sprawling 'department store' of weird and wonderful independent retailers, just on the edge of the Northern Quarter. I've been in a million times and never once escaped without getting lost or ending up in the Rubber Plantation condom shop, frantically trying to find the exit before I buy a multipack of ribbed, Calpol-flavoured contraception.

Jordan says to meet him 'out front', but Afflecks has about thirty thousand entrances, so I parade the perimeter nervously, looking out for his trademark waist-length hair.

I'm nervous, but not as nervous as I thought I'd be. Jordan doesn't know me and, apparently, expects nothing from me. He doesn't seem phased by anything I've said over WhatsApp, or my embarrassing hairdresser monologue. I am worried that he'll get bored of me after five seconds and realise what a huge mistake he's made inviting me out, but I'll just be sure to make my excuses the first time he stifles a yawn.

It's ten minutes after our agreed meeting time, and I'm starting to panic. Where is he? I've walked around the building seven times and there's no sign of him. I pull out my phone but he hasn't messaged; I don't want to bother him and seem needy. A man with a foot-tall Mohawk stares at me as I pass him again. I can't see his facial expression under all the piercings. Next to him is a short, stocky guy with a chubby face, wearing a suit. They're smoking and glancing over at me, muttering. I stare at the floor. I'll give it five more minutes and then I'm going to go home and—

'Briony?'

I look up. I can't see him. I turn around.

'No, Briony, over here.'

I look back over and see the chubby guy waving. What?

'It's me, Jordan!' He laughs.

Jordan? I walk a little bit closer and peer at him. Now I've got a better view, I can see his eyes are the same, albeit without the perfect winged liner.

'Fuck, I bet you don't recognise me.' He slaps his forehead. 'I always forget.'

He comes forward and wraps me in a hug. 'Hi! Sorry, it's me, I promise. I've got photos to prove it, if you don't believe me.' He pulls his phone out and shows me a picture of the Jordan I met last week. 'Don't swipe, for the love of god.'

'Oh, hi!' I say, eventually, handing his phone back. 'Sorry, no, you still look like you. I was just . . . I just wasn't expecting you not to have your . . . hair.'

'Happens all the time.' He grabs the guy with the Mohawk by the elbow. 'This is my boyfriend, Aiden.'

'Hi, nice to meet you.' I shake Aiden's hand and he grins at me.

'Nice to meet you, too. I'll leave you to it. Have a good day.' He kisses Jordan on the forehead and shuffles off into the distance, the chains on his trousers jingling.

'So.' Jordan grins at me.

'So . . .' I suddenly feel incredibly nervous. What am I doing here?

'Oh my god, don't mention the fingerprints.' He holds his hand up. 'I'm serious.'

I laugh. 'I won't!'

'Good. Come on, let's go and buy some weird jewellery and a coffee.' He turns on his heel and heads into Afflecks, leaving me to scamper after him.

'So, what is it that you do?' I ask, as we browse rows of necklaces with severed heads on them.

'Do you like this?' Jordan turns around and shows me a hairgrip with a tiny pool of plastic baked beans attached to it.

'I like beans . . .' I start.

'Cool, let's get one each.' He picks up two and takes them to the counter.

'Oh, no, I can't let you buy me that . . .' I reach into my bag for my purse.

'It's literally fifty p—' he hands the woman at the till a one-pound coin '—and you probably don't even want it. You're only saying you'll pay to be nice, and that's just madness.'

I gape at him. He refuses the woman's offer of a bag and turns around, pinning one side of my fringe up with the hairgrip before attaching his own to the short strands of hair on top of his head. The accessory sits in stark contrast to his pristine suit. 'Amazing! Shall we go and get coffee?'

'Thank you. OK, yeah, sure.' I touch my hair as I follow him up the staircase to the cafés on the top floor. What is going on? He moves so quickly from one idea to another, I can't catch my breath.

As soon as we emerge from the staircase, Jordan launches himself at a girl behind the Coiffee counter. Coiffee is a hair-dressers-cum-café. The name works; the pube-like floaters in your latte do not.

'Miranda! Hi!'

'Jordan! Holy shit, how are you?' Miranda squeals as Jordan picks her up and spins her around.

'Amazing. *Amazing.* This is my friend, Briony.' Jordan gestures towards me and I freeze. We're friends now? Is a baked bean hairgrip all it takes? That's obviously why I have no pals and am constantly ruining everything: I don't have the right breakfast-themed accessories.

'Hiya, Briony.' Miranda smiles warmly at me. 'You guys want a drink? On the house.'

'What do you think?' Jordan looks at me. I can't get my words for a second, because they're both staring at me and I'm not used to having friends ask my opinion on drink locations.

'That would be lovely, if it's not too much trouble?' I say, eventually.

'God, of course not. Sit down, sit down.' Miranda chivvies us to a table in the corner, by the window, and sets about with the coffee machine. She didn't take our orders, but I'm sure it's fine.

I'm still not sure what I'm doing here.

'Don't you just love this view?' Jordan is gazing out of the window at the grey, concrete scenery outside.

'It's really nice.' I nod.

He cocks his head at me. 'No it isn't, and you know it. Anyway!' He slams his hands onto the table and I jump. 'Do you want to talk about stuff? How are you feeling?'

I am thrown by his directness. Our drinks haven't even arrived and he's going straight for the jugular. Is he mocking me? I can't tell. Besides, how *am* I feeling? I don't really know.

'I . . . OK.' I nod. 'I feel OK.'

'So why do you come to group, then?'

'I – I'm anxious, aren't I?' I struggle, feeling suddenly frustrated. 'Look at me.'

'You look all right to me.' He holds his hands up. 'But trust me, I know what it's like to have things going on under the surface. It's not always obvious. What do you do?'

I pause again, my head spinning from his sudden change in direction. This was a terrible mistake. I feel like I'm at an interview.

'I'm a software developer.' I try to leave it there, but he smiles at me, letting the silence hang. It's unbearable. 'I mean, I was. I still am, I hope. I got signed off on mental health leave because I had a panic attack in a meeting. I fucked everything up, basically.'

I feel my face redden as I finish talking.

Jordan frowns. 'Sounds more like you *got* fucked to me.'

'What?'

'Well, you can't help it, can you? You didn't do it on purpose.' He shrugs.

'No, I suppose not—'

'Wait—' Jordan holds up his hand '—do you get panic attacks a lot? Or is it only in certain situations?'

'Erm, big groups, generally.' I blush again. I give Jordan a brief background on what happened at work; the promotion, the project, the lies. I expect to see him wince at how awful my behaviour was, but he just listens calmly. 'I mean, I'm not great around people anyway. But the panic attacks only started happening since my promotion, and it's got worse recently.'

I look at him nervously, suddenly desperate for him to give me some advice. Sami always tells me to suck it up and get back in the room, which is quite hard to do, but I do appreciate it. I feel like Jordan might have some really good pointers; he's so confident.

'Well, mate, I have to say—' he holds his hands up '—that is totally shit.'

I wait a second, but he doesn't say anything further. That's *it?* I am thrown. I expected him to tell me to go to the GP, or try power poses. Instead he's just sympathising, which I don't deserve.

'It's all my fault, though. I got myself into this mess. If I had just listened in the first place—'

'Nope.' Jordan interrupts me. 'How are you supposed to listen when your head is like a bag of screaming toddlers?'

I am saved from responding to this by the arrival of Miranda, who has our drinks.

'Here we go. The Coiffee special.' She places a mile-high mountain of whipped cream in front of me. 'Enjoy!'

'What's this?' I whisper to Jordan, as soon as she's out of earshot.

'God knows!' He grins, taking a gulp and giving himself a thick white moustache. 'Tastes dead good, though.'

It really does. It tastes like Angel Delight mixed with melted Dairy Milk. We sip in silence for a few seconds, until I can't help myself any longer.

'Do you mind if I ask you a question? You don't have to answer it.'

'I always answer questions, no matter what they are.' He winks. 'Is it about the drag?'

'No—' I shake my head and notice a chunk of whipped cream in my hair '—it's about the support group. Why did you come? You seem . . . fine.'

Jordan throws his head back and laughs. 'Good question! *Really* good question. I have some . . . things going on. Someone I know suggested I get help. So I'm doing it to prove a point.'

'Social anxiety, though?'

'Yeah, it's probably not the best one I've done. I've been going along to a few; I did *meditation for outcasts* a few weeks ago.'

'Oh. So you won't be coming back?' I feel weirdly disappointed.

'Who knows?' He shrugs. 'Maybe I am socially difficult. Maybe that's my problem. I could learn something.'

'Not from Fran, you won't.'

Jordan laughs again. 'My god, she's mental, isn't she?'

We laugh and talk about Fran's horrific breaches of confidentiality, and I tell him about the biscuit trauma of week one. Jordan decides he is totally obsessed with Fran. We finish our drinks and he puts his hand over his mouth, stifling a yawn.

'That stuff's made me really sleepy. Reckon she's drugged us?' He flashes a wink at Miranda, who mimes throwing a tea-towel at him.

'I'd best be going, actually.' I stand up and grab my bag, determined not to miss the social cue.

'Oh, right, OK.' Jordan looks taken aback. 'No problem. I'll see you around, then?'

'Yep, yep. See you.' I wave awkwardly and leave as Miranda scoots over to clear our table. 'Thank you for the drink.'

116

I try three different staircases before I manage to find the exit, and once I'm out on the street I lean against the wall and prepare myself for the inevitable post-mortem of my latest social interaction. Jordan definitely thinks I'm weird. What was I thinking, going on about work like that? Someone like him would think the way I behaved was completely incomprehensible. I don't *know* myself, and Jordan seems so at home in his own skin that it almost doesn't seem true.

Why did he want to hang out with me, anyway? Is he one of those people that collect waifs and strays, priding themselves on their weird and eclectic associations? Maybe I'm story material: an interaction to laugh about at the pub with his real friends.

I start walking towards the bus stop, and I notice a lift in my mood. Despite how badly that went, I feel stronger for having seen someone and navigated a social situation impulsively.

I wonder how Sarah is doing.

I pull out my phone and fire off a message. I don't want her to feel alone in this, and I promised I'd support her. I can't leave her at the mercy of Geoff and his unwanted fringe digs.

Me: *Hiya! It's Briony. How are you? Just thought I'd pop in for a sanity check.*

Sarah: *Gaaaah I'm fine, same shit, different day. Stayed at my mum's since group which feels like a major setback. Geoff literally won't stop texting me.*

Me: *Not a setback if it's making you feel better. You're joking? I imagine he's being really helpful . . .*

Sarah: *He texts me every day at 9 a.m. on the dot – PUT YOURSELF IN YOUR FEAR AND STOP BEING LIFE'S BITCH. I think he has them pre-programmed.*

Me: *Oh. My. God. You are NOT life's bitch. What a twat?!*

Sarah: *Massively. Anyway, all good. Still surviving. Everything OK with you?*

Me: *Yep, all fine. See you next Tuesday? A few more sessions and we might be able to tell Geoff to go fuck himself to his face.* ☺

16

I am sweating cobs.

I've been slaving over the stove for three hours, and the carrots in the sausage cassoulet I'm making are *still* raw. Why won't they cook? Why is it that carrots in water cook in ten minutes, but in tomato sauce they take six weeks?

I only have an hour until Sami arrives. My plan was to cook everything in advance so I had time for a calming bath before the shitshow begins, but that idea has gone swiftly out of the window.

It took me *days* to convince Sami to come over and have dinner with us. First, she told me she'd rather let Boris Johnson feel her tits, and then she said she'd rather run up the M6 naked (but then admitted she'd probably actually enjoy that) and then she said she'd only come if she could drink three bottles of wine and have a joint. Ben took a few moments of persuasion, but eventually gave in because (I am convinced) he doesn't give a shit what we do any more. Since the amazing night we had when he got back from London, he has been lost to me. He doesn't get home until 10 p.m. sometimes, and when he does he's so tired he just wants to watch TV or go straight to bed. Half of me feels like a bitch for expecting so much of him when he is working himself into the ground, the other half is convinced he's having hard-core sex with someone called Clementine on a glass desk in a skyscraper.

The second half of me is slightly bigger than the first.

I chuck some more water into the cassoulet and put it back in the oven before running upstairs to zhuzh up my hair and put a dress on. Ben comes out of his study as I emerge onto the landing.

'Wit woo,' he whistles, 'you look amazing.'

'Thanks!' I give him a peck on the lips and thunder back down the stairs to decant some olives into a bowl.

I'm unbearably on edge. Sami is under strict instructions not to mention *anything* about my work for the entire evening. She has promised, but I'm going to need to watch how much wine she drinks. She and Ben haven't been in the same room for over a year. Last time they saw each other, Sami called Ben a fun sponge and Ben told her he'd rather be a fun sponge than a destructive mess.

So, yes. I'm a little apprehensive.

The only reason I'm doing this is because it is part of my new plan to become a better person before I go back to work. Despite both Geoff and most of his advice being awful, I am trying to *put myself in my fear* and rebuild the bridges between Sami and Ben. I want Sami to see that my life here is fun, and I want Ben to realise how together and sociable I am. I also want them both to see how great the other is; how all their spats before have just been misunderstandings. If I can fix this rift, maybe everything will be OK.

The doorbell rings as I'm sliding a loaf of M&S tomato bread into the oven. Ben pads down the stairs to answer it but I slide in front of him as he gets to the hallway, blocking his path.

'I'll get it!' I grin encouragingly and usher him into the kitchen. 'You get the wine out of the fridge.'

I wait until he's disappeared before putting the chain lock on and opening the door a crack.

'Hey. What are you doing? Open the door, you weirdo.' Sami pushes on the doorknob.

'No, I will, one sec.' I put my mouth to the gap. 'Do you *promise* not to mention work? Please, Sami. I'm serious.'

'Oh my god, I *promise*. Jesus Christ. Let me in, it's freezing.'

I slide the chain lock off and she bursts into the hallway, kicking her boots off against the radiator.

'I've brought some chocolate wine I nicked from an event we had last week.' Sami brandishes a bottle in front of my face. 'Ben can drink it while we get stuck into the *proper* digestifs.'

She roots around in her pocket and pulls out a Ziploc bag of brownies. I'm sure it's not her grandma's recipe. I start to sweat.

'Come on through!' I take the wine from her and push her into the kitchen.

'Hi, Sami!' Ben tries to smile genuinely as we walk in, handing Sami a glass of wine and offering her a one-armed hug.

'Nice to see you, Ben.' Sami raises her eyebrows at me. I don't know what message she's trying to convey, but I don't like it.

'Sit down, sit down—' I pull two chairs out '—I'll just see where we're at with this cassoulet.'

'Oooh, *cassoulet*,' Sami mimics in a posh accent.

I laugh, 'I know, so boring, right? I saw it on Jamie Oliver's website and thought it looked nice. I bet it's not, though. We can just pick the sausages out and eat those. I can make some mash. Hope your expectations aren't too high!'

I'm shaking a little as I pull the dish out of the oven. I need a moment to check everything's cooked, but Sami and Ben are watching me in silence. I give Ben a pointed look.

He coughs. 'So, Sami, how's work?'

'Fine, yeah.' She nods. 'You?'

'Really good, actually. I got promoted last week . . .'

I relax a little as they chat. The carrots are cooked now, and Ben and Sami are definitely getting on. This could be the start of something! We could become proper couple friends now. All three of us can hang out together, and every time Sami gets a new partner we can do nice double-date stuff. Then I won't be the only one holding it all together.

I plate up and carry the dishes over to the table, zoning back in on their conversation.

'But it's *bullshit*, though.' Sami's cheeks are pink and she's gesticulating all over the place. 'It's hardly a sign of a healthy, feminist society when there isn't a *single* woman above secretarial ranking in the entire company. I don't know how you can live with yourself.'

My heart starts hammering. Oh no. She must have asked how many women work in Ben's department. Why would she *ask* that?

'There are loads in the *company*. Just not in my division,' Ben retorts. 'We have loads of diversity programmes, and—'

'Oh, woop-de-fucking-do,' Sami sings. 'Diversity programmes! Did you hear that, Briony? Ben's a modern man because he supports *diversity programmes*. Oh, wow. I mean, really. Bravo.'

'Dinner is served!' I squeal, slopping stew all over the table as I put the plates down. 'Tuck in, tuck in. Don't let it get cold! Sami, have you told Ben about . . . Julia? Julia is very funny. I'm sure Ben would love to hear about Julia.'

My head is suddenly searing with pain. I scoop a small spoon of cassoulet on to my plate and put it on the table before going back to the counter to slice up the bread.

'Why would Ben want to hear about Julia?' Sami frowns. 'She's just a girl I work with. A *girl*, Ben, did you hear that? A woman with a job. Grab the pitchforks, it's time for the ceremonial drowning. Are the villagers ready? A female has learned arithmetic! She must be a witch.'

'Have we all got wine?' I finally sit down and fill everyone's glasses to the brim. 'You know, these olives are Greek. Isn't that lovely? I like Greek olives. I think Italian ones are OK, too. Depends on the marinade really, doesn't it? Which are your favourite? Ben? Sami?'

'Erm, probably those pesto ones from Aldi,' Ben mumbles, forking a piece of sausage into his mouth. 'This is really good, Bri.' He leans over and kisses me on the cheek.

'Yeah, it's nice,' Sami mutters reluctantly.

I encourage everyone to eat and drink and they sip in silence, the only noise the scraping of cutlery on plates and me, trying every so often to lure them both into a conversation about cannellini beans. I relax a little, and manage to take note of the fact that the cassoulet is actually quite tasty.

This is going well! Yes, conversation is stilted, but of *course* it is. Sami and Ben have a difficult past; this was never going to be warm and fuzzy right from the off. I still kind of wish I was alone with Sami, or with Ben, then there'd be no chance of her outing me for being such a barefaced liar, but all things considered, this is not the worst it could be.

We finish one bottle of wine and silence descends again, so I go to the fridge for another and nudge Ben under the table with my foot as I get up.

'Ow!' he yelps, and then catches my eye. 'Erm, so, Sami. Tell me what Briony was like at school.'

Oh, no. Not that. Let's not do that, ever.

'I'm sure Sami doesn't want to talk about *school*!' I laugh as I fill our glasses. Ben frowns at me, confused. Why would I nudge him to get the conversation going and then shut his topic down? Because I don't want him to know what a freak I am, that's why.

'Aw, baby Briony!' Sami is louder now she's had a drink. 'She was basically the same as she is now. Quiet, nervous, nerdy, you know. A bit of a wallflower. She had her first boyfriend when she was seventeen and he—'

'Argh!' I yelp. Everyone jumps. 'A . . . A spider!' I point to the wall in front of me. 'Oh, it's gone. How weird! It was huge.'

I sit back down.

'You OK?' Ben leans in to me.

'Fine! Great! Anyway, what were we talking about? Erm, oh, what are you planning on doing for New Year this year, Sami? I know it's ages away, but—'

'No, we were talking about your first boyfriend.' Ben winks at me. 'Go on, what was he like? I'm imagining a lot of wild parties and sneaking out of the window so your dad didn't know you were gone.'

'Wild? Have you met Briony?' Sami snorts. 'He was the Gandalf of the school's World of Warcraft club or something. He had a spot on his nose for *three years*. Literally. She was obsessed with him. And then *he* broke up with *her*. And I don't really think Bri's dad would have given a shit where she went, to be honest. If I'd have had that kind of freedom—'

'Right!' I stand up, grabbing everyone's plates, my stomach somersaulting. I think I'm going to be sick. I'm actually going to vomit all over the table and ruin the dinner party. I should never have invited Sami over. How was this a good idea? 'I'll just clear these and then I'll get the dessert.'

'Oh, were her parents pretty chilled?' Ben asks as I turn my back to the table. I want to cry. 'I've still never met her dad, but her mum sounded lovely.'

This is what I wanted, wasn't it? I wanted them to get on. I wanted them to have a nice chat and bond over their common connection to me. Good call, Briony. As usual.

'What? You've never met Steve?' Sami looks over at me as I load the dishwasher. For the first time this evening she meets my gaze and knows when to shut up. 'Well, I'm sure you will. But yeah, Janet was great.'

'I'm going out to the garage to get the cheesecake,' I say, my voice wobbling. I open the back door and step out into the cold, letting the tears dribble down my cheeks. I can still hear Ben in the kitchen.

'So what was she like? Janet? I'm really sad I never got to meet her. It's such a shame . . .'

I walk across the grass barefoot, and unlock the door to the tiny outhouse we call the garage. It has enough space for a chest freezer and a lawnmower in it, and I am so, so glad I decided to put the cheesecake in here this evening.

I sit on top of the freezer and put my head in my hands. Ben has uncovered the truth. I was never artistic and brooding. I

123

was just a nervous outcast who nobody fancied and who got dumped by the least desirable boy in school. There has never been anything special about me, and now Ben finally knows it.

And I really, really miss my mum.

I cry quietly on top of the freezer for a good five minutes. I'm used to crying quietly, because I do it quite a lot. I wouldn't say it's a hobby, but it's definitely something I've become quite good at.

'Briony?' Sami pokes her head around the door and I sniff, jumping off the freezer and lifting it open. 'You OK?'

'Yep! Yep, just can't find this bloody cheesecake,' I say brightly, while literally looking directly at it.

'It's there.' Sami pulls it out and closes the lid again. She grabs my shoulders and turns me around. 'Are you all right?'

'Oh, I'm fine.' I nod, not meeting her gaze. 'I just don't like talking about the past sometimes, that's all.'

'I know. I'm sorry.' She gives me a hug and her hair tickles my nose. She pulls away and looks at me carefully. 'Has he really never met your dad?'

'No.' I take the cheesecake from Sami's hands and walk around her, back through the door and into the garden. 'There just hasn't been the time, really.'

She hurries after me. 'You've been together *four* years, Bri. Have you met his?'

'Yes, of course. He's really nice.'

That's what makes it so much worse.

I ignore Sami's further questioning and let myself back into the house. Ben claps.

'There she is! We thought you'd fallen into the freezer or something.'

Sami laughs. 'Cheesecake was hiding.'

I slide the cheesecake out of its wrapper and hack a knife through it as Sami pours the chocolate wine. I didn't read the packet and it's frozen solid, obviously, and should have been taken out an hour ago. I serve it anyway and put the plates on the table.

'I'm just going to the bathroom.' I'm not ready to sit down and chat as though nothing has just happened. I leave the room, again, and lock myself in the downstairs toilet.

I look at myself in the mirror. *Come on, Briony. Pull yourself together. Your mum has been dead for years; it's time to get over it. You can't have a hissy fit every time someone brings her up. She was a person, she existed, and now she doesn't. End of story. Stop being such a blubbering mess.*

I look into my own eyes for a second, trying to convey some kind of strength in a weird, telepathy-to-myself kind of way, and my mum stares back at me. We always had the same face; even when I was small and pudgy, my dad says you could tell I was hers. Suddenly, I'm back in the kitchen at home, my mum sitting across from me.

'I know it seems hard, Bri Bear—' she's holding my hand and a tear plops down, landing on her finger and dripping down onto the table '—but I need you to listen to me. I can't give you everything I wanted to give you, all the things I thought I would. And I've had a short time here. I know it might not seem like it to you, but before you know it you'll be my age and you'll realise how quickly it all goes.' At this point she holds my face, pulling my chin up to look into her eyes. 'You have to be yourself. That's all. Don't waste time pretending and pushing yourself away. OK? Do you promise you'll remember?'

The one thing she asked of me, and I can't even get close.

I feel my eyes starting to well up again and slap myself lightly across the face. *Stop having a pity party! Grow up!* I can't keep freaking out like this; it isn't normal. I run through where I am in my head, taking note of the bathroom, the evening, the structure of my life. The past is the past, and I need some perspective on what's happening now. Sami isn't going to mention my dad again, and she has sworn on her grandmother's grave that she won't bring work up. It's an evening with my best friend and my boyfriend, and everything is going to be fine. I wash my hands with cold water and pat my eyes, willing the swelling to go down.

What's the worst that can happen?

Everything seems fine when I walk back into the kitchen. Sami is chatting to Ben about the last season of *House of Cards* (it's the one thing they are united on; Ben likes the politics and Sami likes getting outraged at the misogyny) and Ben is nodding encouragingly.

'I'm just gutted there won't be any more. Why did he have to be just another raging abuser? We'll find out David Attenborough's been touching up orangutans next.' Ben grabs a brownie from the plate in front of him and pops it into his mouth.

'*Right?* It's so disappointing. I just feel like, I don't know, I didn't expect it from him. He was so good in *Se7en.*'

I listen to them chat for a moment, feeling warm inside, before something dawns on me.

'Are those Sami's brownies?'

I already know the answer. I'm going to kill her.

'Oh, yeah, they're really good! Try one!' Ben reaches for another.

'No!' I snatch the plate off the table and put it on the kitchen counter. 'Oh my god, how many have you eaten?'

'Calm down, Bri.' Ben laughs. 'We're going for a hike tomorrow, aren't we?'

'Oh, Jesus. A *hike.*' Sami takes a slug of her chocolate wine and stumbles over to the plate of brownies, shoving another one into her mouth. 'Do you two ever do anything *fun*?'

'We really like the outdoors, actually,' Ben says curtly. 'There's more to life than getting fucked up, you know.'

Sami laughs and shoots a pointed glance at the brownies. 'You're a one to talk about getting fucked up.'

Oh my god. Someone has to tell him. We've got about half an hour until it kicks in.

'What's that supposed to mean?' Ben reddens. 'Just because I've had a few glasses of wine? It's called being civilised. Not

126

that you'd know what that means. I'm surprised you get through the day with your manners.'

'Oh!' Sami throws her hands into the air. 'That is fucking priceless. The high-flying man telling me how uncivilised I am. Let me get my camera, this is a real treat.'

'Grow up, Sami.' Ben snatches the half-eaten cheesecake plates off the table and stands up. 'Maybe if you stopped to listen to how annoying the sound of your own voice actually is, you wouldn't love it so much.'

'Oh, fuck off, Ben. Fuck you and your moral high horse. You think you're so *brilliant,* don't you? Well, you're not. We all know you're cheating on Briony.'

Silence rings in the air. The tap drips once and then stops.

'Get out.' Ben's fist clenches.

'Oh, what? You haven't spoken about it? Come on. She knows, I know, *you* certainly know.' Sami laughs coarsely, her face twisted.

I feel like I'm watching a play. It's like I'm not in the room at all. All of this is happening to someone else, and I'm just a spectator.

'GET THE FUCK OUT OF MY HOUSE!' Ben roars, lunging forward and throwing the cheesecake plate at the wall.

I jump. 'Ben, please—'

'Now.' Ben grabs Sami by the elbow and marches her down the hallway. 'You come into my home and say disgusting things, trying to cause trouble. Is your life so void of meaning that you have to ruin your best friend's, too? You're toxic . . .'

I stay standing in the kitchen as his voice disappears towards the front door. I can hear Sami responding, their voices high and angry, but I can't make out the words any more. I don't want to know what they're saying.

There's a final screech, and then the front door slams shut.

17

'She's punishing you, you know.' Ben's head is lolling back on the sofa, his eyes closed.

He is *so* high.

'Punishing me for what?' I'm nursing the last of the chocolate wine. My hands are still shaking.

'For having a life outside of her. For working hard and having hobbies and interests.'

Something in me sags with relief. He still thinks I'm interesting. He thinks I work hard. He thinks I have *hobbies*, for god's sake.

'I don't think so. I think she's just sure of herself.'

This is usually the point when Ben tells me Sami isn't just sure of herself, she's a twat.

'Oh, god, does it even matter?' He smiles up at the ceiling. 'Does any of it matter? The universe is expanding and we're all hurtling towards death. It's magical.'

He starts giggling suddenly. 'Magical. *Magical*. What a weird word.'

He's crying with laughter now. Oh, good. He's even better than me at *weed*.

'Jesus, how much have I had to drink?' he says eventually, his eyes streaming. 'That chocolate stuff is lethal.'

'It is.' I rub his arm. 'Shall we get you to bed?'

'Mmm. Good idea.'

I help him up the stairs and out of his clothes, and his breathing deepens as soon as his head hits the pillow. He's out like a light.

I tiptoe back downstairs and clear up, my phone on the kitchen table, beckoning me.

I should text Sami. I should try to make amends before this spirals. I bet she's so angry with me for not sticking up for her. But why did she have to say that? It wasn't her accusation to make.

I sweep the shards of plate off the floor and into the bin. Or is Ben annoyed with me for not sticking up for *him?* He didn't seem it, but then again he was incredibly baked. We haven't talked about what Sami said; Ben stormed upstairs after she left and when he emerged he was beyond reasonable conversation. He'll remember it tomorrow, I'm sure.

And then we'll have to sit down and address it.

Once all the dangerous pieces of china are safely in the bin, I leave the rest of the washing up and take my phone into the living room. I have a text from Wiggy.

Wiggy: *Why are you ignoring me? Please call me as soon as you get this. I need to speak to you.*

I delete the text and, on an impulse fuelled by a need for distraction, open my chat with Jordan.

Me: *Hey. Weird evening over here. How are you?*

Jordan: *Ooh, drama? Hope you're all right. Call me if you need me.*

Jordan: *Or better still, come out! I'm in town.*

Me: *Drama, YES. Feel awful, going to stick it out here. Thanks for the offer, though. Another time?*

Jordan: *Oh, I guarantee it ;)*

I smile. I feel better, suddenly. There's something about Jordan. It's not that he doesn't make me nervous – he does – it's that the nerves I feel are stripped back. There's a removal of expectation.

But can I trust him? And is it wrong of me not to tell Ben that I've got these new friends? There's nothing remotely romantic between Jordan and me, but telling him would mean explaining the group sessions and why I had to leave work. He'd think I was the worst person on the planet.

I pull out my laptop and do some more work on my personal project. It's important that I keep coding; just a small amount of time off and you forget almost everything. It's like a muscle you just have to keep exercising. Plus, doing this keeps me distracted and motivated – it gives me a purpose outside of hating myself.

I manage an hour of work before my phone buzzes with a text from Sami.

Sami: *Total shit show this evening, hey? Cheers for the ASS-oulet.*

I lock my phone again. I don't know if she's joking, or whether she's angry with me, but I suddenly can't be bothered trying to figure it out.

It's Tuesday again, and I'm on my way to group.

My emotions are mixed and weird. I'm happy, because I'm going to see Jordan and Sarah, and because Ben hasn't mentioned Sami's allegations once since Saturday night. But also I'm sad, because, while him not mentioning it means I get to avoid a horrible conversation and the potential demise of my relationship, it also means he hasn't denied it. He hasn't flat-out told me it isn't true.

I'm also sad because I woke up to a text from my dad this morning.

It said: *Happy fathrr day to the biggist disapointment of a daugeter.*

It isn't even Father's Day.

The church hall looks different when I walk in; all the chairs have been pushed against the wall and everyone is hovering around the huge expanse of carpet in the middle of the room. I spot Jordan and Sarah next to the biscuits and hurry over.

'Briony!' Jordan booms, looping his arm around my shoulders. I feel awkward and stiff, and suddenly desperate to leave. 'What are we in for today then, do you reckon?'

'Hiya.' I look at Sarah and she smiles weakly back at me from under her fringe. 'Where's Fran?'

'She's gone to get "the props", apparently.' Jordan laughs. 'Honestly, I've never been so excited.'

My stomach twists. What props? Why don't we have seats?

'Hello, Sarah.' Geoff has sidled over to us, a chocolate bourbon between his fingers. 'Why haven't you been replying to my messages?'

Sarah stares at the floor.

'I've had a really difficult week, you know. I had a panic attack at the butcher's. All those *ribs* . . .' He shudders. 'And where were you? Hiding, as usual.'

'Woah, come on, mate.' Jordan takes his arm from around me and steps forward. 'Maybe she wasn't feeling up to it.'

'That's because she's *avoidant*.' Geoff wags his finger. 'You haven't been here long, son, I'll ask you to keep your nose out until you understand the way this works.'

'The way this works is however Sarah *wants* it to work, Geoff,' Jordan seethes. 'Leave her alone.'

'Excuse *me*! I've never been spoken to so rudely in my entire *life*—'

'Good afternoon, everybody!' Fran emerges from the back room and stops Geoff mid-flow. Her arms are full of ribbons. 'How are we all today?'

There is total silence, broken only by Jordan saying, 'Good, cheers.'

'Great! Now, you'll have noticed things seem a little bit different today. We are shaking up the usual circle format and moving on to the next level.'

Fran starts walking slowly around the room, depositing pieces of ribbon around the floor.

'Now, I know that most of you have trouble with public

131

speaking. *Performance anxiety.* Addressing a room full of people, holding a conversation in a busy environment. It's a common manifestation of social anxiety and many of our preoccupations can centre around the voice, or non-verbal cues. Today, we are going to alleviate those worries by not speaking *at all.*' Fran beams and everyone stares back, nonplussed and, undoubtedly, panicking.

'Interpretive dance!' she wails, throwing her arms out to the side. 'You are each going to perform a dance to demonstrate how it feels to live with social anxiety.'

No. No, no, no. I won't. I can't and I won't.

I feel Sarah shrink beside me.

'Now, who wants to go first?' Fran scans the group. 'Not entirely surprising that there are no volunteers! I must remember that I'm not at my *Amateur Dramatics for ADHD* class. Geoff! What about you?'

Geoff balks. His judgmental demeanour disappears and leaves him looking like a rabbit in headlights. A slight twinge of satisfaction nudges against my anxiety.

'Come on, you can choose the song!' Fran squats down next to a laptop, which is hooked up to the speaker system. I am suddenly reminded of school discos. 'What's your favourite?'

'Erm, "Eye of the Tiger",' Geoff mumbles.

'Confident! Good!' Fran loads the song up and the familiar opening guitar riff fills the room. 'Come on then, show us what your anxiety feels like.'

Geoff stumbles shakily forward and stands, stock-still, in the middle of the carpet. I cringe so hard I think I might faint.

'Grab some ribbons, let's see what you've got!' Fran cheers.

Geoff bends down and picks up a long, pink ribbon. He wiggles it limply at the floor in time to the beat.

'Good! Good, I'm getting depressed, demotivated, de-energised.' Fran nods encouragingly. 'Now, get that body moving!'

The speakers pulse – *dum, dum dum dum* – and Geoff whips his ribbon half-heartedly in unison. He starts jerking his knee as the song screeches about the thrill of fighting, and his shoulders bob awkwardly.

This is the worst situation I have ever been in.

'Come on!' Fran shouts. 'Use the space, use the floor!'

Geoff slowly slides down until he is lying flat on his back, and then holds the ribbon in the air, wafting it about for the chorus. Fran claps along.

Geoff nods his head uncomfortably, bashing the back of his skull against the carpet with every beat. It's like watching a beetle try and roll over. He maintains this pose for a very long time, occasionally lifting the arm that isn't holding the ribbon and doing a half-hearted jazz hand.

As the song fades out, Fran stabs the pause button and we are plunged into silence. Geoff remains on the floor, the ribbon clutched limply in his outstretched fist.

'Good job, Geoff. A little more energy next time, perhaps, but a great try.'

'Oh my god,' Jordan whispers.

'Now, who's next?' Fran picks Stuart out of the group and he gyrates uncomfortably to Beethoven's dramatic fifth symphony. He is followed by an older woman, who actually does a pretty good job and obviously has some kind of dancing history. She does a full routine to 'The Fast Food Song', which I'm not sure demonstrates anxiety in any way, but Fran seems pleased.

'Sarah!' she croons, as soon as the older woman has left the stage.

Sarah doesn't budge.

'Come on, then. What's your pick?' Fran goes back to her computer. Sarah stays still.

'You OK?' I lean into her. 'You don't have to.'

'She does!' Fran screeches. 'Everyone has to participate. You can't expect progress if you don't try.'

'I don't want to,' Sarah mumbles. 'I'm sorry. I can't.'

'Of course you can!' Fran waves her over. 'Come on, come and choose your song.'

'No.' Sarah stands still, her face bright red.

Fran tuts. 'Sarah, we haven't got all day.'

'She doesn't want to,' Jordan says. 'I'll go.'

'No, Jordan, it isn't your turn.' Fran dismisses him. 'You'll have to *wait*. Now, Sarah, come on.'

What happened to *assertion*? I'm tempted to step in, and remind Fran that 'saying no' is apparently very important. But I can't. I hate myself for it, but I can't.

'No. Thank you.' Sarah moves backwards and her legs knock into the biscuit table.

'Sarah.' Fran sighs and comes towards us, reaching out her hand. 'Let's just get it over with.'

'NO!' Sarah screams, pushing Fran hard on the arm and running across the carpet, out of the door.

Fran gasps and holds her shoulder dramatically. 'She pushed me! Did you see that? She pushed me!'

I run after Sarah, Jordan right behind me. We burst through the main doors, Fran's wailing fading behind us.

Sarah is pacing the car park, her head in her hands.

'Are you all right?' I put my hand on her arm.

'No! No, I'm not fucking all right,' she snaps, moving away from us. 'It's never going to be all right and I'm sick of it.'

We watch her for a few moments as she walks back and forth. I can't tell if she's angry or anxious or both. Probably both.

'You know,' Jordan starts, taking a deep breath. Sarah looks up hopefully, ready to receive wisdom from somebody so obviously *not* ailed with whatever it is we've been cursed with. 'I'm just really gutted I didn't get to have a go.'

Sarah laughs and smacks him on the arm. 'Why do you even come here? There's nothing wrong with you.'

'Bleh, long story.' Jordan waves his hand. 'Why do *any* of us come here?'

'It's better than doing nothing, isn't it?' I say, and Sarah shoots me a smile.

'Yeah, but is it? She gives you a panic attack every single week, Sarah.' Jordan cocks his head.

'I can't just *give up*,' Sarah hisses, more to herself than to either of us. 'I can't just . . . *sit* there, and let this drown me. You wouldn't understand.'

Jordan looks hurt for a second.

'I didn't think you were coming back,' I blurt, feeling embarrassed as soon as it comes out of my mouth. I bet he thinks I've been obsessing over our conversation.

'And miss *this*?' he gasps. 'Never.'

'How are you feeling?' I try again with Sarah, who looks calmer.

'Better. Still pissed off, though.'

Jordan suddenly grabs us both by the arm. 'What are you both doing later? Let's go out.'

'I can't,' Sarah and I say at exactly the same time.

Jordan raises his eyebrows. 'Interesting. What are you doing? Briony?'

'I'm . . . I've . . . my boyfriend is expecting me, and—'

'Text him. Sarah?'

'I've got, erm, I mean, I need to do some washing, I think, and—'

'Great! So I'll see you at mine at eight? Can't wait.' Jordan winks and saunters out of the car park and up the street.

Sarah gawps. 'Has he just . . . gone?'

'I think so.'

'We can't go.' She looks at me worriedly.

'No, definitely not. I don't know what to wear. Or who will be there.'

'Exactly. We don't even know his address. Let's not go.'

'Yeah. Let's just go home.'

We stand in silence for a second and watch as Jordan disappears around the corner.

I should get back now. Ben will be home at seven and we should really have a chat about what Sami said the other night. I want to intercept him before he locks himself in his office again. I can cook some dinner and then when we've talked he can work and I can do some more bits on my project. If we haven't broken up by then, obviously. If we have, I'll just pack my stuff and go to Sami's.

My stomach feels like it's being wrenched out of my mouth at the thought of it.

'Or . . . you could come back to mine?' I say.

Sarah pauses. 'Yeah, I think I could do that. We could have a drink, maybe. And then go and meet Jordan if we feel like it.'

'If we feel like it, of course.' I nod.

Music starts pumping out of the open church hall door, and I glance inside to see Dom, an almost mute seventeen year old, shuffling awkwardly with a ribbon wrapped around his head.

'Let's go,' I say.

18

'I love your house,' Sarah says, as I run around picking up dirty mugs and launching them into the sink.

'Sorry, it's such a mess. I'm off work at the moment, and you sort of lose sight of the crap when you get used to it.'

'Honestly, it's fine.' She stacks the two toast-crumbed plates on the coffee table and carries them through to the kitchen. 'How long have you lived here?'

'Two years now. Only thirty-three left on the mortgage, which is exciting.' I rinse the cups out and load them into the dishwasher. 'Do you want a drink? I think we've got some wine somewhere . . .'

'Sure.' Sarah hovers awkwardly by the table as I fill our glasses, and I suddenly realise that my horror at having another human being in my space is probably nothing compared to her discomfort at being here and not knowing what to do with herself.

'Come on, let's go and sit down.' I lead her into the lounge and she perches on the sofa, taking one of the glasses from my hand.

'So what's Jordan's deal, do you reckon?' She nibbles on her fingernail.

'I don't know. I had coffee with him the other day and he said he was proving a point, or something. He said he was difficult.'

'I don't reckon he is. I'd kill for his confidence.'

'Same.' I take a sip of my drink and wonder whether Sarah is offended that Jordan and I got coffee without her. He was assigned as my support, though, and it was before he created the group WhatsApp a few days ago. 'Sorry I didn't think to invite you with us, I would have done—'

'Oh—' she waves me away '—don't worry about it. So what is it that you do?'

'I'm a software engineer,' I tell her. 'Well, I was.'

I explain the whole story and Sarah nods in sympathy.

'That sounds awful. I left work off my own back because it was all too much. I sort of wish I hadn't, though. The idea of going back is, like . . . terrifying.'

'God, I know.' I check my watch. It's half-past six. 'So, do you think we should go out? It's just, my boyfriend is due back at seven and he doesn't know about the group. So, obviously, he doesn't know about you. He doesn't know anything, actually.'

Sarah laughs. 'Fran would call that *conflict avoidance*.'

'Fran is even nuttier than we are.'

'True. But no, don't worry, I'll get out of your hair.' She stands up and puts her half-finished glass down. I suddenly don't want her to leave.

'You know, that wasn't me trying to get rid of you. I always think people are trying to get away from me, but I promise I'm not. Maybe we could go out with Jordan? If you're feeling up to it?'

Sarah pauses, twisting one of her rings around her finger. 'I don't have anything to wear.'

I open my mouth to offer her something of mine, but then I worry that she'll see my wardrobe and hate everything in it. Or that I'll lend her a dress and it'll have armpit stains on it and she'll think I'm disgusting. But she won't want to come out if she's in her jeans, and I really don't want to see Ben.

'Come on, I'll lend you something.'

She follows me up the stairs and I apologise again for the unmade bed and pyjamas on the floor.

'Right, so do you think a dress? Or a skirt? Or what?' I pull the wardrobe open.

'Oh, god, I don't know. What will Jordan be wearing? What will his friends be wearing?'

'I have no idea. It's Tuesday night, so maybe let's go smart-casual? Then you can wear your boots and borrow one of my dresses?'

I feel calmer about the clothes situation with Sarah here; we can wear similar things and then I won't stick out.

'OK.' She nods.

'Have a look through, choose anything.' I stand back to let her see.

'This is nice.' She pulls out the dress I wore for my date with Ben last week. The quirky, vintage dress that made him cringe at the sight of me. 'But I don't want to take something you like,' she says, misinterpreting the expression on my face. 'You wear that; I bet it looks lovely on you.'

'No, no, please. Wear it, I don't mind at all. Keep it, in fact.' I take it from its hanger and give it to her. 'It'll suit you better anyway.'

Sarah goes off to the bathroom to get changed and I change into a simple black dress; the kind of thing that no one can have an opinion about. As I'm pulling a pair of tights on, my phone buzzes.

Sami: *Out tonight with Julia et al. Come meet us in Font?*

I hesitate before messaging back.

Me: *Can't do tonight, sorry. Will call you tomorrow.*

She doesn't reply.

Sarah comes back into the bedroom. She looks incredible.

'You look amazing!' I enthuse. 'Red lipstick goes well with it; do you want to borrow some?'

'Do you reckon?' She studies herself in the mirror and laughs. 'Yeah, go on then.'

I go downstairs to get us some more wine and we patch our make-up up in the bathroom. By the time we're done it's almost seven, and I quickly remove all traces of Sarah from the house before we leave. I grab the bottle of wine for the road and we head out of the front door.

Sarah peers at her phone. 'Jordan's sent his address. It's in town. Why does he come all the way out here for a support group if he lives in town?'

I want to know the answer, too. I also want to know why Jordan wants to hang out with us both so badly. But bringing that up with Sarah would imply that I think *she* isn't worth his time either, and I don't want to do that.

'Let's ask him. Come on, we'll get an Uber round the corner just in case Ben sees us.'

I feel like I'm having an affair. I messaged Ben in the taxi to say that I was going round to Sami's, and I am now knocking on the door of an apartment in the middle of the city centre.

What if something happens to me? What if I'm abducted and nobody knows what my last movements were? They'd be able to track me on GPS, I'm sure, or the phone towers or something. But what if Ben tries to track me *now,* and thinks I'm bonking someone else or buying weed?

Or, more likely, what if he's annoyed with me for going round to Sami's? Her name hasn't been mentioned in our house since the dinner party. Would seeing her be a betrayal? What if he drives over there to bring me home?

'Hey!' Jordan is suddenly standing in the doorway in front of us, and for a second I don't recognise him again. He's wearing a long, brown, curly wig and his lips are over-lined, giving him a gigantic pout. The shimmering mini dress and platform silver heels he's wearing put mine and Sarah's outfits to shame.

'Come in, come in.' Jordan steps back and ushers us into the hallway. The walls are vibrating with the sound of a heavy bass coming from a room up the corridor. Oh my god. There are going to be so many people here. It all makes sense now; we're just additions. Jordan is the kind of person who can invite everyone he meets to his house, because the boring ones will just get swallowed up in the crowd anyway. I'm going to end up perched on the edge of an armchair looking lost and awkward for the entire evening. All of Jordan's cool friends will stare at me and whisper about the odd girl in the flat boots with the middle-aged-Karen hair.

I drain the last few drops of wine from the bottle.

'Come on through!' Jordan leads us down the corridor but Sarah hangs back.

'You OK?' I murmur, and Jordan stops and turns around.

'I don't think I can do it.' Sarah shakes her head.

'I promise it's not a scary living room.' Jordan laughs kindly. 'The sofa's a pretty alarming shade of green, but you really can't blame me for that; it's a rental.'

'We can go back if you like? I can call you a taxi?' I try, touching Sarah's arm.

'No, it's OK. Sorry, it's just all the people.'

'What people?' Jordan frowns and then raises his eyebrows. 'Oh, don't worry about that.'

He opens the living room door and the bass gets louder.

'Look!' he shouts over the noise.

I peer inside.

There's nobody there.

The entire room is empty, save for the furniture and a pulsing speaker. Jordan walks over and turns the volume down. 'It's just me! No party.'

I feel my shoulders drop. Thank *god*. Sarah steps into the room and sits down on the infamous acid-green sofa.

'See! No problem. What do you want to drink?' Jordan sets about with an expensive-looking cocktail mixer in the kitchen, and I wander over to the windows. The view is incredible; he lives right in the centre of town, thirteen storeys up, and a sea of twinkling lights stretches out as far as I can see.

'Here.' Jordan hands me a glass. 'My secret recipe.'

'Oh my god, what do you *do*?' I blurt, looking around me. Now that my fears have been squashed I am noticing how posh this place is. There are solid wood floors, faux-beams and exposed brick. It's apartment porn.

'Ha. Nobody ever asks me that until they come here.' He slurps on his cocktail.

'Sorry. God, that's really rude, isn't it? I don't know why I didn't ask earlier.' Heat rushes to my face. I assumed that Jordan did drag professionally, which was so narrow-minded of me. But maybe I'm right? It must be a bloody good gig. 'If it's any consolation, I don't know what Sarah does either.'

They both know what I do, don't they? I'm so selfish. I bet they've both thought I'm totally self-involved since the day they met me.

'I worked at NatWest.' Sarah rolls her eyes. 'Please don't try and be polite by asking about it; it really is as boring as it sounds.'

'I'm a lawyer,' Jordan says, and me and Sarah stare at him. 'Surprised?'

'No! No, not surprised. Not surprised at all,' I flap, even though my jaw is on the floor. 'You're very . . . lawyer-y.'

He throws his head back and laughs loudly. 'No, I'm not. It's fine, honestly, I love the look on people's faces when I tell them. You've given me a gift.'

'What kind of law do you practise?' Sarah asks.

'Family law. Custody, child protection, divorce, that kind of thing,' he nods.

'Do you get to wear one of those grey wigs?' I say, regretting it immediately. What kind of ridiculous question is that?

'No—' he pulls at his hair '—I save that for the evenings, sweetie.'

I laugh.

'Do you usually go out on weekdays?' Sarah asks, and I remember it's a Tuesday. I remember last week, meeting him outside Afflecks in the middle of the working day.

'Sometimes.' Jordan sits down on a high-backed armchair. 'So. The interpretive dance.'

Sarah shudders. 'Don't even talk about it.'

'What planet is that woman on? Honestly?'

'She calls it flooding.' Sarah sighs. 'Apparently if you're over-whelmed by something that scares you, it snaps you out of it.'

'Oh, wow. Tell that to ex-soldiers.'

'Right? It's Freudian, apparently.'

'The same Freud who thinks we all fancy our mums and like tidiness because we couldn't shit when we were babies?'

Sarah laughs. 'The very same.'

'I know I said this earlier, but why do you keep going back?' Jordan flicks a stray hair out of his eye. 'There must be other groups.'

Sarah shoots me a glance. Now would be the time to ask why Jordan doesn't find support round here. There must be tonnes of it. But it takes me too long to figure out a way to ask, so Sarah jumps in.

'There aren't any other groups within walking distance from me.' She shrugs. 'I was thinking of trying to get referred some-where, maybe.'

'So you weren't referred to the group by your GP?' Jordan asks.

'No, why? Were you two?' She looks at us both.

'No,' we respond at the same time. I wonder how an NHS-funded group can run without GP referrals.

'Are you getting anything from the sessions, Jordan?' I ask. My voice sounds very loud.

'I'm getting some first-rate entertainment.' He smiles, and then shakes his head. 'Sorry, it's not funny for you guys, I know.'

'Why do you even come?' Sarah asks kindly.

There's an almost imperceptible beat of silence before Jordan responds. 'Not sure, really.' He stands up, plucking our half-full glasses out of our hands and taking them to the kitchen. 'Things aren't as . . . *rosy* as they seem. You have to try one of my caipirinhas. They're legendary.'

'What do you mean?' I press. I want answers. I want to know what problems he could possibly have.

'Oh, nothing. I'm just trying a few things out, that's all. Bits and bobs here and there.'

He starts shaking the cocktail mixer, drowning out any further questions we might have had. He isn't making any sense.

'Why don't you go to a group in town?' Sarah asks finally, once he's poured the drinks. I feel a swell of relief that it's finally been said; I won't be the one who has to ask now.

Jordan brightens, as if the question is easier somehow. 'Won't bump into anyone I know, will I?'

'Does Aiden know you go to group?' I wonder.

'Of course. I tell Aiden everything.' He looks at Sarah. 'My boyfriend.'

'Sorry,' I say, realising how rude we're being. 'We're really quizzing you.'

'Don't apologise!' He laughs, and raises his glass. 'Cheers. So, what do you fancy doing?'

'I don't mind,' I say, glancing at Sarah. I'm quite happy here, but I don't want to be a party pooper.

'Me neither,' she says.

'Well, I didn't get all dressed up for nothing.' He throws his cocktail back and swallows it in three big gulps. 'Drink up, let's go.'

19

I think Sarah and I may have developed the same coping strate-
gies. I'm on my fifth shot of tequila; she's on her sixth.

We're in Tasha's, a gay bar on Canal Street, and even though
it's Tuesday the place is packed. Jordan has managed to wangle
us a booth in the corner and he is getting attention left, right
and centre.

He's in his element, chatting and laughing and batting away
anyone who tries to come and squeeze into our sofa seats.
There's only us three, Aiden and a girl called Priya, who is
shouting into my ear.

'So how do you know Jordan?'

'We met through a friend!' I scream back, not knowing how
much Jordan would want me to share. It's sort of true; Fran is
a mutual acquaintance.

'Oh, cool!' She nods in time to the music.

'What about you?' I try.

'We've been friends since primary school. And yes, before
you ask, he's always been a total enigma.'

I laugh, imagining a tiny, four-year-old Jordan, confidently
telling the teacher he thought her alphabet book was bollocks.
I can't think of anything more to say, so I go back to staring
into my drink while Priya watches the dance floor, tapping

her foot. Does she want to dance? I glance around the group. Sarah is talking to Aiden, and Jordan is resisting being dragged towards the stage to give an impromptu performance, shouting, 'If you're not paying me, I'm not doing it, Andy. I've *told* you!'

I feel really boring. If I were another version of me, a better version, I'd grab Sarah and Priya and head over to the dance floor, not giving a shit about anything but the music and having a good time. But I'm not in a parallel universe, and I'd probably end up on an epic fail video on YouTube.

I wonder if I'll *ever* be fun. Maybe this is just me; maybe trying to be better is pointless. Perhaps it's something in my DNA. I'm just a wallflower. But surely the fact that I feel like I *want* to dance means that there's something inside me pushing against my fear?

Sarah has stopped talking to Aiden, so I lean into her ear. 'Drink?'

We slide out of the booth and head over to the bar, ordering four more shots of tequila and knocking them back. I feel quite drunk now. I've had one and a half cocktails and seven shots of tequila in under an hour.

'I feel like I want to dance,' shouts Sarah.

'Me too!' I squeal. 'But I can't. I'll make a tit of myself.'

'Ugh, god, don't you *hate* it?' She leans in and blasts my eardrum. 'Don't you just fucking hate feeling like you've got to censor yourself all the time for no reason?'

'YES!' I nod, wanting to cry with how right she is. 'It's so, so shit. Who are we doing it for?'

'I don't know! I don't bloody know!' She runs her hand through her hair and I see her face for the first time, released from the veil of her fringe.

We watch as Jordan finally shakes Andy and weaves his way towards us. 'Come on, let's dance!'

'No, no,' I protest, and Sarah shakes her head.

'OK, no pressure.' He grins. 'You can just watch, you'll enjoy it more anyway.'

He snakes onto the dance floor, moving to the beat with such incredible rhythm that I'm almost sad Fran didn't give him a chance at his interpretive dance performance earlier on. His heels are higher than any I've ever worn, but he moves as though he's barefoot. It feels like everyone in the bar is watching him and – the most alien concept of all – he seems to be loving it.

'*Fuck*,' Sarah groans next to me. 'He's making me feel even *worse*.'

'No!' I cry, grabbing her by the shoulders. 'We're cool, Sarah! We're really cool. We're women in our twenties so we're literally in, like, the top ten per cent of coolest people on the planet by definition.'

She grimaces. 'Not true.'

'Girls!' Jordan calls over to us from where he is gyrating with Priya. 'Come on, give it a go!'

I shake my head fiercely. I can't. I suddenly feel like I'm watching myself from above; a girl standing next to a dance floor, young and free, an open invitation to step forward and enjoy herself with two kind people. A chance to just *let go*.

I imagine what might happen if I joined them. I could dance and move and get out of my own head for a second. Or, I could jerk my arms about, fall on the floor, have everyone pointing and laughing at me. The image of people sneering from the corner of the room is suddenly so vivid, my heart starts hammering.

'I'm doing it!' shouts Sarah, rushing over to Jordan.

I'm alone. I feel like a contestant on *I'm a Celebrity*, the last one to be picked for a terrifying bushtucker trial. Not doing it will let my teammates down; I'll look sour and boring. Isn't boring everything I'm trying not to be?

Maybe one more shot of tequila.

I turn around to get the bartender's attention, but, before he sees me, a man is by my side.

'You looking?' He keeps his head forward, but his eyes dart towards me.

'Sorry? No, I'm not looking for anyone. My friends are over there.' I gesture behind me, where Sarah is shuffling self-consciously, a little smile playing on her face.

'Mandy?' He edges a little closer to me.

'No, I'm *Briony*,' I bellow into his ear. The music is so loud, he's obviously struggling to hear me.

'No. Are you looking for *Mandy*?' He holds his hand out under the bar and I see a small white pill nestled in his palm.

I freeze. No, this is bad. I need to get away from this man as soon as possible.

I shake my head and make to move away, but then I remember Sami and Julia. Dancing like nothing mattered, getting cross with me the next day for moaning about my hangover when I hadn't touched anything harder. What use is being assertive and sticking to your values? It's got me nowhere. I glance over to my group again; Jordan has Sarah by the hands and is spinning her round and round, her head thrown back and her mouth wide open, laughing. Why can't that be me? The tequila isn't helping, and after seven shots I'm not sure adding more to my system will be any use.

Maybe I just need a boost?

I reach into my bag for my purse. 'How much?' I ask.

'Twenty.' He rolls the pill between his thumb and forefinger.

This is good. This is definitely what I should be doing. I'm twenty-eight and my shoulders are so tight I feel like I might snap. I'm in a bar with new friends and taking drugs is just commonplace; it's normal. It's what people do. I want to be part of the crowd, like Sami and Julia, not overthinking everything and worrying about cheating boyfriends and disastrous meetings. I want to live in the moment.

'Here.' I reach out to give him two ten-pound notes, but before he has time to take them, a hand reaches between us and snatches them out of my grasp.

'What the fuck are you doing?' Jordan is looming over us, his face red and angry.

The guy turns on his heel and disappears quickly into the crowd.

'I was just buying some drugs,' I say, my voice thick.

'Are you joking?' He pushes the notes back into my hand. 'You think that'll make you feel better? You think that's a good path to go down?'

'No, I—'

'How do you think you'll feel tomorrow? You think you'll wake up cured?' He's livid. 'You'll feel fifty times worse than you do now, trust me.'

'What's going on?' Sarah has appeared and is peering at us nervously.

'Briony was buying shit off some guy.'

'What?' Sarah looks horrified. 'Do you . . . do you do that a lot?'

'No!' I feel like crying. They're not reacting like I expected them to. I thought they'd think I was brave and carefree. Instead, they're looking at me like I've just murdered someone. 'I've never done it before. I just wanted to dance.'

'We're leaving.' Jordan takes Sarah and me by the hand and pulls us towards the door, stepping around the bouncer and depositing us out on the street.

'I'm sorry.' I can't stop the tears now; they're streaming down my cheeks. 'I've ruined your night.'

And I have. I've ruined everything, *again*.

'*My* night?' Jordan looks at me, his expression softening. 'Fuck my night, Briony. You'd have ruined your own head for days. You can't do things like that, not when you've got an anxiety disorder.'

'I don't have a disorder!' I shout, suddenly angry. I'm so fucking angry, I could punch something. 'Nobody knows what's wrong with me! I'm messed up and that's never going to change.'

Sarah crushes me into a hug. 'No. No, that's not true.'

'It is!' I wail. 'This is never going to get better. I'm missing out on everything. I'm missing work, a career, a healthy relationship, an entire *life*.'

149

I walk over to the railings overlooking the canal and bury my head in my hands. 'I just wanted to dance,' I sob.

'I'm sorry.' Jordan wraps his arms around me, leaning his head on my shoulder. 'This was too much for you.'

'It shouldn't be too much, though.' I feel weary, and I suddenly just want Jordan to hold me and hug me and transfer some part of himself into my brain. His comfort with physical contact is alien to me, and I long for it. I'm tired of going rigid when someone gets too close. 'Going out with friends shouldn't be too much.'

Jordan releases me and steps back. I turn around and lean against the railings.

'You wanted to dance?' he says, a glint in his eye.

'Yes, but—'

'Then let's dance.' He holds his hand out to me.

I look at him, and then survey the street. It's middle-of-the-week empty apart from a bouncer every couple of doors, most of whom are on their phones.

'I can't, it's weird.'

'We're all weird, Briony.' He keeps his hand held out to me.

I look at Sarah. She nods. I glance around me again, checking for people, for cameras, for potential danger. I can't do this. I can't, I can't, I can't.

I'm sick of saying *I can't.*

I step forward and take his hand, my heart pounding. My stomach flips as my skin makes contact with his. When was the last time I held someone's hand? Ben barely comes near me any more. It's a balm, the touch of another person. Without the lust and expectation, it's a safety net. A physical manifestation of 'I'm here'.

Jordan lifts his arm up and spins me round, grabbing my other hand and stepping, twice forward, once back, up the street. He moves his hips and I copy. He lets go of me and shimmies, all the way to the floor and back up again, his face alive and happy. I laugh, instinctively, and do the same.

150

'Yes!' He grabs my hands again and we move up the street, two steps forwards and one step back, the music changing every time we pass a different bar. I feel my boots tapping against the cobbles under my feet, and I move from side to side, swaying. Sarah follows us, laughing.

We keep moving, up and up, left onto a bridge. We reach the middle, where the moonlight is sparkling on the water and the music is faint and muddled. Jordan lets go of my hands and stands back.

'Go, Briony. Go!'

I stand on the bridge, throw my head back, and dance.

20

I swap my usual coffee for peppermint tea; my head is pounding and caffeine will only make it worse.

Last night was incredible. Sarah, Jordan and I danced on the bridge until Jordan nearly toppled into the canal, and then we sat, swinging our legs over the water and chatting about Sarah's job and the irony of someone with social anxiety having to deal with people all day.

Ben was asleep when I got home, and when I woke up at seven thirty, he'd already left. I want to feel upset about it – he's obviously avoiding me – but mainly I just feel relieved; we can't address the inevitable if we're never in the same room.

I move over to the sink to pour myself a glass of water, but I stop as something catches my eye. There's a note next to the tap.

Morning! We keep missing each other. Shall we go for a hike on Saturday? I think it'd be good to talk. Love you, B x

I sit at the kitchen table, cradling my tea. This is it, then. I've received my summons; my day of execution has been scheduled. At some point on Saturday, when I am up to my knees in cow shit, being battered by the wind, Ben is going to tell me he's leaving me for a woman with shiny hair who has never had a spot in her life. She probably thinks spots are a life choice, they're so alien to her. Maybe he'll bring her along for support? Perhaps he'll hide her in a stable somewhere, and then take me inside and produce her, like a prize pig, before he asks if we can still be friends.

How will I react? It won't be good. I'll cry, and then probably throw myself off the nearest cliff. I can't live without Ben. Ben is everything. He's the only thing that keeps me tethered to a better idea of myself. I'll have to walk back down the hill alone, falling on my arse in front of them both, and then where will I go? I don't have anywhere but here.

I picture myself rattling around Sami's flat while she's at work, wearing one of Ben's old shirts and making voodoo dolls of his new girlfriend. But would Sami even have me? She isn't texting me as much, and I won't have the money to pay rent once I'm finally, inevitably, fired.

It's less than a week until I go back to work now. The thought jolts into my head, breaking my thought process, and a faint pain shoots across my stomach. I can't think about it.

My phone is lying on the table where I dumped it last night. I unlock it and find three missed calls from my dad, stamped 00:23, 02:46 and 03:02. It was a long night for him, then. I should have been there for him. The guilt is overwhelming. But then, I know how it ends.

No. I will not let myself drown in this again. I finally felt like myself last night, and I can't let whatever that feeling was slip away. I quickly reply to another text from Wiggy, asking him to leave me alone, and go onto the group chat.

Me: *Such a good night last night, guys. Sorry I nearly ruined it by trying to buy Class As.*

Jordan: *I'm hanging out my arse. Can we get food?*

I wonder briefly why he isn't at work, but then remember that he can probably meet us on his lunch break.

Sarah: *Only if we can get burgers. A burger is the only thing that will save my soul.*

Me: *Just let me know when and where, and I'll be there.*

We agree on 12:30, at Almost Famous. I smile. This is good. If I've got something to look forward to, I can get through the day.

I go to lock my phone, but another message comes through. It isn't from the group chat.

Sami: *Hey, stranger. Why do I feel like it's been ten years since I've spoken to you? What are you doing? Come and meet me on my break?*

Oh, god. What am I supposed to do? I've just agreed to meet Sarah and Jordan, but I don't want Sami to feel like I'm palming her off for something better. I need to see her. We should talk about what she said to Ben the other night, and then we can move on from it and go back to how we were. I hope she isn't angry with me. If Ben leaves me, she's all I've got.

But I really want to see Jordan and Sarah, too.

Me: *Hiya! I can meet for half an hour at 12ish? I've got some stuff to work on.*

I hope she buys it. I don't want her to know I'm meeting other people.

Sami: *OK, meet me outside my building.*

I look at the clock. I need to be on the bus in four hours. That's plenty of time to catch up on last night's soaps.

I wander through to the living room and reach for the TV remote. It's sitting on top of my laptop, and I pause. I can watch *Coronation Street* later, can't I? I should do something productive; something that will take make me feel strong and purposeful, so I can hold on to the slither of myself I found last night.

I put the remote down and pick up my computer.

Balls to Wiggy; I've got my own project.

Sami is ten minutes late.

I'm standing in the lobby of her building, trying desperately not to look like a terrorist. Sami works in some top-secret, high security building. She does marketing for GCHQ or something. I've already paced around outside, but it's freezing, and now I'm standing in the foyer next to the radiator, willing her to emerge.

One of the security guys looks over at me. I move to the left, half-hiding behind an indoor plant. He frowns. I reach out and

154

stroke its leaves, as if I'm here to inspect the foliage. What is wrong with me? Why don't I just tell him I'm waiting for a friend? This is like the airport security queue. Even though I know I'm innocent, I always panic that I've got ten grams of coke up my bum that I've forgotten about.

'Can I help you?' the security guard calls, moving towards me.

'I'm meeting someone!' I shout, panicked. Oh, good. Now I look totally normal.

'Who is it? I can call up.' He studies me warily.

'Sami Jones, she's in marketing, she's my friend and we've known each other for ages. Since primary school. She said to meet at twelve but she's late. I don't know where she is. Is this Barrow House? Am I in the right place?'

Oh my god. *Stop talking!* One of my biggest fears is that I'll one day be interviewed by the police and will somehow manage to incriminate myself despite all the overwhelming evidence that it wasn't me.

'Briony!' Sami strides through the lobby, flashing a smile at the security team. 'Sorry, she's waiting for me.'

'I thought he was going to taser me,' I murmur, shakily, as she loops her arm through mine and walks me outside.

'What, Greg? Why would he taser you?'

'Because it's suspicious, me hanging around your building like that.'

Sami lets go of my arm and turns to face me. '*How* is it suspicious? What is wrong with your brain?'

'Nothing, no, never mind,' I say, my face getting hot. 'Shall we get a coffee? I've got to go soon.'

'Where do you have to go?' She narrows her eyes at me.

'I've got some stuff to work on . . .'

'Do it later.' She smiles, pleased with herself, and then links my arm again. 'Let's get our favourite.'

My heart swells. This feels like old times, me and Sami heading off to get caramel lattes on our lunch breaks. We used to do it most weeks, when she had time.

'OK, come on then.' I start walking but she pulls me back.

'Wait, Julia isn't here yet.'

'Oh. I didn't realise Julia was coming,' I say, my stomach sinking.

'Yeah. Why, is that a problem?' Sami raises her eyebrows at me, daring me to slag off brilliant bloody Julia.

'No! No, of course not. It'll be lovely.'

'Sorry!' Julia comes tearing out of the building, her hair following close behind. 'I'm here, I'm here.'

She pushes herself between Sami and me, and begins. 'So, where are we going? Did you say caramel lattes, Samuel? Do you think I could get hazelnut? I always think hazelnut has that slightly salty edge to it, don't you? Caramel can get a bit sickly. Have you ever tried orange syrup? You should have it in a mocha; it literally tastes like a chocolate orange. Which café are we going to? I've got until one o'clock; shall we get a panini, too?'

'Oooh, yeah, let's get lunch,' Sami says.

I want to scream. 'I can't, actually.'

'Why? Just do your work later,' Sami mutters as we round the corner.

'I'm . . . I've got to meet someone about the project,' I lie. I need a fixed time or I'll never get away.

'What project?' Julia gasps as we push through the doors and into the warmth of the café. 'Did you get your job back?'

I never lost my job, you annoying, insensitive dick! I almost shout, but I hold my tongue, shocked by how strong my internal reaction is. 'I've still got my job. I just haven't gone back yet.'

'So who are you meeting?' Sami sits down at a spare table and digs around in her purse, pulling out a few pound coins. 'Here, Bri, would you get me a caramel latte, if you're going up?'

'Oh. OK, yeah, of course.' I take the money.

'Get me a hazelnut one.' Julia thrusts a fiver into my hand.

'OK.' I start to walk over to the counter, but Sami calls after me.

'Actually, Bri, make mine a hazelnut, too.'

I nod, and join the back of the queue. Emotion is swirling around inside me. What am I, the skivvy? And since when do

156

we drink hazelnut lattes? I try to tell myself it's fine, Sami can have whatever she wants, and I was the last person to sit down, but I am suddenly electric with anger.

I order and pay, and watch as the barista loads three tall glasses onto my tray. *Come on, Briony, get some perspective. Someone has to get the drinks, and someone has to keep the table, it's the way it works. And Julia wasn't being rude before, she was just taking an interest in you. Don't burn your bridges; you haven't got many left.*

I take the tray over to the table and divvy up the change, and Sami and Julia sit back and sip their lattes, continuing their conversation.

'God, you're right, hazelnut *is* better.' Sami nods appreciatively.

I sting from the dig. Was it intentional? I want to bring up what happened the other night, but I can't, not with Julia here.

'How's Ben?' Sami asks sweetly, as if she's read my mind.

'Fine, yeah.'

'Oooh, did you find out whether he's cheating on you?' Julia pipes up. 'I'd go mad if Dan cheated on me. I'd literally rip his balls off. Can you imagine? The fucking *shame* of it—'

'He's not cheating on me,' I say loudly, surprising myself. My hands are shaking. How dare Sami talk to Julia about this stuff? How could she do that to me? No, I mustn't get wound up. They're friends, of course they talk about things. It's normal. And I'm their friend too, aren't I?

'Briony.' Sami cocks her head at me, a pitying smile on her face. 'He didn't even deny it.'

'Well, he isn't,' is all I can say. How do I know? I'm almost certain that he is.

Sami tuts. 'Always in denial, this one.'

They fall back into conversation about a girl at work whose boyfriend had an affair with her best friend for three years without her noticing. I try to block out the noise and lean forward to take a sip of my drink, not trusting myself to use my hands; they're shaking so much it'll slop all over the table. It's too low down,

I can't reach. Sami watches me through the corner of her eye.

'If he's not cheating on you—' Sami turns to face me '—then you'll be introducing him to your dad soon, won't you?'

My heart stops. She didn't, did she? She didn't bring my dad up. Not in front of Julia. I must have misheard.

'Aw, yeah, your dad.' Julia pouts at me, her eyebrows crinkled in sympathy. 'Are you worried he'll see what he's let himself in for?' She laughs.

Time seems to stop. I feel sick. Am I the office gossip fodder? Is my entire life just a big, juicy titbit to divulge around the water cooler? My entire body starts to shake. She's *discussed* me. She's told Julia something only she knows about, something I have never had the guts to show anybody else, not even my own boyfriend. And it evidently meant so little to her, she hasn't even bothered to tell Julia not to bring it up. How could she do that to me?

My head is singing with pain. My breath comes in sharp, short gasps, and radio static crowds my ears. My vision closes, slowly, from the sides, until I can't see at all. All I can feel are the eyes, everywhere, staring.

'Are you OK?' Julia's hand is on my back. I can't breathe.

I can hear them asking me questions, but it's like I'm underwater. I tuck my head between my legs, struggling, my heart slamming against my ribs. *Come on, Briony. You've done this before. It's OK. You're OK.*

Gradually, everything seems to melt. My teeth are chattering and my hands are limp and sweaty in my lap. I sit up; Julia and Sami are staring at me in horror.

'What was *that?*' Julia asks.

I reach for my latte, spilling it everywhere as I raise it to my lips. I drink it down in four shaky gulps, feeling the soft sweetness ping against my tongue, reminding me that I am here.

I stand up. 'Don't *ever* talk about my father,' I hiss, leaning over, slamming my glass back down on the table. 'And for the record—' I shrug my coat on and swing my bag onto my shoulder '—caramel is better than fucking hazelnut.'

21

'Bloody hell.' Jordan is staring at me, his mouth hanging open. 'You actually said "caramel is better than fucking hazelnut"?'

'Yes!' I'm shouting a bit, and I keep bouncing up and down on my chair like I've got a UTI. I walked into Almost Famous on a colossal adrenaline high, which has peaked again as I've told Jordan and Sarah what happened at the café. I left out the part about my dad, obviously.

Sarah sighs. 'I think I might be in love with you.'

'I'm so *angry*,' I seethe, waving my burger around. 'How dare she? How dare she talk about my private life with other people?'

Jordan claps his hands gleefully. 'I'm obsessed with you when you're like this. Actually obsessed.'

'I didn't know you were worried about Ben.' Sarah frowns. 'That must have been really difficult.'

'It was. It is.' I ram a handful of chips in my mouth and wave her sympathetic look away. I don't want to think about Ben, or my dad, or any of it. I feel angry and that feels powerful; I didn't know I could feel this much. I didn't know I could feel anything except worry and hollowness. 'Anyway, *fuck her*. I'm done. I'm actually done. I'm bored of it all.'

'Good for you!' Jordan bumps his burger against mine. 'Look how strong you are.'

'Yep,' I mumble, my mouth full. I take a huge sip of my piña colada and swallow. 'I don't think we should bother with the group any more. We don't need it.'

'Well . . .' Sarah glances at Jordan.

'I'm serious—' I lean forward to make sure they're listening to me '—it's doing literally nothing for us. We'll be fine! Look, I'm fine now! I actually think I might have fixed myself.'

Jordan smiles at me, but it's indulgent; he doesn't buy what I'm saying.

Sarah carries on. 'I think I still need the group, Bri. And I know you're feeling really fired up at the moment, but it might be worth just sticking it out? I don't think there are any quick fixes . . .'

'I agree.' Jordan nods at Sarah. 'Let's stick at it together, for now? You might not feel this strongly tomorrow.'

I consider this. Right now, I really don't feel like I'll ever have a problem standing up for myself ever again. I could go and start an argument with the waitress just because. Plus, the group really has done nothing for me, for any of us. Why are we wasting our time?

'Think about it.' Sarah says, her eyes pleading. 'Just sleep on it.'

'All right.' I nod. 'But only to keep you two company.'

The adrenaline is already draining out of my system, and reality is nudging against my bubble. I shake it off.

'Shit.' Sarah looks at her phone.

'What's up?' Jordan peers over her shoulder.

Her eyes fill. 'Someone . . . I tweeted something about the fires in California. All those animals, you know? It feels like everyone's forgetting about them. Someone's just commented saying I'm a heartless bitch for not thinking about the human cost.' A single tear plops down her cheek and onto her jumper.

'Oh, Sarah.' I reach forward and rub her arm. 'That's horrible. What a nasty thing to say.'

'Ha!' Jordan reaches over and plucks Sarah's phone out of her hands, reading what's on the screen. 'I don't think so.' He pulls his own phone out of his pocket and starts typing furiously, giving one final, dramatic tap before he locks it and puts it on the table, picking up his burger again.

Sarah's phone chimes.

'Hi Karen – thanks for your constructive and helpful input! I hope your cheap hair extensions aren't flammable. #byebitch.' Sarah slaps her hand over her mouth. 'Jordan!'

'Is she serious? Did she make them herself out of her dead dog's pubes?' Jordan wails.

'Her name isn't even Karen.' I giggle, reading it on my own phone.

'Oh, Briony.' Jordan shakes his head at me pityingly. 'She's a Karen.'

'What if she replies?' Sarah has stopped eating and is nibbling on her fingernail. 'What if she attacks me?'

'So what?' Jordan shrugs. 'Who cares? You don't know her.'

'Well, no, but—'

'You can't be scared of people on the internet. You can't be scared of people full stop. They're just . . . people.'

'But I *am*,' Sarah murmurs, her eyebrows creased.

'Why?' Jordan rests his chin on his palm and studies her. 'What is there to be scared of?'

'I – I don't know.' Sarah shakes her head. 'I've always been like this. Since school.'

'What happened at school?' I ask.

'The usual stuff. Being the odd one out all the time. Being laughed at. People pulling my hair, throwing rocks at me. Telling me I was a freak because my dad left. They called me "bastard" until the last day of year eleven.' She's clenching her fists now, her face red. She takes a deep breath and calms herself. 'Sorry. It's just hard not to feel like everyone's out to get you sometimes.'

'Oh my god.' I am horrified. 'Sarah, that's not "usual stuff". That's abuse. It's *assault*.'

'I know that now.' She sniffs.

161

Jordan leans over and wraps his arms around her, apologising into her hair. I think about my time at school, bearable only because of Sami. Without her, what would have become of me? Would I have been the bastard without a mother? Maybe I owe Sami something after all. But shouldn't we be stronger for it, me and Sarah? Wiser and mightier because of what we've been through? We experienced more than most people before we could even understand what any of it meant.

'My mum died,' I blurt, suddenly. I feel my face heat up. 'Sorry, that sounded like I was trying to make it a competition. But – I mean, I understand. Living with one parent. It's – well, it's hard.'

'Oh god, Briony.' Sarah's eyes well up again. 'I'm so sorry. Thank god you had your dad.' She looks worried suddenly, her face slackening. 'Sorry, shit, he's not . . .'

'No, no. I had my dad, yeah.' I nod.

'I had no idea.' Jordan looks at me with such pity that I want to run far, far away. 'What happened?'

'She died,' I say, my jaw set. I don't want to talk about it. I don't know why I opened my mouth.

'Well, yeah. I gathered that.' Jordan cocks his head at me, his eyes kind. 'Were you close, afterwards? You and you dad?'

'Not really,' I mutter quickly. I turn to Sarah. 'Anyway, we shouldn't let these things define us. We should be stronger in *spite* of them.'

'Yeah.' Sarah nods, and I feel a sudden closeness with her, for all the things we've endured separately, but can now endure together. How is it possible that she doesn't like herself? How could anyone not like Sarah? 'We should.'

Jordan raises his glass. 'To being fucked up. Every single one of us.'

'Morning, stranger.' Ben pads into the kitchen and rests his head on my shoulder.

'Sorry, who are you?' I laugh, twisting round to kiss him.

He cups my face and smiles at me, his eyes searching mine. 'You OK?'

'Yeah.' I nod, actually meaning it. I'm fine. I'm *good,* even. I stood up to Sami, I've got Jordan and Sarah, and I spent the whole of last night working on my project.

I stare at the sunlight bouncing off Ben's back as he fills the kettle: his broad shoulders and strong neck. I'm sure everything is going to be fine; we can work through this. We haven't spoken properly in so long, so maybe Saturday's hike is just a chance to catch up with each other, to regroup and come back together.

'Looking forward to the weekend?' he says, as if he's read my mind.

'Yeah, I am.' I beam up at him as he turns around with his coffee. 'It'll be nice to spend some time together.'

'It feels like we haven't seen each other in weeks, doesn't it?' He pulls a chair out from the table and hesitates, leaning on the back of it instead of sitting down. 'Sorry I've been . . . well, so busy. You seem better, though.'

'Better?' What does he mean? Shit, did I tell him I was ill as an excuse in case he found me bunking off? Or does he know? Did he see me skulking around the house when I should have been in the office?

'Yeah. Well, not better. Happier. You seem . . . brighter, I suppose.' He frowns, as though he's confused.

'Do I?' I do feel better today, but I wasn't aware I'd ever let him see me down. 'It's the sun; it makes everything look nice.'

He looks at me for a second and something passes across his face, but as soon as I notice it it's gone. 'I'd best be off.' He dumps his half-full coffee on the draining board. 'I'll be back late most evenings, so I'll probably see you Saturday morning?'

'I can't wait.' I stand up and hug him hard around the waist. He freezes for a second, almost imperceptibly, and then hugs me back.

I watch as he leaves the room, and then pull my laptop towards me. I flick through my project. It's good – really good

– and I feel a sudden rush of pride. I'm back in work next Monday, and I'm ready to go in all guns blazing. I've kept myself in the loop since my little soap opera hiatus, lurking in the background on Slack, and I feel fresh and competent.

I pick up my phone and reply to a couple of the messages on our social anxiety group chat. Jordan keeps changing the chat name to 'Fran Fan Club', but every time Sarah changes it back to 'SA Group <3'. I upload a selfie of us all from the other night as our group icon, and Jordan immediately changes it to a photoshopped picture of Rod Stewart on a horse. I laugh, but I can't keep up, so I go onto Instagram and leave them to battle it out.

At the top of my feed is a picture of Sami and Julia, taken in the café yesterday. I can see myself in the background, standing in the queue. I've never seen my whole body from this angle before, and it feels strange to get a third-person perspective from across a room. My shoulders are hunched and my face is taut as I count the change in my hand. I look . . . miserable. Sami has written a caption under the photo: 'Hazy lattes with the best girl in the world' followed by a string of emojis: two girls with a love heart between them, a coffee cup, a hazelnut, and a sunshine.

I feel the pain like something physical. It's a representation of my life, of everything that's wrong with me. Sami and Julia, grinning up at the camera, and me, also there but not really, relegated to the background and forgotten. As if I didn't even exist.

I lock my phone and drop it onto the table, but it buzzes again with a new message. I go to turn it to silent, but it isn't WhatsApp. It's a text.

GP-NOREPLY: Your smear test was CLEAR. Next test due in THREE YEARS.

A sharp jolt of pain shoots across my stomach.

22

I am marching down the road, my teeth grinding and jolting with every step.

I am *furious*. I feel like there's a bolt of electricity running through my body, right from my toes up to the top of my head. My eyes are wide as I barge through the crowds of people, my fists clenched.

How could they have got it so *wrong*? What do I pay my taxes for, if the NHS is only going to make me wait over three weeks to get an incorrect result? And *then*, as if that wasn't bad enough, they leave me on hold for thirty-six minutes listening to Queen's 'Radio Ga Ga' on repeat before cutting me off. Maybe if they stopped funnelling money into Fran and her shitty, unhelpful groups, they could buy another phone and pay for an extra receptionist.

My thoughts keep flitting from one thing to the next. My head feels fuzzy and wired.

I reach the surgery and shove the door open with my shoulder, marching up to reception.

The blonde woman behind the desk smiles. 'Good morning, can I—'

'I need to see a doctor. Immediately.' I put my hands against the counter and lean forward. She rolls back slightly on her chair.

'If it's something pressing, you should call one-one-one or go to a walk-in centre. If it's life threatening, we advise you to—'

'*No.* No, I don't want to call one-one-one. I don't want to go to A and fucking E. I want to see a doctor. *My* doctor. Right now.' I'm shaking. I feel like I'm outside of my body, as though this is happening to someone else and the real me is sat in the corner, watching on in horror.

The receptionist points her long, sharp fingernail at a sign above the desk. 'If you continue to be aggressive, I'm going to have to call the police. We're here to help, not be abused.' She looks smug, as though she's been waiting to say this her entire career. 'We have no more appointments today. You should have called this morning for an urgent telephone triage—'

'I *TRIED* calling this morning!' I shout, the panic making my chest feel tight. My vision starts blurring. 'Nobody answered!' I point at the phone, which is ringing on her desk. 'Why aren't you helping that person? Why won't anyone *help* me?'

I suddenly can't hear anything. My breathing is coming short and sharp, and everything slowly fades to black. I feel hands drag me by my armpits. I'm deposited on a chair, and then someone is pushing my head down, between my knees.

'Breathe. Just breathe, that's it.' The voice swims in my ears. 'No, slower. Try to breathe slowly. In and out. There you go.'

The room comes back, inch by inch, as my heart rate slows. I stare at the linoleum floor under my wet feet. I lift my head to find the receptionist, crouched in front of me.

'I'm sorry,' I whisper.

'That's OK.' She furrows her eyebrows. 'How are you feeling?'

'Like a dickhead.'

She laughs. 'I think you need to go to A&E. I'm going to call ahead.'

'No!' I shout, and she flinches, looking worried again. 'No, no. I don't want to go to hospital.'

'Wait here.'

She returns to reception and I put my head back between my legs. I can't bear to see everyone gawking at me.

What the fuck is *wrong* with me? I've never, ever spoken to anyone like that before in my entire life. I just verbally abused someone. I feel like I can't remember it; like it happened to somebody else. She could have me arrested. I could be banned from this practice, or get a criminal record, or be sectioned and put on medication. My heart starts hammering again. Why won't anyone just tell me what's wrong with me? I need to know. Maybe they're not telling me because it's too awful. Maybe whatever it is, the tumour or the disease, has wormed its way into my brain and is changing my personality, making me reckless. I'm dying. I just want to know *why*.

'Sorry.' The receptionist is back, and I lift my head up. 'The only appointment we have is tomorrow morning. The doctor can't see you today. I strongly advise you to take yourself to A&E, or we can call an ambulance—'

'I'll come back tomorrow.' I stand up and look around the room for the first time. A sea of faces, all silent, all looking angry, sympathetic or embarrassed. Embarrassed for me.

I turn around and leave.

'No, Geoff! Opposite! Oh, my lord. Opposite Stuart. Yes, like that.' Fran is standing in the middle of the room, squawking instructions at us all.

'You OK?' Jordan peers at me as I drag my chair across the carpet.

'Fine.' I drop it opposite Jane, as instructed by Fran, and sit down. Jordan hovers and then moves away.

'Right!' Fran claps and then surveys us all. 'We're working with our hearts today. We're *opening up*. You've all tried speed-dating before?'

In what world would a room full of introverts be familiar with speed-dating? Nobody answers.

'Good! Now, you're going to sit opposite each other and talk about your deepest, darkest secrets. You're going to tell each other the things that upset you and haunt you at night. The things that make you wish you'd never been born. And there will be *no judgement!*' Fran shouts, and I jump. 'I'll start, to give you an example. I once lost a fingernail in a bowl of cake batter and didn't tell the bride. Somebody probably ate it.'

Silence.

'Well, go on! Your turn! Get spilling.'

I look at Jane as Fran prowls the room, her ears open for gossip.

'Hi, Briony.' She smiles.

'Hiya.'

'I don't know what secret to tell you.'

'Don't tell me a secret, Jane. Don't tell anyone your secrets. How is that going to help?'

'But Fran said—'

'Fran hasn't got a clue what she's doing.' My eyes feel dry and heavy. I don't want to be here. I suddenly hate myself and my life and everything in it so strongly, I think I might scream. How am I sitting here, talking to a woman I barely know, having spent my morning attacking a receptionist? Is this how most twenty-eight-year-olds live? Is this normal? No, of course it isn't. I'm royally fucked up.

'So . . . what should we—'

'Just make something up.' I shrug.

Jane squirms, chewing her lip. I stare at my hands. 'I'm sorry Fran told everyone about your hairdressing thing,' she says suddenly.

I smile at her. 'Me too. I'm sorry she told everyone about your rosemary bush. Did you manage to get another one?'

'No, not yet. I was thinking—'

'No thinking!' Fran has appeared and is looming over us, her face angry. 'No thinking, just *telling.*'

'I don't want to tell—' I start.

Fran blows the whistle hanging around her neck. Someone gasps. 'Move on! Next seat!'

I stand up and leave Jane to talk to Sarah. I sit opposite Geoff.

'I wet the bed until I was forty-two.' Geoff's eyes are red as he leans forward, staring at me. 'Forty-two. I loved a girl once. I loved her so much . . .' He hiccups. 'But she left. They always leave. Once I wet the bed.'

'Geoff . . .' I lean forward and rub his arm. 'You can't – you don't need to tell me that. It's obviously not making you feel any better.'

'Oh, what would *you* know?' he spits, his eyes flashing. 'You haven't even lived. And you're not exactly *trying*, are you? Look at you, always breaking the rules. Never doing what Fran says. She's trying to *help* you. But you just don't care. You're a selfish little madam—'

Fran blows her whistle.

I stare at Geoff for a second. 'That wasn't very nice.'

'Briony!' Fran taps me on the arm. 'Come on, quickly!'

I stand up. The only seat left is opposite Jordan.

'So,' he says, as I sit down, 'tell me *your* secret. What the fuck is up?'

'Nothing.' I shrug. 'I'm tired.'

'Tired of what?'

'Tired as in I need sleep.'

'Nope.' He shakes his head. 'Try again.'

'It's *nothing*, Jordan.' I sigh. 'I'm tired of making a dick of myself.'

'I've never seen you make a dick of yourself.'

'You're lying. I just want to be normal.' I look over to Fran, hoping that she'll blow the whistle. She's standing next to Stuart and Sarah, pretending to study a Tai Chi advertisement on the wall. Stuart is speaking energetically.

'What do you mean, normal?' Jordan is staring at me, his perfectly lined eyes boring into mine.

'Normal like, normal. Like you.'

Jordan throws his head back and laughs. 'Like *me*?' He spreads his arms. 'You think *this* is normal? You think this has been *easy*?'

'Well, what's your fucking secret, then? Go on, if you're so eager to know what's going on with me. What's up with *you*? Where's your dirty little piece of shame?'

Jordan sits back as though I've slapped him. I want to take the words back immediately. 'I'm sorry.' I lean forward. 'I'm sorry, that was awful. I'm not – I'm really sorry.'

'No. It's fine.' He smooths his hair. 'You're upset.'

'I am. I am, I'm not thinking straight—'

The whistle blows.

Jordan stands up and leaves.

23

I am sitting in the doctor's waiting room, nervously twiddling my ring around my finger. The receptionist from yesterday isn't here, and I'm sure none of the patients are the same, but I can still feel every eye boring into me.

I flip my phone over in my hands. Nothing on the group chat. I wonder if Sarah and Jordan are talking about me in another conversation. I bet Jordan messaged Sarah after he went, telling her what a horrible person I am. She tried to catch me on my way out of group but I left, scared of what I might say to her if she pushed me for an explanation about Jordan's departure. She messaged me afterwards, asking if everything was OK, so obviously they've been talking. They'll cut me off soon enough.

A searing pain flashes in my temple, and I grab the armrest of my chair. I need the doctor to see me *now*, right this second, while this is happening. If he could test me while I can feel this, maybe he could get to the bottom of it.

Do I want to be friends with Jordan, anyway? Thoughts are flitting around my brain like trapped birds. Why is he even bothering with me? Am I a project to him? Something to fix; an anecdote?

A ping sounds from the speaker above my head, and my name is displayed on the screen on the wall. Room 3. The same room I had my smear test in. How fitting.

I make my way down the corridor and tap lightly on the door before opening it.

Dr Patel is typing on his computer, so I sit down.

'Hi, Briony. How are we today?' He looks at me with kind eyes, and to my horror, I feel a tear leak down my cheek.

'Fine,' I say. I don't know why, because I'm sat here crying, so obviously I am *not* fine.

He hands me a tissue gently. 'What can I do for you?'

I cough. 'I keep – I have these pains. In my head and my stomach. And my smear test result came back clear, but I'm sure it's not. I'm certain there's something wrong with me. I don't think they checked it properly; I think I might be dying of something but I can't figure out what it is. I think it needs doing again, or maybe some blood tests, or an ultrasound? Just to check?'

Dr Patel watches me carefully as I speak. When I finish, he nods. 'Let's have a look at your notes.' He types something and then clicks. 'Your test was clear, so there's really nothing to worry about there. They're remarkably accurate. Tell me some more about these pains.'

'It's my head. Here.' I gesture to the space above my eyebrows and at the top of my hairline, and then down to my abdomen. 'And my stomach, too. They come on suddenly. Really sharp.'

'OK. And are you doing anything when you experience these pains? Have you noticed a pattern? Is it when you move, for example?'

I shake my head. 'No. No, there's no pattern.'

'And do they disappear at any particular time? Any situations where you don't feel them?'

I rack my brains. I can't think, now I'm here. 'Maybe when I'm asleep?'

'So you've never been woken up by this?'

'No.' I suddenly worry that I should have said yes, that he won't take this seriously if he doesn't think it's affecting every hour of my life.

'OK. Just hop up on the bed and I'll have a feel of your tummy.'

I lie down and he presses different parts of my stomach. I suddenly need to fart and my heart rate soars. Do *not* fart on the doctor, Briony. You will not receive fair treatment if you trump on Dr Patel.

'Not painful to the touch at all?' He frowns at me, and I shake my head.

'All right. Let's take some blood tests.'

I sit up and hold my arm out, and he gently pierces my skin. I need him to understand how serious this is. He needs to send these bloods first class, tracked, urgent response required. I'm dying, and he needs to find the cause.

'It's got a lot worse recently. The past few weeks, since I left my job. It's progressing really quickly.'

'What happened with your job?' he asks casually, swapping the vials.

'I was signed off for a while. Anyway, it started out of nowhere and now it's most days. I think it's something serious.'

'Why were you signed off?'

'Erm, my manager didn't think I was coping. Long story. So what tests will you be doing? Do you have any idea what it could be?' I roll my sleeve down and hold the cotton ball tight in the crook of my elbow.

Dr Patel smiles and gestures for me to take a seat on the chair again.

'Now,' he says, when I've sat back down, 'let me put these in their little bags . . . why didn't your manager think you were coping?'

'I'm not very good with people. Groups. Big situations. Which is funny, because now I *go* to a group to try and help my fear of groups.' I laugh, but I actually want to cry.

'What group is that?' He writes my name on the bag and I tap my foot impatiently, desperate to stop making small talk and get back to the more pressing issue of my impending death.

'It's a social anxiety support group. Run by a woman called Fran. NHS funded. Have you heard of it?'

He finishes writing and looks at me. 'Who referred you there?'

'No one. I just walked in. So how long will my results take, do you think?'

'Hm. Where is it? What's it called?'

I answer his questions about group but I want to scream. Why isn't he taking this seriously? Why isn't he acting? I'm on borrowed time, here.

'Briony,' he says, finally, looking at me with concern. This is it. He's going to tell me what his prognosis is. 'We'll have to wait for the blood results to be sure, but it seems to me like you might be suffering from what are called *psychosomatic symptoms*.'

Oh my god. What is that? It sounds horrible. Will it be slow, or will it take me quickly?

'Have you heard of these before?'

These what? Is it multiple diseases? I knew it. I *bloody* knew it. 'No.'

He rustles around for a leaflet and passes it to me. On the front is a picture of a man looking pained. 'Psychosomatic symptoms are physical manifestations of psychological disturbance,' he says.

I must look horrified, because he continues. 'When we're feeling anxious, or depressed, we can lose our appetite, or have trouble sleeping. We can feel the effects of our mental ill-health in our bodies as well as our minds. For some people, anxiety – which I believe is the case with you – can cause physical symptoms, like stomach pain and headaches.'

Wait, what? What the fuck is he saying to me? That my nervous disposition is literally making me ill?

'No. I mean – but it's so painful . . . I'm not imagining it, it's not in my head—'

'Of course it isn't.' He nods, and I can tell he believes me. 'It's real pain, and real symptoms, but they're a *result* of what's going on up here.' He taps his head. 'Now, this is in no way saying that we're not going to investigate this properly to make sure there's nothing else going on. I'll send your bloods off, and we'll go from there. But in the meantime, as you've told me you're struggling with your anxiety, I'm going to refer you for counselling and prescribe some propranolol. It'll help ease any panicky symptoms you might be feeling—'

'I'm not taking any medication,' I say, my voice wobbling. I can't believe what I'm hearing. My brain is attacking me. How is this happening?

A little voice in the back of my head whispers through my shock: *you knew this, though, didn't you?*

'OK. That's fine. I can send you for some extra tests at the hospital, just to check everything is all clear. It's always best to be safe.'

'I don't want to go to the hospital,' I say, and on cue, my hands start shaking. I can't go to hospital. What did I expect to happen, though? If he finds out there really is something wrong with me, it's the first place I'll have to go.

He studies me. 'I'll just do the counselling referral now, then, and you'll receive a letter in the post. I'll mention the effect it's having on your work and you should be high-priority.'

He taps at his computer again and I stand up. 'Thank you,' I say, out of habit rather than actually meaning it. What if he's *wrong?* Can't he send my blood sample as high-priority, too?

'You know—' he looks at me, that sympathetic face again '—it's not uncommon for anxiety to migrate around the topics it chooses to worry about the most. Health anxiety is a really tricky thing; be kind with yourself.'

I suddenly realise that he knows. He knows about my performance in the waiting room yesterday. My face flames, and he smiles kindly.

'When will I hear about my bloods?' I touch the handle of the door, desperate to leave so I can process.

'It'll be a week or two, hopefully sooner.' He nods. 'Come back if the pain gets worse, or if you change your mind about having further investigations.'

'OK. Thank you.' I open the door.

'Oh, and Briony,' he calls after me as I leave. 'I've never heard of that support group before. It's certainly not one anyone I know has ever referred to. Just watch out.'

24

So that's it then: I'm officially mad.

I'm so bonkers that my body is rebelling against me. It literally cannot cope with the brain it was given. It's like looking in the mirror and hating your face, but in reverse. My body is looking in the mirror and wishing it had been given a better-functioning mind to run it.

I knew this, though, didn't I? I didn't want to believe it, but some part of me knew.

But what if it isn't that at all? I rummage through my memories of the pains I've been feeling. The first one at work, when all the project drama started. And then more frequently, as I tried to figure out what to do. Since being signed off, I've had them randomly, it seems. Or was there something that triggered them? I can't remember.

I get off the bus and unlock my phone to message Jordan and Sarah about the group. They need to know. But just before I hit send, I delete it all. They don't want to hear from me. What am I offering them, anyway? Maybe Sarah is getting some comfort from knowing there's someone else out there suffering like she is, the same way I've felt relieved being around her. But what about Jordan? I can't trust him. I don't know anything about him.

They don't deserve someone so unstable in their lives, anyway. Both of them have been nothing but kind to me, and I've repaid it by shouting at Jordan and running away from Sarah, leaving her on her own with Fran and Geoff. And now it seems I'm unravelling so rapidly, what kind of support could I be? What kind of friend have I ever been?

Sami realised it; it won't be long before they do too. It'd be better to just nip it in the bud right now.

My phone starts ringing in my hand. It's Dad. I hover over the red icon, but what do I have to lose, really? Everything is utterly fucked; I almost invite him to try and make it worse.

'Hello?'

'Briony?' He's sobbing, his breath coming in gulps.

'What's the matter, Dad?' I ask carefully.

'Oh, don't sound so concerned,' he wheezes, his voice taking on an edge. 'Don't you bloody worry.'

'Look, I—'

'No, no. You go back to being a busy little princess; you've got far too much going on to give a shit about anyone else.' He snorts, his nose thick and snotty. 'My daughter, my flesh and blood. What a blessing *you've* been.'

'Why don't you just tell me what's the matter? Maybe I can help?' I ask, but my heart is whooshing in my ears. He *is* making it worse. He always manages it, somehow.

'Don't bother. Wouldn't want you wasting your precious breath on me.'

'It's not—'

'Just don't go crying when I do something stupid.'

The line clicks, and he's gone.

The house feels so empty. I've spent days drifting from one room to the next, like some kind of bored and purposeless ghost. An old episode of *Coronation Street* from the 1970s is playing on the TV. I've already seen it; I've seen them all.

Ben is upstairs in bed, but I've been down in the lounge

177

since 5 a.m. I barely slept, and we're going for our hike in a few hours, so there's no point in trying to drift off now anyway.

I'm preparing myself for the break-up. I wonder if Ben will let me keep the TV. Where will I go? I'll probably have to find a hostel; one of those women's refuges. Or a homeless shelter. Maybe I'll live on the streets forever and get into heroin. I could get a dog; I've always wanted one. I'd probably make more friends out there anyway, there might even be people who feel worse than I do.

Maybe I should get myself imprisoned. Then I can retrain as a chef for free and never have to talk to anyone ever again. I'll just cook and cook and cook and nobody will bother me.

I'm a bit worried about how dark my thoughts are getting. I feel like someone has sucked the joy out of everything, and my life has been split in two. On the one side are all the things that terrify me; on the other is everything that makes me sad. The grey area seems to have disappeared.

I hear creaking upstairs, and two minutes later Ben looms in the doorway, wearing just his boxers.

'Morning.' He gives me a lopsided smile.

'Hello.' I try to smile back.

'Coffee?'

'No, thanks.' I point to my full cup. It's my sixth of the day.

'I'm just going to grab a shower; shall we leave in about half an hour?'

'Perfect.'

He heads back upstairs and I hear the pipes groan through the ceiling. There was a time, a few months ago, before my promotion, when I'd have gone and joined him in there. Now the thought makes me feel sick. It's like I need him, but I know I don't deserve it any more.

Also, he'd probably reject me, seeing as he's about to chuck me anyway. And that would be mortifying.

Eventually, he comes downstairs and we set off, through the back garden and up onto the hills. Every step feels like I'm edging closer to some new kind of territory: a single life, the final tether to my old existence severed. No more job, no more Sami, no more Ben. Nothing to grab on to.

'Phew, it's too long since we've done this!' Ben stops at the top of the hill and rests his hands on his knees, panting.

'I know, it's been weeks.' I'm breathless too, and I dump myself down onto the grass.

'Don't sit down, you'll get a wet bum.' Ben holds his hand out to help me up.

'No I won't, it's dry,' I say, as I feel the dampness soak through to my skin.

'All right.' Ben sits down next to me. 'Jesus Christ, it's soaking.' He laughs, and pushes me gently on the arm.

'I know.' I laugh too. 'Sorry.'

He takes a deep breath and looks out at the expanse of green in front of us. 'God, I love it up here.'

'Me too.'

'Do you?' He looks at me suddenly, and his face crinkles into an expression I can't read. 'Do you actually?'

'Of course! You know I do.' I try to smile at him but it sticks to my face. I can't bear this.

He sighs and starts picking at the grass under his shoes. 'I think we need to talk, Bri.'

My stomach drops. I feel sick. The tears I've been holding back for weeks spring to my eyes. Here it is, then. He's done. He's been done for ages, and now he's letting me know. Where is she, I wonder? The woman who's better than me. Is she at home, checking her phone, waiting for him to text and say he's finally free?

'I get it,' I say, my voice thick. 'I'm sure she deserves you more than I do.'

His head snaps up. 'What?'

'Does she have a bush?' I'm gulping, the tears coming thick and fast. 'Is she like Matilda? Did Matilda have a bush?'

'What the fuck are you talking about?' He's glaring at me now, his eyes angry.

'You know what Sami said at ours the other night. Don't pretend you don't remember. I've had my suspicions for a while, but—'

Ben lets out a roar and smacks the ground with his fist. A chunk of soil jumps up and lands on his sleeve. '*Fucking* Sami. I'm sick of Sami. Why do you let other people make you miserable, Briony? Why is everything suddenly so *dark?*'

I stare at him, my crying momentarily halted with the shock. 'What do you mean?'

'You think *I'm* cheating? You think I'd do something like that? You think I have the *time?*' He's ripping grass up from the ground so ferociously, there's a bald patch between his legs. 'What is this, a ploy? A diversion tactic?'

'I don't understand . . .'

'Yes, you do. It's not me who's been playing away, is it? What have you been doing with all your secret messaging and sneaking about? Why are you so . . . why aren't you . . . *talking* to me—' His voice cracks and he puts his head in his hands.

I stare at him, my head spinning. What is happening?

'Ben . . .' I throw my arms around him. 'Oh god, don't cry. Don't cry. I'm not cheating on you. Of *course* I'm not cheating on you . . .'

'Then what the fuck is happening?' He shrugs me off and looks at me, his eyes red. 'What's going on with you? Where *are* you?'

'I'm here!' I say, waving my arms in the space around us. 'I'm here! I'm not sneaking around. I'm—'

I stop myself. I can't explain about the group, and Jordan and Sarah. Not now. If there's any chance of salvaging this, I can't have him thinking I'm a liar *and* a nutcase.

He watches me as my sentence trails off, his face sad and crumpled. 'Who are you? I don't feel like I know you any more.'

The pain comes immediately, cracking across my skull. 'Neither do I!' I scream, suddenly, standing up. 'Who am I, Ben? I don't know who I fucking am!'

He sits back on his elbows, looking up at me, his mouth open. 'What? I'm so . . . I don't get it, Bri. I don't know what you're doing, who you're with, where you are, *who* you are—'

'Well, maybe I've never been anything, Ben,' I say, my voice cold and level. 'Maybe I've never been fucking anything at all, and you just saw what you wanted to see.'

'What are you even talking about?'

My phone starts ringing in my pocket. Ben looks at it, and then at me, as though daring me to interrupt whatever it is we're doing by answering.

I pull it out.

Unknown number.

'I have to get this,' I say, apologetically. I desperately want to end this now, to apologise, to move on, but this might be the doctor's, and there's a part of me that's glad for the interruption, the delaying of the inevitable.

Ben sighs and flops onto his back as I put the phone to my ear.

'Hello?'

'Hi, is this Briony Cox?' The voice is unmistakably Manchester, and I can hear a phone ringing in the background.

'It is.'

'And you're a relative of Mr Steven Cox?'

My heart stops. This is it. He's finally done it. It's all my fault.

'Yes,' I whisper. 'What's happened?'

'I'm calling from Pendleton Police Station. We've got your father in a cell here, and we need you to come and pick him up.'

25

It's not the first time I've been to the police station.

It's not even the fifth, or the tenth. I've lost count. I'm surprised the desk sergeant didn't have me on speed dial. He must be new, not knowing who I am.

At least I'm not at the hospital.

I'm sitting on one of the plastic chairs in the waiting area. I left Ben at the top of the hill and just ran, full-pelt, until I got to the car. My phone is vibrating constantly in my pocket.

I'm aware that I'm making things worse.

There's a woman screaming at whoever has come to pick her up. He's shouting back, his face red and blotchy. My heart pounds in my ears. The Saturday morning crowd; I'm used to this, but it's been a while, this time.

'Briony Cox?' The desk sergeant looks up from his computer and waves me over. My chair squeaks against the floor as I stand up.

'Where was it this time?' I ask, picking at the thin layer of plastic peeling off the counter.

'Ah, yeah, I've just had a look at his track record. This isn't your first rodeo, is it?' He looks at me kindly. 'Outside Morrisons. Relieved himself up a wall and then swung for a PCSO. Missed, thankfully. You wouldn't be picking him up today if he'd made contact.'

My insides twist. 'How long has it been?'

The desk sergeant puts his pen down and studies me, interpreting my question the way I intended it. 'Perhaps not long enough. He's a different man after eight hours, by all accounts. Watch yourself.'

I nod.

'He'll be out in a second.'

I go to walk back to my seat, but the door opens and suddenly, there he is.

He's filthy, his hair matted and his face sunken. His eyes are bloodshot. He looks like he's aged another ten years since I last saw him on Market Street with my stupid bag of lingerie.

'Briony!' he gasps, when he sees me. 'Oh, god.'

He falls at my feet and sobs noisily, clutching onto my ankles. People turn away, embarrassed.

'Dad, come on.' I reach down and yank him by the armpit. 'Get up.'

'Oh, love.' He gets to his feet slowly. 'I knew you'd come for me. It's all a big misunderstanding. I've told them, I wasn't even in Piccadilly Gardens. I wasn't there.'

I glance over at the desk sergeant, who shakes his head. They probably *picked him up* in Piccadilly Gardens.

'All right. Come on, let's get you home.' I clutch his elbow and walk slowly towards the door. My legs are like jelly. My entire life is falling apart.

We emerge onto the street as an ambulance rushes past, sirens blaring. I jump, my eyes wide.

'Whew, always a scaredy-cat, weren't you?' Dad chuckles and clucks me under the chin. I don't stop myself from recoiling in time, and he notices, shrugging his arm out of my grip. 'Where are you parked?'

'Just here.' I unlock the car and the lights flash. Dad gets in and sits, seatbelt off.

'Put your belt on.' I put the key in the ignition.

'Pft, what's the point?' He crosses his arms. 'Bloody nanny state.'

I pull out of the space and onto the road, and the car starts pinging. 'Dad, please put your seatbelt on.'

'Oh, stop here, won't you, love?' He points to the Tesco coming up. 'I'll grab us some pizzas for lunch. Do you want garlic bread?'

I haven't got the energy to fight it this time. I can't go home, anyway. 'Fine.'

'Oh, damn,' he mutters as I pull into a space, 'I've lost my wallet somewhere. Bloody pigs probably nabbed it.'

They didn't, of course. He probably hasn't had his wallet for weeks. I've got a twenty-pound note in my hand before he's even finished the sentence.

'Cheers, love. I'll treat us to something nice, just wait here.'

I lean my head back against the seat and watch him walk through the automatic doors. My knee is jiggling against the clutch, and I put my hand on it to stop it. It gets worse.

Eventually, he comes out, carrier bag swinging. He gets in the car and slams the door, gently putting the shopping by his feet.

We set off, and the seatbelt sensor pings again. We're in slow-moving traffic, and it stops every time I go below five miles an hour.

'What flavour pizza did you get?' I ask, as the lights change and we start moving again.

'Hm? Oh, cheese and tomato.' He sniffs.

'Can't get much pizza for twenty quid in Tesco these days,' I say, more to fill the silence than anything. I can't bear the silence.

Ping. Ping. Ping.

'Nope.'

'Did you find any garlic bread?'

I see his head turn towards me out of the corner of my eye. The traffic starts clearing.

'Course I did.'

We speed up, nearing the dual carriageway. The pinging speeds up, more insistent now.

The road slopes upwards, and as it does, I hear the unmistakeable clink of glass on glass.

'Dad,' I say, quietly.

'What?'

'Did you get any pizza?'

'I just told you, didn't I?' He shuffles in his seat and my stomach sinks. I shouldn't bring it up. I should leave it. I press my foot down onto the accelerator and the pinging gets louder, faster.

'You told me you'd stopped. I can't come to the police station any more, Dad. Why do you do it? Why do you have to pretend you want to get pizza with me when—'

'What's with the twenty fucking questions?!' he explodes, smashing his hand against the dashboard. 'You want pizza? Here's your fucking pizza.'

He launches the carrier bag onto his lap, a small bottle of vodka rolling into the footwell. He pulls a tiny, child-size pizza out of the bag and frisbees it across the car at me. I scream.

PING PING PING PING PING

'Put your seatbelt on!'

'Don't pretend to give a shit about my safety,' he growls, wedging a beer cap between his teeth. It opens with a hiss.

'Dad, don't drink in the car.' My heart is pounding so hard, I think it's going to burst out of my chest.

He holds the bottle up and drinks it down in one. 'Who the fuck do you think you are? You're nothing, Briony. Nothing but a waste of fucking space. Couldn't wait to be shot of me, could you? Couldn't wait to piss off and leave me for your perfect little city life.'

The pinging is suddenly all I can hear. My vision starts to cloud. We're driving at seventy, in the right-hand lane. My knuckles are white on the steering wheel, and my airways start to close.

Not now. Please, not now.

The pain across my stomach is suddenly so severe, I yelp.

'Oh, grow up. Can't take a little bit of criticism, can you? Never could. Whinging over the tiniest of things. You're an embarrassment. A complete joke.' He opens another beer bottle. I move into the left-hand lane, my scalp prickling. I try to catch my breath, but I can't. Our junction comes up and I veer off, our speed far too high for the roads we're now on. I swing into the housing estates and lift my foot off the accelerator slightly.

PING PING PING PING PING

'No need for me any more, have you? Don't need me to buy your clothes for you, so I'm irrelevant, aren't I? You're a selfish little bitch. I bet your mother's glad she's dead so she doesn't have to put up with you.'

I slam my foot down hard on the brake, yanking the steering wheel left and onto the pavement. Dad's beer flies out of his hand, bouncing off the car door and bubbling all over the carpet. A horn sounds behind me.

'LOOK WHAT YOU'VE DONE NOW!' he roars, his face crimson. 'LOOK WHAT YOU'VE FUCKING DONE!'

The pinging has stopped. I put my head between my legs, wedging it under the steering wheel, and wait as the panic washes over me. I can't hear properly, but he's shouting. Once it's over, the tears come.

I sit up.

'. . . and what are *you* crying for? Do you know how much that beer cost? You think you can just piss money up the wall, don't you? You're a bloody—'

I push him, hard.

He stops and looks at me, his mouth open. 'Did you just lay your hands on me?' His face clouds, his eyes darkening.

'Get out of my car,' I choke, my voice thick with tears.

He laughs. 'We're still five miles away. I'm not going anywhere.'

'Get. Out. Of. My. Car.' I shoot my hand down into his footwell and grab the bottle of vodka.

'Give me that back! That's *mine*. You don't touch what's not yours.'

186

I reach behind me and lower his window.

He looks behind him as it opens, and then to the bottle in my hand. 'Don't you dare.'

'Get out of the car,' I say again.

'No.'

I pull my arm back. 'If the police have nicked your wallet, you're fucked, aren't you?'

He gawps at me, his eyes flitting between my face and the bottle.

'All right, all right. I'm getting out.' He holds his hands up. 'You mental bastard.'

He opens the car door and stands on the slither of pavement between the car and someone's front lawn.

'Shut the door,' I say.

'What? Come on, you're not going to leave me here, are you?' His eyes look panicked now, his head weighing up the options. Get in the car and lose the vodka, or drink on the street with no money? 'Don't be like this, Bri. Let's go back and have that pizza. You know I'm only messing with you. It's tough love, darling! That's what you have to do as a parent. I'm just looking out for you, trying to make you the best you can be.'

I feel my resolve wavering. I can't really leave him here, can I? I can't do this to him. He's my father. That would make me the most selfish, reckless person on the planet. And I'm sure he does love me, in his own way. He just struggles to show it.

I bet your mother's glad she's dead so she doesn't have to put up with you.

My hand tightens around the bottle. 'Close the door.'

'All right, OK, but then pass me the bottle and let me back in?' he pleads, his eyes round and sad. I feel my heart fight with my head like a physical battle.

'Yeah.'

He closes the door.

'Move back.' I reach my arm out of the window and dangle the bottle by its cap.

He takes a step backwards, his feet sinking into the grass, and holds his hand out to grab it. I unfurl my fingers a second too early and watch, slow-motion, as it drops, past his hands, and onto the pavement.

I move quickly, jabbing one finger onto the auto-lock and the other onto the window button. He pummels his fists against the car. 'You've smashed it!' he screeches, his eyes wild and his jaw slack.

I put the car into gear, check my mirrors, and pull away.

26

I can't breathe.

I've just got home to a note from Ben:

I couldn't get in touch with you. I don't know where you went or what's going on. I've gone to stay at my parents' for a bit. I'm sorry, I just can't deal with this. We'll talk soon. B x

Everything is ruined. I have literally, single-handedly, destroyed every good thing in my life: I have no job, I've lost Sami, Ben has gone, my own father hates me and my body won't obey me; it's turning on me more and more every day.

What was it Fran said? *Assert yourself.* Well, I've given that a shot. I basically told Sami to fuck off, and dumped my dad five miles away from where he lives. I shouted at Jordan and told Ben I didn't know who I was, and where has it all got me? I'm even more bonkers than I was to begin with and I'm completely and utterly alone.

I walk around the house slowly, looking at all of Ben's things. His personality is injected into every part of this house. I imagine if it was all gone. What would be left? Not a lot. The IKEA coffee table – that's mine. And the YouView box. My orthopaedic pillow in the bedroom. That's about it: bare bones, zero character.

God, have I even *built* a life? Or just tagged on to everyone else's? Do I have an identity at all?

On autopilot, I start running the bath, and sit in it as the water pools around my feet. I'm shivering. I take the Radox from the caddy and upend it, pouring half the bottle under the tap. Once the bubbles are around my neck, I turn it off and lie down, submerging everything but my nose under the water.

I can hear my heartbeat. It's slow and steady. Why can't it always be slow and steady? I clench my fists under the water, digging my nails into my palms. It's all my stupid body's fault. If it hadn't fucked me up by making me terrified of everything, none of this would have happened.

The water starts to cool around me. I can hear the creaks of my spine making tiny movements without me telling it to. Do I have any control?

Distantly, from outside the water, I can hear my phone ringing.

I listen to it for a second, and then slip further down until I'm completely underwater, and start humming so I can't hear it any more.

It stops, and then starts again.

I stay under for as long as possible, and then surface, gasping. I reach my wet hand over to the toilet seat and swipe to answer the call, putting it on speaker.

'What?' I don't even know who it is.

'Briony? Are you OK?'

'Who is this?'

'It's Wiggy.' Shit. Shouldn't have answered.

'Oh. Hi.'

'You haven't been answering my calls.'

'Nope.' I trace a pattern in the bubbles with my fingertip.

'Are you at the swimming pool?'

'No, I'm in the bath.'

I can hear him go red. Good. It isn't me, for once. I don't give a shit any more. 'Oh, sorry. Should I call back later—'

'I won't answer.'

'Right. Well, I really wanted to speak to you. Can we meet?' he asks, speaking quickly. 'Please?'

'Fine,' I say. Why not? I'll see him on Monday anyway. He can speak to me then. 'Catch me before work.'

'Oh . . . haven't you heard from Jason?' He sounds awkward now.

'No. Why?'

'Erm, well, he wanted you to – well, he thought you could come back a bit later, maybe. There's some restructuring, and he said maybe you'd be better working from home until we figure out where to put you. Hmm.'

While we figure out where to put you. We. I'm the one being 'put'.

'All right.' I'm like a broken robot. I can't process any more shitty events.

'So can we meet tomorrow, maybe?'

'OK.'

'For the record, I think Jason really should have contacted you about this sooner. I'd really like to have you back ASAP, you know, but it's been tricky—'

'Where shall I meet you?'

'Oh. Erm, Nero again? Eleven o'clock?'

'Sure. See you there.' I hang up before he can respond, and sink back into the water.

I am tottering down Canal Street in the highest heels I own (three-inch). I've drunk an entire bottle of wine, and I am ready to meet new friends.

I have very specific criteria for these new acquaintances. I can't just let any old nobody into my cool and sophisticated circle. They've got to tick all the boxes. I am choosing, because I am in control. All potential candidates must be:

1) Totally fucked up. They must be mentally scarred and/or functioning

nutjobs. Friends have to be able to relate to you! Empathy is the key element of any successful relationship.

2) Objectively unlikeable. Getting on with your social circle and sharing common interests is overrated. If you actively dislike someone, it's a lot easier when they decide to fuck off and leave you on your own.

3) Totally devoid of any personality. It is vital that friends add value to your life. If your life is totally meaningless, that value really is unquantifiable.

I stagger into a bar and buy a bottle of beer, tucking it into the inside of my jacket and walking back out onto the street. I spot a girl slumped by the bridge where Jordan, Sarah and I danced just a few days ago. I sit down next to her.

'Hi.' I take a swig of my beer.

'Hmph,' she replies. Seems like my kinda gal.

'Do you hate yourself?'

'I'm going to be sick,' she says and, on cue, throws up all over her shoes. She wipes her mouth and looks at me blearily. 'Are you OK?'

'Yup.' I sway slightly and lose my balance, landing on my elbow.

'Are you on your own?' She blinks and looks around me.

'Yep.'

'Do you need me to call you a taxi?' she slurs.

Ugh, for god's sake. She's *nice*. I don't need someone nice.

I stand up and keep walking. I'm going to find the drugs man. The drugs man is a total dickhead. I'll have a chat with him.

I go into the place we were in last time and stand by the bar, waiting to be approached. Nobody comes. I buy another drink and then look around, scanning the crowds. It's Saturday night, and it's a lot busier than it was last time. The beer slides down too easily, considering how much I've drunk. I order three shots of tequila and throw them back, keeping one bleary eye on the crowds. Is this how it feels, being my dad? A day in the life of Steven Cox. I feel the booze melting into my brain until

I can't summon the faculties to worry. My wiring is sluggish, the quick-firing zaps of my thoughts muted. It's nice.

I vaguely note that usually, standing here at the bar alone would unnerve me. I'd feel seen. But I can't clutch the sensation long enough for it to take hold.

I'm about to order another beer when I spot a guy over by the cloakroom, passing a small baggy over to a girl in a bun.

I make a beeline.

'Hi,' I say, once she's wandered off.

It's not the same drugs guy as before. This one has long, sandy hair and sunken cheeks. He looks at me like he hates me.

'What?'

'I just said hello,' I say, my voice thick with alcohol. My vision bends until there are two of him looking down at me.

He looks around him and then leans in. 'You looking?'

I nod. Am I? Why not? Honestly, literally, genuinely, why not? What do I have to lose?

He passes me a baggy with a pill inside, and I fold a twenty-pound note into his hand. 'Will you take it with me?' I ask, my head lolling slightly. 'I've never done it before.'

'Fuck off.' He backs away. 'Freak.'

He disappears into the crowd and I stare at the pill in my hand. I think I'll take it out on the street.

I buy a mini bottle of wine, leave the bar and head over to the bridge, sitting myself down and dangling my legs over the edge. One of my shoes falls into the water with a *plop*.

'Oops.' I giggle. I don't care any more. I'm the sad, weird woman, sitting on a bridge and taking drugs on her own. Is this fun? Is this what happiness is?

I tip the pill into my hand and turn it over, squinting. My head won't stay straight on my shoulders. I prop it up with the heel of my hand, holding the pill up to my eyes. It's nondescript. Maybe it's paracetamol? Ecstasy, LSD, paracetamol. Who cares, really?

I rub it against my lips. Maybe it'll cure me. Maybe I'll have a colossal panic attack. Maybe I'll die and be found with only one shoe. Then Dad can come to my funeral and give a speech about how much he loved me, all the while knowing that he was right: I'm even more fucked up than he is.

Maybe I'm the *same* as he is. Maybe he had a moment, after Mum died, where he went out and drank a mini bottle of wine, eight bottles of beer and three shots of tequila, and realised that the oblivion of it all was too fucking good.

I open my mouth to take the pill, but I suddenly spot a familiar head of long, brown curls over on the street. I lean forward.

'Jordan!' I scream. He doesn't hear me. He's talking to someone, his head bowed. 'Jooooordan!'

People stare at me. The wild woman on the bridge in one shoe. I stand up and shout his name again and he turns, eventually, his eyes widening when he spots me. He strides over.

'Briony?' He holds me by the shoulders. 'What are you doing?'

I take a noisy glug of my wine, toppling slightly to the side and scrabbling for the railing for balance. 'I'm about to do my first drug. Would you like to watch?'

'What?' He looks down at my hand and his face darkens. He plucks the pill from my fingers and tosses it into the canal. 'What is going on with you? Where have you been? We've been worried sick.'

'Is Sarah here?' I look over his shoulder.

'No. Sit down. Where's your shoe?' He ushers me gently to the floor.

'In there.' I point to the canal. 'With the pill.'

He sits opposite me, crossing his legs under him. 'What's going on, Bri?'

'Oh, nothing, really. I fucked my entire life up, but no big deal.'

'What are you talking about?' He touches my arm.

'Well, my boyfriend has gone. Ben's gone. He's got sick of

194

me, just like everybody else.' I laugh, and even to my own ears I sound mad.

'Nobody's sick of you.' He looks at me with concern. 'Why have you been ignoring us?'

'I'm out of control, Jordan. I'm not in control of anything.'

'Of course you are!' He shakes his head. 'You're in control of *everything*. You just don't see it.'

'I just wanted to be powerful. I wanted to feel *empowered*. Like Sami.'

'Sami who told your secrets to everybody? Sami who made you feel like you were worthless?'

'The very same!' I cheer.

'Why would you want to be like her?'

'Because she's *fun*. She has wild sex and does drugs and owns a room. She's a boss bitch and she knows it.' I sing the last two words.

'You think that's empowerment? Shagging people and taking drugs? Even if you don't really feel like it?' He plucks at his tights. 'Empowerment is whatever makes *you* feel powerful, Bri.'

'How am I supposed to know what that is?' Everything is blurring into one big mass. My stomach churns.

He stares at me, his mouth sad. 'I'm sorry you feel shit.'

'I'm sorry I shouted at you at group. You deserve better,' I slur, knowing it's a cliché but really meaning it. He deserves better, and I should go. I can't see, though. Everything is moving slowly to the left, and my eyes dart lazily, trying to catch up.

Jordan shakes his head again.

A figure looms over us. 'You guys OK?' It's Priya.

'Yeah, will you watch her a sec? I'm going to go and grab some water.' Jordan stands up gracefully and makes a beeline for the bar.

'Get me a beer while you're in there!' I shout, throwing the rest of my wine back and sloshing it down my front.

'Good to see you again, Briony.' Priya smiles kindly at me.

'No it isn't.' I roll my eyes and the world tilts. I slump

backwards, my head bumping softly against the cobbles. 'I'm ruining your night again.'

'No, you're not!' She laughs gently and rubs my arm. 'You stay there and rest a second. I'm going to order a taxi.'

'Why is Jordan so nice to me?' I mumble.

'He's nice to everyone. He likes fixing people.'

Through the fog, something clicks in my mind. I *knew* it.

'Here we go.' Jordan has reappeared and is brandishing a bottle of water at me. I can't see him properly; I can't really figure out what's going on any more. Everything is so heavy. My eyes roll back, and I struggle, but it's too tempting. I can feel hands on my arms, on my face, water splashing against my neck; someone is saying my name.

And then nobody is saying anything, and I'm nowhere, and I don't have to do anything any more.

27

I wake up when my face presses against something cold and smooth. I peel my eyes open, and the pain comes immediately; my stomach burns, my head sears and my throat feels like it's been microwaved.

I'm in bed, I realise, at home. Ben isn't here, but Ben left, didn't he? Ben isn't coming back. I reach my hand up to my face and pull a piece of paper from my cheek. I read the note, my eyes half-closed.

I had to go, but I've left you breakfast on the side. I'm so sorry you feel like this. We're here. J x

   P.S. Your clothes are in the washing machine – they should be ready to hang out by the time you're up.

Jordan. Last night comes back to me in pieces. The shame and dread threaten to overwhelm me. I lift the duvet and look down; I'm wearing my pyjamas, with last night's underwear underneath. I smell like alcohol and vomit.

I have to meet Wiggy. The thought wafts towards me like a horrible smell, and I groan, burying myself under the duvet. I'm not going. There is no way I can face Wiggy and his pompous snorting on a day like today. I'm going to stay here, alone, under the duvet, until every drop of alcohol has left my system and I can sort my head out.

It's hot, and I'm struggling to breathe, so I roll over onto my side and poke my head out of the duvet. The full-length mirror glares at me, showing me a pale woman with bags under her eyes and frown lines between her eyebrows. My eyes don't look like my mum's any more. I look like my dad.

I sit up suddenly and swing my legs out of bed, clutching my head as a wave of nausea and wooziness washes over me. I am *not* him. I refuse to be him. I will not lie here in my own filth and let my world turn to shit.

My head is throbbing. Every speed bump the bus drives over feels like a personal assault.

Jordan must hate me. I am a prize liability and a total fun sponge. How do I manage to be a total mess and a party pooper at the same time? I'm the worst combination of traits; not fun and carefree, not aware of my own limits, just blackout hammered and morbid.

Little sparks of memory keep darting around my mind. Lying on the bridge, all the things I did, all the things I said; I bought drugs off a seedy stranger and screeched down the canal. There was a girl who looked at me and asked me if *I* was OK, while she vomited into her shoes. The shame squeezes around my throat and pulses behind my eyes.

And Priya's comment.

He likes fixing people.

I pull my phone out onto my lap to type a message to Jordan, but my fingers pause over the keys. *He likes fixing people.* Maybe that's all I'm worthy of being – somebody's pet project. After my behaviour last night, it feels like anything more sincere would be wasted on me.

Jordan will have told Sarah what I've done now. I'm not good enough for them.

Or maybe I'm too much.

A fire bolt of pain courses through my stomach.

There! I remember what Dr Patel said. I need to remember what happened before the pain. I open up the notes app on my phone. *Thinking about: Not being good enough/being too much for people/people leaving. Pain: Stomach.*

I pocket my phone and step off the bus. I can hear the logical voices of Ben, Jordan and Sarah, ricocheting around my brain: *you had a low moment. It was a mistake. Everyone fucks up. You just have to learn from this.* None of it sticks, though – the shame is drowning everything.

I'm nearing Caffè Nero when my pocket vibrates with a message.

Jordan: *Are you OK? We're so worried about you. Come and stay at mine if you need it – door's always open.*

My heart drops a few millimetres in my throat. He doesn't hate me. Or maybe he does, but saw what a mess I was and is worried I'll do something stupid and doesn't want it on his conscience?

Or . . . what Priya said last night swims into my mind again. I pocket my phone.

Wiggy is already waiting at the same table by the window when I get inside. I join the queue and order a vanilla latte – the idea of caramel or hazelnut still makes me feel sick. I take my drink over to him and sit down.

'Hi, Briony.' Wiggy smiles weakly at me.

Christ, he looks *awful*. Now that I'm up close, I can see the dark grey bags under his eyes. His hair is greasy and the corners of his mouth have sunk down towards his chin. I'm probably not looking much better.

'Hiya, Wiggy. You OK?' My mind keeps flitting back to last night, my heart racing with the beer fear and humiliation, and I breathe deeply to calm it. I need to remember where I am, what I'm doing. Wiggy wants to tell me something. I'm here to listen – I must stay in the moment.

'Yes, yes. Fine.' He nods enthusiastically.

I wait for him to start, but he keeps nodding, almost manically, his eyebrows raised and a smile plastered on his face.

I frown at him. 'You sure you're all right?'

The corners of his mouth start to twitch, and his lip wobbles.

Suddenly, his face crumples and he erupts into noisy, wet sobs. The woman on the table next to us stares.

'Oh, god, Wiggy! Don't cry!' I reach over and rub his back, feeling weird. What is happening? 'What's going on?'

'I can't do it, Briony. It's a mess.' He sucks air in loudly and lets out a long *wheeee* sound. The barista coughs uncomfortably.

'It's all right. Let it out,' I soothe. I shoot a glare at the woman next to us, who is still staring. I pat him and make little *shh*-ing sounds.

Eventually, when he's all cried out, he lifts his head and gives a big, wet snort. He gets out a tissue and blows his nose. The noise almost deafens me.

'I do apologise.' He coughs. 'That was completely inappropriate.'

'It's not inappropriate!' I object. 'If you're upset, you're upset. What's happened?'

'Oh, god.' His eyes fill again. 'I'm drowning, Briony. I just can't *do* it. I've tried a million different ways, but I can't figure it out. I tried to call you, but . . .'

'I didn't answer,' I suggest. I don't quite feel bad – I was on mental health leave, after all.

'No. Sorry, I'm not blaming you. It wasn't your place. I'm just – I'm completely at a loss. Mmm.'

'With the project?' I ask, my head spinning. Was it that hard? Did I dodge a bullet? I swallow down a wave of nausea and dizziness and try to concentrate.

He nods. 'It's due in a month and we've got nothing. No, less than nothing. We've fucked up a load of the existing code as well.' He gasps as he finishes talking, as if the idea of it is actually painful. 'I just wanted to know what your plans were before you . . . left. I know it's not fair, wanting a leg-up, but . . . I really needed your help. I don't know what to do.'

I stare at him.

Oh, god.

Fuck it, what have I got to lose?

'Wiggy.' I lean forward. 'I don't know what the project is.'

Wiggy stares at me, his eyebrows knotted. 'What?'

'I don't know what it is. I pretended to know, because I freaked out in that meeting and didn't want to admit to everyone that I hadn't heard. I'd just agreed to a four-week timeline and it would have completely undermined my position to go back on it.'

'Wait . . . what? So you . . . you gave your job up instead of saying anything?'

'Jason signed me off,' I explain, 'but yes, essentially. I was going to hand it over to you regardless.'

Wiggy looks out of the window, his mouth open. After a second, he turns back to me. 'Well, fuck. *Fuck*. What are we going to do, then?'

'We?' I raise my eyebrows, wincing as my head pounds. 'Wiggy, you're in my job. I'm not even technically supposed to be working.'

'I don't *want* it!' he wails. 'I only wanted to give it a shot for a month or so. I thought maybe they'd create a new role for me if they saw how well I did, but—'

'Hang on, you didn't want to be Tech Lead?' I say suspiciously. 'You went for the promotion at the same time as me. Don't tell me you weren't secretly hoping I'd never come back.'

'I wasn't!' He shakes his head. 'I promise. I thought it might give me a fighting chance in the next rounds, but I never thought you wouldn't step back into it. I swear.'

My head is reeling. I sit back in my chair and cradle my drink in my hands. What the hell is going on? Wiggy *was* after my job, I know he was. He ran for promotion against me. But then, what was he supposed to do? Sit back and accept defeat just because I'd put my name forward?

But he jumped at the chance to take over from me when I gave him the project. Didn't he? I try to take my mind back to our conversation in this exact same place just a few weeks ago. He was . . . doubtful, at first. But obviously he was, I was more senior than him and I was offering him a chance, he couldn't have shown his cards straight away.

Unless he was being . . . genuine?

No. Impossible. If there's one thing I know, it's that people always want to fuck you over.

He's staring at me with watery eyes.

I sigh. I am far too hungover for this.

'Right, show me what you've got, then.'

Wiggy jerks forward in his chair, scurrying around in his bag for his laptop. 'Oh, thank you so much. Thank you. Now, look, like I said, we don't have anything, really. It's all a bit of a mess.' He dumps the computer onto the table and snaps the lid open, tapping in his password. 'So you can see here, we've got the geotagging code that already exists from the partner matching—'

'Wiggy,' I interrupt, 'do you fancy explaining what we're supposed to be doing first?'

'Of course! Sorry.' He slaps his forehead. 'So, before, we matched users based on their location, right?'

'Right.'

'But that was based on their home addresses. It'd tell you how many miles you lived from someone.'

'Yep.'

'Well, Carl and the guys wanted to start matching people based on where they were in *real time*. So, say you love walking your dog on the beach at Formby, but you live in Blackpool. You're only going to match with other Blackpool residents, right? Carl wanted people to be able to stroll along their favourite beach, or their weekly camping spot, and see who was around in that moment.'

'Like Tinder?' I ask.

'Yes, exactly like that.' He nods, and looks at me hopefully. 'The thing is, we haven't got very far. We're basically a team of four juniors and me.'

'What about the seniors?'

'They're on other projects.' Wiggy frowns, and I guess the unsaid.

'And you didn't want to ask for help because it'd undermine your position?' I smile in spite of myself.

He sits up in his seat. 'No!' But then he reddens, and slumps forward again. 'Yeah. OK, fine. I can see why you legged it.'

'I didn't *leg it*,' I protest, but he's right. I legged it so fast I nearly broke my neck.

'So . . . what are we going to do?'

I study Wiggy. He's already looking more alive now that he's got an ally. The geotagging is complex, but it's not impossible. I could have done this in four weeks if I'd just spoken out and asked for clarification. Although technically, we still have four weeks left . . .

'We're going to fix it,' I say.

It's dark when I finally get home. There's an email in my inbox from Jason.

Hi Briony,

I hope you're feeling better? Just wanted to drop in about your return to work tomorrow. I wondered if you might prefer working from home on some basic coding tasks for the time being? We're having a restructure and the kitchen is being refurbished, so there isn't a lot of space. Shall we say four weeks, until the project is complete?

Do feel free to call if you want to talk this over.

Best wishes,
Jason

I was expecting it, but my heart still sinks. Another blow. All my suspicions were correct: they don't want me back. Has Wiggy instigated this? Is he using me to secure his place while trash-talking me to Jason behind my back?

For some reason, I can't make the thought stick. It doesn't fit right with the Wiggy I saw today.

God, why can't people just be *honest* with me? Why couldn't Sami tell me she didn't want me any more back in high school? Why doesn't Ben just sever our ties? Why won't Jason just send me packing and stop dragging me along?

I hit reply on the email before I even know what I'm doing.

Hi Jason,

Thanks for reaching out. I'm feeling much better, thanks for asking. I'd rather not work on basic coding at the moment. I'm keen to get back into things at my previous level ASAP. Could we schedule a meeting to chat about this further?

Kind regards,
Briony

I hit send.

Holy fuck. Did I just *schedule a meeting*? I regret it instantly. What am I going to say? What if he asks the entire company to come along to hear my speech and buys a sandwich platter for the occasion? What if Carl and the others are all still so angry with me that they throw an egg mayo at my head? What will I *do*?

Jason's reply pings back quickly.

Hi Briony,

Sure. Shall we say 9 a.m. next Monday? Please take the coming week as further leave.

Best wishes,
Jason

Shit.

28

Sarah is looking absolutely incredible. Her hair is shiny and her eyes are bright. She's practically glowing.

'Oh my god, why do you look so good?' I stoop down to give her a hug, stopping her from standing up.

'I don't know!' She laughs, covering her mouth and glancing around to check that no one is looking at her.

I pull a chair out and sit opposite her. Sarah messaged me asking me to meet her for lunch today. It was the last thing I felt like doing, but I promised I'd be her support, and I didn't want to leave her hanging in case she was upset, or there was something she wanted to talk about. It seems that the opposite is true; she looks better than I've ever seen her.

'How are you?' Sarah peers at me sympathetically. 'You haven't been answering our messages.'

'Yeah, yeah. Fine. Not bad.' I nod, shuffling the menu about. 'I mean, Ben's left me, and my job is basically dead, and I can't shift this feeling that I'm going to fuck everything up for you and Jordan and you'll suddenly realise that I'm a waste of space and block my number, but apart from that, yep. All good. What about you?'

'What?' Sarah shakes her head. 'Why would we think you're a waste of space?'

'Because I'm a nightmare. I fuck everything up.' I purpose-fully don't tell her about the other night. If Jordan's mentioned it, she'll bring it up.

Sarah looks cross for a second. 'Now you're just being pathetic.'

I raise my eyebrows. I've never heard her speak like that before. It kind of hurts, actually. Great, now she thinks I'm pathetic. This is brilliant.

'I'm sorry!' She covers her face with her hands. 'I'm really sorry. I was trying out a Jordan tactic and it didn't work. I can't do it. Shit, I'm sorry, Bri.'

'No, you're right.' I laugh. 'I was being pathetic. I *am* pathetic.'

She narrows her eyes at me.

'Gah, OK, sorry! No, I'm not pathetic,' I say, not meaning it. 'What's a Jordan tactic?'

'You know, straight-talking. To the point. No eggshells.'

The waitress comes over and takes our order. While Sarah is requesting olives instead of mushrooms, I message Ben. I've been WhatsApping into the void with him since he moved in with his parents.

When I look up, the waitress has gone.

'Who's that?' Sarah asks.

'Oh. I was just messaging Ben.' I flush slightly.

'Ah. What happened there?' she asks kindly.

So it looks like Jordan hasn't told her everything. I sigh. 'He said he didn't know who I was any more. He thought I was *cheating* on him. Because of our WhatsApp group.'

'What, cheating with me *and* Jordan?'

'No, he didn't know who I was messaging. He just noticed me being secretive.'

'Oh, yeah. I remember you didn't want us to bump into him when I was round at yours. Why didn't you just tell him?'

'Because then I'd have to tell him *everything*. If I told him about you guys, it would mean I'd have to tell him about the group, and *then* I'd have to tell him about being anxious and the reason I was signed off work and that I basically just *lied* about everything.' How did I get myself into this hole? Hearing it back, it sounds even more ridiculous.

'Jesus, Briony.' Sarah looks worried. 'Couldn't you have just been honest with him?'

I feel annoyed for a second. Surely Sarah knows how it feels? But then I remember how easy it is to see someone else's problems and a simple solution, and how hard it is to turn that pragmatism onto yourself. I can't see how Sarah could dislike herself, but she does, and I'll never be able to wrap my head around that.

I lean forward suddenly, a thought occurring. 'Sarah, do you ever get any pains?'

'What?' She looks confused by my sudden change in topic.

'Like, stomach pains. Headaches. Stuff like that.'

'No? I mean, no more than the average person, I guess. Headaches when I'm tired, stomach ache when I've eaten too much. Why?'

I sit back in my seat. 'I went to the doctor and he told me I have psychosomatic symptoms of anxiety, or something. Like physical symptoms of my thoughts.'

'Shit. That's horrible, Bri, I'm sorry.' Sarah knits her eyebrows together.

'I don't know, maybe it's something else? Something actually physical.'

'Have you noticed a pattern with it?' she asks.

'I'm trying to write down my thoughts every time it happens.' So far, I've got six notes, and each time, the pain comes when I've wound myself up over something.

'Well, don't feel alone in it. I've been reading up about anxiety a lot, trying to see what I can do to make myself feel better.' She looks thoughtful for a second, as though she's weighing something up in her mind. 'Do you do weird things, like turn a light on and off five times before bed?'

'No.' I shake my head.

'Oh.' Her face reddens and she flips her fringe further over her eyes.

'Why? Do you?'

'Yeah. I mean, I've always done it, though.' She shrugs, looking down at the table. 'I thought it was just . . . something I do.'

'But it turns out it isn't?'

'It's a symptom of anxiety. But it's OCD, and I thought mine was social.'

I pause a second, thinking. 'The doctor told me anxiety can . . . manifest in different ways. Like picking a target. I get really het up about my health. Like, I'm convinced I'm dying *all the time*. But it's recent, really. Maybe yours has done the same.'

Sarah nods. The waitress appears with our pizzas, and we start cutting into them.

'Have you seen Jordan much?' I ask.

'Yeah. Most days, actually.' She forks a piece of pizza into her mouth and avoids my eye.

'Oh, right.'

'You weren't answering,' she gabbles, suddenly. 'It wasn't because we didn't want you there. He's helping me work through things. Taking me out of my own mind a bit.' She pushes a stray olive around her plate awkwardly. 'Honestly, Briony. I promise, it's not been social stuff.'

I feel stung. I knew they'd have hung out without me, but almost every day? I have ignored them both for ages, but they still could have invited me. And Sarah looks so much happier. Does she even want to be here with me? Is she counting the hours until she can go back to laughing with Jordan? I'm hardly good company; I just put myself down and moan all the time.

Was I too hasty in cutting Sami off? She hasn't tried to get in touch with me, so she obviously hates me. Why did I push her away when she's my only real friend? I feel overwhelmed suddenly, and desperate. Why does everyone keep leaving me?

'I spoke to Priya the other night,' I blurt, regretting it before I've even said it. 'She said Jordan likes fixing people. People are like projects for him.'

Sarah's face drops. I feel sick. That was nasty and spiteful.

'That makes sense,' she says eventually, when the silence has dragged on for so long I think I might just throw myself into the pizza oven. 'It's not like he'd be hanging out with me just because he enjoyed my company.'

'No—' I shake my head '—no, I'm sorry. I'm sure it's not true. I was being defensive and horrible – that wasn't fair. He loves hanging out with you! I do, too.'

'It's all right.' She puts her cutlery down and her face darkens. 'This is obviously all some kind of game to him, isn't it? Well, I don't want to be somebody's pet project.'

'You're no one's pet project!' I wail. I want to cry. Why have I started this? 'You're brilliant, Sarah. That's why he likes spending time with you.'

'Don't worry about it.' She flashes me a weak smile. 'Shall we get the bill?'

29

It hasn't escaped my attention that I still don't know if my dad got home safely. Is he still sat on the side of the road? He wouldn't have stayed anywhere without booze, but there was a pretty hefty amount of vodka sitting on that tarmac, so maybe he licked it up and went on his way. I've seen him do worse.

The most likely thing to have happened is that someone saw him stranded there and pulled over. He'll have given them the puppy-dog eyes and probably told them about his witch of a daughter who chucked him out of the car for buying the wrong size pizza. They'll have given him a twenty and dropped him home.

I'm sure I'll get another call from one of the emergency services at some point. My bet is on an ambulance, this time.

I'm *exhausted*. I'm lying on the sofa, staring unseeingly at an episode of *Hollyoaks*. The constant overthinking and resulting pain has finally wiped me out, and I don't have the capacity to use my brain any more. It's quite nice, actually. Maybe I could just stay like this forever, staring at the TV, until one day Ben comes home to pick something up and finds me, skeletal and deranged, probably wearing an old, dirty wedding dress and ranting about UFOs.

I'd be happy, I imagine, safe in my living room bubble. I could get a cat. I could drop slowly into madness until I believed the cat was a person – my husband, maybe – and made three-course dinners for us both. I could never wash my hair, children would egg my house, and then the cat would die and I'd run naked through the streets, wailing.

What the fuck is wrong with me?

I come to, checking the time on my phone. 16:10, and still nothing from Ben. I shoot him another text. My WhatsApps are staying grey-ticked.

Hiya. Me again, via the medium of good old SMS. I miss you so much and I'm sorry. Please, please talk to me. X

I stare at the screen once I've sent it, but there's no way to tell if he's read it.

Group starts in an hour. I'm not sure whether I'll go; what would be the point? Sarah will be upset, Jordan will find out what I said, and Fran will make us do something weird that will cause us to all feel ten times worse than we did an hour earlier.

Is there any coming back from this? From the shame? I saw a new side to myself yesterday: a vindictiveness I didn't know I had. Is this my rock bottom? Something lifts in my mind. Every shitty event before this has seemed like rock bottom – losing my job, falling out with Sami, Ben leaving – but I can somehow feel that this is it. Unless the house burns down, I have nothing left to lose. I have to move forward, now. I have to make sure none of this ever happens again. Aside from the cat/wedding dress plan, there isn't another option. I have a brain, don't I? I learned how to read and write and run and listen; I can learn to get over this. I can pull myself together and do better.

I flip my phone over on the sofa and slide my laptop onto my knees.

I've been putting a lot of time into Wiggy's project. It's a complete mess, and it's taking longer than I thought it would to untangle it all and get the system set up. We're nearly there now, and working on it makes me feel calm. I can lose myself in it for hours and then the day doesn't feel so long and lonely.

I'll get nothing from this, of course. Not unless I out Wiggy to Jason. I still haven't figured out what I'm going to say, or whether it's even worth going to this meeting.

Time slips by, and by the time I've got the geotagging framework in place it's twenty past five. Before I even stand up I know I'm going to go to group; every week I have this dilemma and I always trot back there like I don't have a choice. Even now, when I've pushed everyone away, I keep running back for the connection. For the hope. Maybe there's something in me still fighting.

Jordan and Sarah are nowhere to be seen when I enter the building. Ominously, the chairs have been arranged in rows, like a theatre, facing a wooden lectern I imagine Fran has stolen from the altar of the church next door.

I take a seat at the back and wait as everyone files in and sits down. Still no sign of them. I imagine that this is it; that I'll never see them again. They've had a private chat and decided that I am totally nuts, nasty and/or boring, and therefore never want to be in my company ever again.

I don't want to be here, now that they're not with me. But equally, I don't want to go home and watch Pat Butcher swing her earrings on the *EastEnders* reruns for the rest of the evening. I am literally alone.

I pull out my phone and apologise to Sarah again, and then tap out a message to Sami. She still hasn't spoken to me since the latte incident, and I know she's annoyed with me. It was upsetting, but I definitely overreacted. We've been friends for over twenty years; I can't throw all of that away over one little spat, can I?

Me: *Hey. Are you OK? I'm sorry about the other day. Can we go back to normal now? I miss you. Sorry x*

My phone stays silent. The group chat has been inactive for a couple of days; neither Jordan nor Sarah have told me they're not coming this evening. I check to see if I've been blocked, but I haven't.

Fran coughs loudly and I look up. She's standing at the lectern, her arms spread.

'Welcome back, everybody! How are we?'

Silence.

'Good! I'm glad you're all well.' She pulls at the sleeves of her cardigan and tucks a stray, wispy hair behind her ear. 'Now, today we're going to practice *mantras*. Mantras are very important. The premise is, if you say something enough times, you'll start to believe it.' She nods encouragingly. 'You're all going to create your *own* mantras today, and then we're going to SHOUT them from the rooftops!' She tilts her chin towards the ceiling and roars. Jane shifts uncomfortably in her chair a few seats down from me.

'As usual, I'll go first.' Fran clears her throat and raps her knuckles against the lectern. 'I am stunning and sexy,' she says.

What?

'I am stunning and sexy. I am stunning and sexy. I am stunning and sexy I am stunning and sexy I am stunning and sexy. I. Am. Stunning. And. Sexy. I. Am. Stunning. AND! Sexy. I am stunning and *sexy*. I am stunning and SEXY! I AM STUNNING AND SEXY!'

She carries on, screeching as she leans further and further over the lectern. I stare, my mouth open. What the actual fuck is happening? I look around me. Jane looks genuinely traumatised, her eyes wide and scared. Stuart is staring into his lap. Geoff is looking at Fran, nodding and licking his lips. I bet *he* thinks she's stunning and sexy.

'Isn't that a bit . . . much?' A familiar voice comes from my right, and I look up to find Jordan sliding into the seat next to me. My heart lifts.

Fran stops, breathing heavily, and glares at Jordan. 'Excuse me?'

'Well, it's a bit . . . self-obsessed, isn't it? Isn't the point of a mantra to get yourself over an insecurity?' He's wearing a long, blue wig today, and he flips it over his shoulder.

'That's right,' Fran huffs. 'And I'm *very* insecure. Do you know how difficult life is when you're led to believe that you are not at *all* stunning or sexy?'

'Must be tough.' Jordan nods.

Jane giggles quietly.

'Right!' Fran squeaks. 'Who's first? Stuart?'

Stuart slips out of his seat and walks to the front. 'I don't know what to say,' he mumbles.

'What's your biggest insecurity?' Fran prompts.

'Erm . . .' Stuart scratches his eyebrow. 'That I'm a mediocre carpenter.'

'There you go!' Fran cheers, bafflingly. 'Say, "I am an above-average carpenter".'

'I am an above-average carpenter,' Stuart says.

'Good, now louder.' Fran claps.

Stuart repeats his mantra, louder and louder, as Fran eggs him on. Jordan is in pieces beside me. 'An above-average carpenter?' he whispers. '*What*?'

Jane is next, and Fran makes her say 'I am a perfectly adequate wife and mother' twenty times.

'Jordan, you're next.' Fran beckons Jordan as Jane sits back down.

Jordan strides to the front, laying his hands on the lectern as if he were the director of our strange, surreal company.

'Now, Jordan—' Fran starts.

'I am stunning and sexy,' Jordan says. 'I am stunning and sexy. I am—'

'No! You can't take *my* mantra,' Fran protests. 'That's not how it works—'

'I am *stunning!*' Jordan puts a hand on his hip. 'I am *SEXY!*' He leans forward and blows a kiss to the room. 'I am stunning and sexxxxxy!' He sashays along the front of the room, before turning around and doing a hugely inappropriate slut-drop.

'NO!' Fran squeals. 'Stop that right now!'

Jordan slinks over to Fran, his hips swaying, and puts a hand on her shoulder. 'I, babe—' he purrs '—am stunning and sexy.'

214

'Sit back down!' Fran stamps her foot, her face the colour of beetroot.

''Kay.' Jordan winks, and shimmies back to his seat.

'Oh my god,' I whisper, my shoulders shaking and tears forming in the corners of my eyes. 'Oh my god, that was so good.'

'Born with it, bitch,' he murmurs, and I lose it again.

'NOW!' Fran pants, wiping the back of her head with her hand. 'After that . . . *performance*, it's someone else's turn. Briony, up you come.'

'I can't,' I say instinctively, my heart lurching.

'You can.' Jordan grabs my hand and squeezes.

I stand up shakily and make my way to the front of the room. *Come on, Briony. If Jordan can slut-drop in Fran's face, you can say a simple sentence.*

'Right, Briony, what's your biggest insecurity?' Fran peers at me. Everyone is staring. I feel my face start to flush.

'I don't know.' I shrug, my fingers fiddling with my necklace. What would my mantra be? I am fun and confident? My boyfriend loves me and his phone is just dead? All my friends think I'm wonderful and simply can't cope with my brilliance?

'Of course you do. Come on, let's get to it.' Fran snaps her fingers.

I am fantastic at my job and Jason was right to promote me? I own a room and command respect? My dad loves me really and is glad I exist?

'I've got one for her.' Jordan raises his hand at the back of the room.

'No, Jordan, you've done enough. Briony needs to choose her own.' Fran tuts and turns back to me. 'Well? What'll it be?'

'I – I want to hear Jordan's,' I say.

'No, the point of this—'

'I want to *hear* it,' I say, more forcefully this time.

Fran sighs. 'We haven't got time for this.'

I look at Jordan. 'Tell me.'

He smiles at me. '*I am enough*,' he says.

'Right, well, that's very nice, Jordan,' Fran starts, 'but you can't just—'

'I am enough,' I murmur, quietly. 'I am enough. I am enough. I am enough.'

Fran sighs and throws her hands in the air. 'What is the point?'

'I am *enough*,' I say, louder now. 'I am enough. I *am* enough.'

Jordan nods at me, smiling.

'I. Am. Enough.' I twist my necklace between my fingers again. 'I am enough.'

'Right, let's move on to the next person now . . .' Fran scans the room.

'I am enough.' I smile, looking at Jordan again. 'I'm enough.'

Jordan grabs me by the shoulders as soon as we get outside.

'That was amazing!' he shrieks. 'You smashed it.'

I laugh. 'Thanks.'

'Did you see Fran's face? She was *so* annoyed that you went with my idea.'

A thought briefly flits across my mind: was Jordan genuinely encouraging me, or was he using me to get a rise out of Fran and create a bit of mischief? Is he trying to fix me, or is this all entertainment for him? Or is it both?

'I think your performance got a better reaction.' I nudge him, batting the thought away.

'Oh my *god*.' He links my arm as we walk through the car park. 'She had such a hard-on for me, didn't she?'

'No!' I splutter, remembering. 'I think she was terrified.'

Jordan looks at me out of the corner of his eye. 'So . . . where you been?'

'I'm sorry.' I shake my head. 'I'm – I can't even explain. I'm sorry about the other night. I feel—'

Jordan lifts a hand. '*Please* don't apologise. You were in the fucking pit, Bri. I'd have been far worse.'

'I don't deserve that. I've behaved so—'

My phone buzzes in my pocket, and I jump, thinking it must be Ben. I unlink with Jordan and pull it out.

Sami: *Come round mine now? We can hash it out.*

'—so, yeah. You fancy it?' Jordan is looking at me enthusiastically.

'Sorry, what?' I lock my phone and pass it from hand to hand.

'Mine, tonight? We can do a sleepover. I've got homemade face masks and everything – don't judge, I'm a walking cliché.'

I weigh up the options in my mind. Take a risk on Jordan, who might be using me as an entertainment/self-satisfaction project, or try to patch things up with Sami, who knows me better than anyone and has looked after me all these years?

'Ah, I'd love to,' I say, eventually. 'I can't though, I've got plans.'

'Who with?' Jordan asks, very directly.

'Erm, just a friend,' I lie. Again. What is wrong with me?

'Oh, OK!' He smiles. 'No problem. I'll see you next week, then? Message me if you need anything. I'm serious. One call and I'm there.'

And he's gone, leaving me staring at my phone and wondering whether I've made the right decision.

30

Sami answers the door wearing dirty sweatpants and an off-the-shoulder jumper. Her hair is scraped back and her eyes are red.

'Hey.' She doesn't stand back to let me in.

'Hiya.' I smile weakly. 'You OK?'

'Fine.' She studies me for a second and then steps into the hallway, leaving me to follow and close the door behind us.

We go into the living room, where Maja is rolling a joint. It already stinks of weed in here, so the red eyes make sense.

'Hello, Briony.' Maja waves her hand limply at me. 'Would you like some spliff?'

'Oh, no.' I shake my head. 'No, thanks. No . . . spliff. Thank you.'

'All right.' She lights her finished joint and stands up, before drifting slowly out of the room.

'Sit down, then.' Sami gestures to the sofa and I perch on the edge. I'm unnerved; she's being cold and distant with me, which I expected, but not to this extent.

'I'm sure you must be angry with me . . .' I start.

'You think?'

'I know. I said some horrible things—'

'You screamed at me and Julia in the middle of a café.' She stares at me, her eyes dead.

Did I scream? I remember being angry, but I didn't think I'd raised my voice. I must have forgotten, or not noticed in the heat of the moment.

'I'm sorry,' I say, leaning forward. 'It was out of order.'

Something feels wrong as soon as the words are out of my mouth. Was I out of order? Of course it isn't good to scream and swear and shout at people, but it wasn't exactly uncalled for. Was it? I can't get the facts and emotions straight in my head; Sami is angry, which means I must have done something bad, but am I angry, too? Do I have a right to be angry?

I replay the café scene in my head. Was I just het up because they'd asked me to get coffee for them? Did I overreact because I was already worked up? But she told Julia about my dad, and she knows that's a sore spot. No, more than a sore spot – a big red button that nobody ever presses. Do I *deserve* not to have that button pressed? Or am I oversensitive?

'It's fine.' Sami rolls her eyes. 'You're so dramatic.'

Something shifts inside me. I don't think I was being dramatic. In fact, I *know* I wasn't being dramatic. It was a horrible thing to do, and she hasn't apologised. *I've* apologised, again. And she posted that picture of her and Julia, when I was there too. She knows me, and she knew that would hit hard.

'Aren't you sorry, too?' I say suddenly, surprising myself.

She laughs. 'Jesus Christ, Briony. For what?'

My face starts to heat up. 'For telling Julia about my dad.'

'What Julia said is Julia's problem; I'm not going to apologise for it.'

'But you told her in the first place. You told her something you promised you'd never tell anybody.' To my horror, I feel tears gathering in the corners of my eyes.

'For god's sake. You don't think everyone has *always* known about your dad? You think it was some well-kept secret you'd done a top job of hiding?' She snorts. 'Briony, *everybody* knows about your dad. Everyone at school knew, and Ben probably knows too. It's not a big deal.'

A tear leaks down my cheek 'And *how* would they know, Sami? How would everyone at school have known about that?'

'Because it was common knowledge! He never picked you up, he never came to anything; you never had a clean uniform, you never brought lunch. The teachers had to lend you money for sandwiches, for fuck's sake. And everyone knew about your mum, didn't they, so it wasn't exactly well-hidden.'

My eyes are streaming at the memories. Figuring out the washing machine at age thirteen; burning myself on the iron; thinking I'd covered my tracks and that nobody would know that I had no one in the world who cared about me. Taking twenty pence a day out of Dad's wallet, clubbing it together and buying a tiny weekly shop of own-brand bread and ham to make dry sandwiches so no one would suspect that all of our household benefits went on vodka.

Sami is still talking. 'You'd be out on the streets until midnight most nights, unless you stayed at mine. People *saw* you. Maisie Buckshaw's mum drove you home one night, remember? News travels.'

Walking around the housing estates until I was sure he'd passed out and wouldn't start on me when I got home. Begging Sami's mum to let me stay another night, climbing up through the window so he wouldn't intercept me.

'You're not a child any more, Briony. You can't keep burying your secrets and pretending you're someone else. It's caught up with you, and you knew it would eventually.' Sami sighs.

'It's only caught up with me because you told Julia. It wasn't your secret to tell.' I wipe my face with the back of my sleeve.

'Ugh, god, what does it *matter*?' Sami throws her hands up. 'Honestly, Briony, you need to move on.'

'*How* am I supposed to move on?' I shout suddenly, my hands shaking. 'How, when I'm picking him up from the police station most weeks? Or visiting him in the hospital where he's having his stomach pumped? How do I move on when that's hanging over me?'

I'm so angry, my teeth are chattering. Why can't anybody understand? Why can't Sami just support me? Am I so unlovable that I don't even deserve a friend who won't out me to everyone she knows?

'I can't do this any more, Sami,' I whisper. 'I can't do it. You make me hate myself.'

Ben's voice swims into my memory: *She makes you feel like shit.* The pain of losing him as an ally feels physical.

'Oh, shut up.' She wafts her hand as though what I'm saying is irrelevant. 'You need to chill out.'

'No, I don't,' I say, calm now. 'But you're right. I need to move on.'

I pick up my bag and stand up.

'Where are you going?' Sami rolls her eyes.

'If you can't apologise to me, and you can't respect my privacy, then I don't want to know you.' I walk through the living room door. 'Bye.'

'All right, see you when you text me begging me to forgive you!' Sami shouts after me.

I open the front door, and leave.

I knock tentatively on Jordan's door, my overnight bag swinging from my shoulder. What if he isn't in? I mean, obviously he's not going to be in. He'll have immediately found plans with interesting, fun people and is probably out dancing as we speak. Or he's invited someone else over here? Maybe he's watching *Mean Girls* with Sarah on the acid-green sofa. Or maybe Aiden's over, and I'm interrupting—

The door swings open.

Jordan has removed his wig and has a chunky, vom-like substance all over his face.

'Briony!' he cheers, and grabs my elbow, pulling me into the flat. 'Did your friend bail? What happened? Do you want some face mask?'

'Oh . . . maybe in a minute?' I put my bag down in the hall.

'Sorry, please tell me to piss off if you want to. I just thought, because you'd offered . . .'

'Are you joking? Come in, sit down.' He ushers me through to the living room and deposits me on the sofa. 'Wine?'

'Yes, please.' I watch as he pours a glass and brings it over to me.

'Right. You drink that and tell me what's happened, and I'll put your face mask on.'

I tie my hair back as he goes into the bathroom and emerges with a dessert bowl and a spoon. He sits beside me and starts lathering something cold and slimy all over my cheeks. 'OK, spill.'

'I went to see Sami,' I mumble, careful not to open my mouth too widely in case a chunk of fruit falls in.

'Ooh, like *Sami*, Sami?'

'Yep. I went to apologise, and—'

'You went to *apologise*?' Jordan stops, holding the spoon in mid-air. A piece of orange gloop drops onto the carpet with a muffled splat.

'Yeah, but when I got there she was just so . . . like, she didn't give a shit. She was angry with me. And I understood that, but then I sort of . . . didn't, any more. It's like I realised that it was actually quite shitty what she did, even though time has passed and usually I feel guilty. I just stopped feeling guilty. I felt kind of . . . right? If that makes sense.'

'You felt like she'd done you wrong and you weren't going to be guilted into believing you were the baddie again?' Jordan raises an eyebrow.

'Yes, exactly that!' I nod, but then a thought occurs to me. Jordan only knows about Sami from what I told him about the café incident. 'Wait, what do you mean "again"?'

'I know the type.' He sighs. 'Gaslighting bastards.'

I laugh. 'We're not in a relationship! She can't gaslight me.'

He looks at me kindly. 'Oh, Briony. She bloody well can. Let me guess: she makes out like all your problems are your fault? She hurts you and then twists it so it's like it didn't happen the way you remember? She puts negative thoughts in your head and then behaves like you're overreacting when you get upset?'

Something flashes through my mind.

You don't think he's cheating on you, do you?

I'm sure he's not bonking anyone, Bri. You're being paranoid again.

'Yeah, I know, it's shit,' Jordan says, seeing my face. 'Toxic, toxic, toxic. Have you chucked her?'

'I told her I didn't want to know her,' I whisper, my mind reeling.

'Excellent!' Jordan pats a final spoon of gunk onto my face and sits back. 'I think you did the right thing. It's important not to cave in and go running back, though. You have to sever all ties.'

'How do you know all this stuff?' I ask.

'Family law.' He smiles. 'You see these kind of arseholes all the time. It's usually partners, looking for control because they're so insecure. But a friend can control you just as easily if you're dependent enough.'

He's right. I *am* dependent on Sami. I have been since I was a child.

'She used my vulnerability against me,' I muse.

'Yup.' Jordan nods. 'But absolutely, one-hundred-per-cent, totally *not* your fault. If you remember one thing, remember that.'

I sit back and close my eyes, feeling the face mask hardening between my eyebrows. I reach down for my wine and lift it to my mouth. 'Have you seen Sarah recently?' I ask, half terrified of the answer.

'Not the past few days, no. We hung out loads when you went . . . AWOL, but she's gone quiet all of a sudden.'

I open my eyes. 'I said something awful to her.'

'What?' Jordan looks at me.

I sit up and put my glass down. 'When you found me . . . that night on Canal Street . . . you went to get me some water and Priya said something to me.'

'What did she say?' He doesn't look worried, just confused.

'She said you like fixing people.'

Jordan raises his eyebrows. 'Oh.'

'I don't think she said it in a horrible way. Just . . . in response to something I'd said. But when I saw Sarah the other day, she was saying how much you guys had been hanging out, and I felt so low and shitty about everything, I just – I told her what Priya said to me. I was trying to hurt her, and make myself feel better, I think. I felt awful about it as soon as I'd said it.'

I feel awful now, too. Now I've exposed myself to Sarah *and* Jordan as a nasty and vindictive person. A dull pain flares in my stomach and then disappears.

'Ah. Do you think she was upset?' I can't read Jordan's face.

'Yeah. She seemed it. I'm sorry, I hope I haven't caused anything. I mean, I know I have, if she's gone quiet on you. It was a horrible thing to say. I really hate myself for it.'

'Don't hate yourself!' Jordan turns to me, his eyes blazing. 'You're *human,* Briony, and you were feeling crappy. We all do stupid things. You've apologised. I'll speak to Sarah.'

My eyes fill. 'I don't deserve that.'

'You do! You deserve the right to make mistakes without your world falling apart, just like the rest of us.' He stands, picking up my half-finished glass, making his way into the kitchen to top it up.

Do I deserve that right? Up until now, it's seemed like every mistake I've made has made its home on my shoulders, and I haven't been able to shrug it off. And because I kept everything to myself, I didn't even open up the possibility of another perspective. Jordan's forgiving attitude has immediately made the fuck-up seem ten times smaller. If I can't open up, and accept and forgive myself, how can other people?

'So . . . do you like fixing people?' I ask, as Jordan comes back over.

Jordan laughs and then shrugs. 'I don't know. I've never thought about it like that.'

'I don't feel like I know much about you,' I muse.

'No.' Jordan looks down into his glass, his smile gone. 'No, I don't suppose you do.'

'So tell me?' I push. 'What's going on with work?'

He looks at me. 'What do you mean?'

'Well, you're a lawyer, aren't you? How do you make it to a support group six miles out of town at five every Tuesday?' *And why are you always free to have long lunches on weekdays?* I want to add, but I don't want to push the point too hard.

Jordan stares past me, out of the window at the city beyond. 'It's . . . a long story.'

'You know, for someone so big on self-acceptance and openness, you're doing a pretty shitty job.' I nudge him.

He laughs, but it's hollow. 'I know. I'm a massive hypocrite. I'm sorry.'

I think back to what Sami said earlier. *You can't keep burying your secrets and pretending you're someone else. You need to move on.*

'Shall I tell you about me?' I say, my voice shaking slightly. I haven't ever put my life story into words, not even in my own head. But I trust Jordan. As little as I know about him, I feel safe in his company.

'Only if you want to.' Jordan sits back and watches me.

I take a deep breath. 'You know my mum died. When I was twelve. Cancer. I feel like my life's split into two, really. The before and after.'

Memories flood my mind. Paddling pools in the garden. Sticky fingers icing buns in the kitchen. Mum's hair, wild and curly, tied up in a big clip that looked like a spider. Her soapy smell as she lay next to me, reading *Mog's Christmas* as my eyes grew heavy. The warmth of the kitchen in the mornings, beans on toast for tea.

And Dad. Dad coming home covered in paint, grinning, picking me up and spinning me around. Him in the middle on the sofa, wedged between Mum and me as we watched *The Lion King*. His cuddles when I cried when Mufasa died. Telling me, when I asked why I didn't have a baby brother or sister: *You're all we need, Baby B.*

'Things started changing, even before,' I continue. 'Obviously. She was so poorly. We spent months in hospital, but really, it was quick. I always wonder, if we'd had more time to prepare ourselves . . .' I shake my head. 'And then my dad started drinking. He stopped going to work. He smoked a lot of weed, went out and did other drugs, but mainly it was the booze. It was like a switch flicked. I had nobody to look after me any more.'

Jordan is staring at me. I keep going.

'Some weeks he wouldn't move at all. He'd be on the sofa all day, and would sleep there all night. It was like time stopped existing. I suppose I was grieving too, looking back, but I couldn't – not really. I had to be the strong one for us both, because he was falling apart. I didn't want anything else to change; I thought if I could keep up the pretence that everything was fine, keep going to school, keep turning up, nobody would interfere. They wouldn't take me away.'

Jordan is crying now. Big, silent tears are rolling down his cheeks. My eyes stay dry.

'But now I think, wouldn't that have been best? He turned nasty. He told me he hated me, that he wished it'd been me instead of her. I know it was the drink talking, but . . . I don't know. In the end, I was just scared of him. I ran away to university as soon as I could, and I've never been back. Or, at least, I've never been back inside. I drop him home when I have to pick him up from the police station, or the hospital. He doesn't have anybody else. He calls me all the time. Sometimes he's kind and sad, and it breaks my heart and I hate myself for not going to him, for not looking after him, you know? But mostly he hates me. He hates me so much, and it's because I'm bad, and everything is my fault.'

Jordan is silent for a long moment. He leans forward and grabs my hands, his face wet. 'It is *not* your fault. None of this is your fucking fault.'

'How do you get that thought out of your head, though?' I ask. 'I mean, I can *see* that. I'm questioning myself, finally, and I can see that *of course* my mum dying wasn't my fault. But how do I stop myself from feeling it, and having it underline everything?'

'You don't,' Jordan says sadly. 'At least, not just overnight. It's years of work, and providing yourself with evidence that what you believe isn't true.'

'How do I do that?'

'You're doing it right now.' He smiles. 'Sitting and telling someone all of your shit and having them listen to you and actually care.'

I lean in and wrap my arms around his neck. Chunks of papaya crumble off my face and onto his T-shirt.

Jordan laughs away my apologies. 'Don't worry about it.' He sits back and picks up his wine again. 'You know, it's so easy to see why you got yourself into this web of lies with Ben.'

'How do you mean?'

'When you've got something like that in your history, something so scarring and impactful that you want to leave behind, it's easy to tell little white lies to people so they don't uncover the truth. And little white lies build up, until you're founded on a story that isn't even true.'

'You sound like you're speaking from experience.'

Jordan looks at me. 'You know why I got into family law?'

I shake my head.

'My brother—' He stops and runs his hands through his hair, and then sits up straight. 'My brother was a drug addict. *Is* a drug addict. He had two kids in a fucked-up relationship and their mum couldn't handle it. She left. Me and my parents . . . he distanced himself from us. Wouldn't let us see the children, wouldn't speak to us at all for months on end, and when he did it was only to ask for money.' He takes a deep breath. 'Next thing we knew, there was a call from social services. My nephew hadn't been registered for school, so they'd turned up at the house and found my brother . . . well, he was out of it. High as a kite. The kids were both filthy and terrified. They were starving; the police didn't think they'd eaten in days.'

It's my turn for my eyes to fill now. It hits so close to home. 'God, Jordan. I'm sorry.'

'My parents fought for custody, but his partner showed up again and took them both away. We didn't see them for a while, but we knew it was bad. She wasn't a good mother. Anyway, after a couple of years, social services gave them back to him. Just . . . handed them back over. Like it had never happened. I was already training to be a lawyer, and I knew right then that I had to go into family law. To stop shitty parents having the opportunity to fuck their children's lives up. But before I qualified, they—' His voice cracks, and he coughs. 'They called us again. The youngest – Tommy – he'd fallen down the stairs. He was four, and my brother had left him home alone to go out and score.'

'Oh my god. Jordan, I can't even imagine—'

'He survived, with a head injury and some broken bones. But how does it take that? How does it take a child being hurt to get them a good home?'

'It's awful.' I thank god that my mum stuck around long enough for me to have a safe childhood.

'Anyway, my parents got custody, then. They're good kids, really sweet and funny. So clever.' He smiles as he talks about them. 'My brother did a stretch in prison. He's been out for six months, and he's already knocked someone up. They're living together, and social services are crawling all over them, waiting for her to pop so they can take the baby. And guess which law firm he's hired to fight his corner?'

'No,' I gasp.

'Yep. Mine. The place I show up to every day to try and make a difference.'

'Can't they reject the case?'

'They could, but it's money, isn't it?' Jordan looks tired, as though letting the façade down is physically draining. 'My brother's got everyone he knows chipping in for legal fees. Crowd funders, sob stories, the lot.'

'So you quit?' I ask.

'No, I didn't quit.' He shakes his head. 'They gave me a paid sabbatical. Until it's all over.'

I nod. There don't seem to be the right words. This explains Jordan's anger at me when I was trying to buy drugs, and his fierce protectiveness of people he cares about. It must be impossible having to fight someone you love.

'So do you come to group for the . . . escape?' I try. Despite him telling me his story, I still can't wrap my head around why he feels like he needs that particular brand of support.

He looks at me, and then stares across the room. 'No.'

'If you don't want to talk about it—'

'My parents are the most important people in the world to me,' he says, his jaw set. 'The *most* important. But I hid myself from them. I never showed them who I am – you know, with the drag – I just couldn't.'

'That must be so difficult,' I try. 'But they sound like wonderful people. I'm sure they'd just be happy that you're happy.'

'I ran into my dad in town a few months ago. Just after we found out about my brother's new baby,' Jordan continues as though I haven't spoken. 'I was on my way to Tasha's in *all* the gear. I'd gone all-out. He didn't recognise me, but he heard my voice. And he looked at me . . .' Jordan trails off, his eyes glazed.

'What happened?' I whisper.

'He looked at me, and his eyes were so . . . there was this look. As though he was disgusted by me. And then he walked away.'

'God, Jordan. That's so hard.' I reach out and squeeze his hand. 'Have you talked to him about it?'

'No. We haven't spoken. But that's the problem, isn't it?' He turns to look at me, his eyes desperate. 'That's the problem, Briony. When you know people disapprove of who you are, you hide it before they've even had a chance to look. And then they catch a glimpse, under everything, and prove you right.'

'And then you hate yourself,' I say.

He nods. 'And then you hate yourself.'

31

When I get home the next day, there's a letter waiting for me on the mat.

I rip it open and scan through it quickly.

*An **assessment appointment** has been made for you at Bridgegate Mental Health Services . . . Please fill in the attached questionnaires and bring them with you . . . For more information about Cognitive Behavioural Therapy (CBT), please go to the NHS website . . .*

I check the date. It's next Wednesday, at four. I'll have had my chat with Jason by then, so I should know where I stand. But what will this therapist be expecting from me? I flick through the questionnaires.

Using a scale of zero (0 = not at all) to ten (10 = extremely) please answer the following questions:

Parties and social events scare me

I avoid doing things or speaking to people for fear of embarrassment

Heart palpitations bother me when I am around other people

Trembling or shaking in front of others is distressing for me

The list goes on.

Am I supposed to fill this out and hand it over to a stranger?

Someone who, by definition, will judge me and want to see all my flaws?

I sit down at the kitchen table and pull out a pen. I think really carefully about each answer before ticking it off. *I avoid giving speeches.* Do I? Maybe I don't *avoid* them. I've never been asked to give a speech, so how would I know? Perhaps I can put a three, or even a two for that one. I don't want this therapist thinking I'm a solid ten across the board.

I sleep badly before a big social event. Well, *yes.* But then I always sleep badly, so maybe that cancels it out? Maybe I actually sleep *better* before a big event, but just haven't noticed because I rarely sleep at all?

But the more I think about every answer, the more I put myself in each hypothetical scenario, the more terrified I feel. I can't lie to myself, and I certainly can't lie to someone who's trying to help me. I've got to be honest, or I'll end up in even more of a mess. I'm *extremely,* in every category.

I fill out another questionnaire asking how much my anxiety affects my relationships, work and lifestyle. I feel a smug sense of satisfaction as I give *hygiene* a one out of ten (*not at all*) but then remember the stench of the house every time I return after days inside, and reluctantly change it to a five.

When I'm done, I put the questionnaires in a pile on the table with the letter on top, so I can't see what I've written. The thought of anyone reading my answers makes my knees feel weak, so I pin the papers to the fridge and go upstairs.

I lie down on the bed, and before I know what I'm doing, my phone is at my ear and I'm calling Ben. There's something in me that feels different, feels like I *need* to speak to him. I've been messaging him since he left, but that was a panicky sort of feeling, like I was reaching out to try and grab him and pull him back so we could pretend nothing had changed.

But now I feel like something *has* changed. I feel like I've got something to tell him, or show him; something important, not just a desperate clutching of nothingness.

The phone rings out. His answerphone message squawks in my ear, and I listen to it, even though it's just the automated Vodafone woman, because it's familiar.

I hang up without leaving a message, and almost immediately a text pings through.

Ben: *I'm sorry I'm not responding. I feel like this space is good for us. I miss you, Bri, but I'm not sure I miss the you you've been recently. I need to get my head on straight again. X*

I brace myself for the sucker punch to the chest, but it's lighter than I expected. My brain flits with images of our old life, before my promotion, and now. It flits to the future, and a mild ache crosses my stomach, and then passes. I feel like I'm taller, somehow, and less hopeless.

Did unburdening myself to Jordan last night actually help? Or is it because I've finally severed ties with Sami? I poke around in my mind for triggers: meetings at work, speaking in front of people, hospitals, dying. The anxiety comes, and bubbles away in my stomach, but for this moment, it feels like I have a hold on it. It feels like, if I wanted it to, it could run away with me, but right now, I am strong enough to take the reins and slow it down.

Do I really need to see this therapist? I remember the last time I felt powerful: when I lost it at Sami and Julia in the café. Was that power? Or was it anger? I remember going to see Sarah and Jordan, and saying I'd never need group again. But within hours, I was back to square one.

No – this is a moment, and while they might be becoming more frequent, they aren't guaranteed.

I pick my phone up again and call Sarah. It rings a few times, and I wonder if maybe she hates talking on the phone, and I've made her feel uncomfortable by trying to contact her in this way. But then the line clicks.

'Hello?'

'Hiya, it's Briony.'

'I know, I have caller ID.' She laughs.

'I'm really, really, really sorry about what I said about Jordan. Like, ridiculously sorry,' I gabble.

'It's OK. I'm sorry I didn't reply to your texts.'

'No, please don't apologise. I was just . . . I was hurt and I wasn't in a good place.'

'Oh. So . . . did you make it up?'

'No!' I yelp. 'No, Priya did say it, but it was wrong of me to throw it in your face like that. And it isn't true. It's not true at all. Well, maybe it is a bit, but he has good reasons for it. Kind reasons. He actually wants to help; it's not like it's a hobby . . .' I trail off, a bit breathless.

'What reasons?' Sarah asks.

'It's not my place to say, but he's been through some shit too. He just knows how it feels to be . . . to be frustrated and like you're fighting something you'll never win.' I feel tears welling in my eyes and I swallow them down. I feel awful for putting Jordan in a situation where he had to prise drugs out of my hand.

How do you think you'll feel tomorrow? You think you'll wake up cured? You'll feel fifty times worse than you do now, trust me.

'I can't imagine Jordan having any problems,' Sarah muses. 'It doesn't seem . . . right.'

'I know. But I guess everybody does.' I sigh. 'Please don't be angry with him. He's such a kind person.'

'Has he got you at gunpoint?' She laughs again. 'Don't worry, I'm not angry. I was hurt, but it's OK.'

'Are you angry with me? You didn't come to group.'

'No, of course not!' she says, in the tone I recognise as the one I use when I don't want Sami to think I feel anything negative about her. 'I'm not angry with you. I just wasn't feeling up to it. Promise.'

'You're allowed to be, you know,' I say, thinking that it might actually be true. Maybe people can be angry with you, or think you've done something shitty, without hating you and wanting nothing more to do with you.

'Well, maybe I was, a little bit,' she mumbles. 'But I'm not now, honest. Life's too short and all that jazz.'

'Yeah.' I nod, even though she isn't in the room.

'Will I see you next Tuesday?' she asks.

'Yeah, I'll be there.' I suddenly realise that I haven't told Jordan or Sarah what Dr Patel said to me about the group. I open my mouth to explain, but I stop myself. I need to do some research first, check it's definitely right. I can't pull Sarah's support rug from under her when I might be wrong. 'Shall we all meet beforehand? Grab a coffee, or something?'

'Yeah.' I can hear her smiling down the phone. 'That'd be nice.'

32

Jordan and Sarah are already sitting at a table when I walk into the café. Their drinks are half-full, so I assume they've been here a while. Sarah looks upset.

'Hey, everything OK?' I sling my bag onto a spare seat and sit down.

'I've just told Sarah everything I told you the other night,' Jordan says.

'Oh,' I say, unsure how to tread. 'How are you feeling? Are you . . . OK?'

He nods. 'Yeah, I am. I felt better after I spoke to you. It really lifted a weight off.'

'So you thought you'd try and lift it some more?' I ask, smiling.

'Exactly.' Jordan laughs. 'And I needed to apologise for what Priya said. I needed to explain.'

'You didn't have to explain anything,' Sarah says, shaking her head.

'You were a bit annoyed with me though, weren't you?' Jordan nudges her playfully.

'All right, yeah, I was a bit.' She laughs.

The waiter comes to the table and I order a tea. 'It's me who should apologise again,' I say, once he's left. 'It was such a dick move.'

Jordan flaps his hand around, dismissing me. 'You were feeling balls, and you've already said sorry. We've all been there.'

'OK.' I smile, relieved. 'I'll shut up.'

'But for the record,' he continues, sighing, 'the reason Priya said that is because I *did* fix her, in a way. Her and Aiden.'

'What do you mean?' Sarah frowns.

'They were both addicts when I met them – a few years ago now, at an LGBT community event in town. I . . . helped them, I guess. Offered a bit of support, let them crash at mine when they needed it. It took a while, but they've been clean for a long time now.'

'That's really good of you,' I say.

'Yeah, I suppose. But maybe it was selfish of me. Maybe I was just trying to control someone else because I couldn't control my brother.'

'I doubt that.' Sarah rubs Jordan's forearm. 'If they didn't want help, they wouldn't have kept coming back to you.'

'Yeah, maybe you're right.' Jordan finishes his coffee and sets the cup down gently in its saucer.

'So . . . if you don't want to fix us, why *do* you hang out with us?' I look at Sarah. 'No offense.'

'None taken.' She laughs. 'We're not exactly your usual crowd, anyone can see that.'

Jordan shrugs. 'I don't know. I like being around you both. You don't . . . I guess you don't push me like the rest of my friends do.'

'In what way?' I ask.

'Like, every time I mention this stuff about my parents to them, it's all "You be you! Fuck what anybody says!", you know? It's like I've got to be *on* all the time.'

'But you're such an advocate of that!' Sarah says, smiling. 'You're always telling us to be ourselves and not give a shit about what anybody else says.'

'Yeah, maybe I should stop.' He laughs. 'It's all great, but it's just words, isn't it? It doesn't stop you believing all the bad things.' He looks at me then, a nod to our conversation last night. 'The point is, I'm just as shit-scared about what the world says about me as you guys are. And when I'm around you, there's no pressure to pretend I don't care.'

'Oh, good – we're all doomed,' I mutter, and Jordan laughs loudly.

'No! No, we're not. I think I've still got the confidence edge over both of you, so we'll get by.'

'So group is less for the social stuff and more for the self-esteem?' Sarah muses.

'I suppose so. I don't know. I try all these things, but I can't really figure out what's going on in my head to begin with. Do I hate myself? Am I afraid that other people judge me? Am I terrified of losing my parents for being who I am? Yes, yes and yes. But where's the line between self-development and just accepting yourself? And what does all that worrying make me? Socially anxious? I don't know.' Jordan sighs.

'I don't know either.' I frown. 'I don't know what I am. Do you think naming it even helps?'

'God, no. I'd rather die than be given a label.' Jordan shudders. 'I think you've just got to do what feels right for you.'

'I think I'd like a label,' Sarah mumbles. We turn to look at her and she scratches her eyebrow self-consciously. 'I mean, I think maybe I'd find it reassuring. You know, just having something to call it. Then I'd at least have a place to start.'

Would I like a label? I think about how desperate I was to find out what was wrong with me, about my abusive tirade at the receptionist at the GP. I *needed* someone to tell me what the problem was, but when I was offered further tests, I refused. Was it my fear of hospitals and the past trauma of living in them when I was twelve, or was I really just scared to find out the answer?

'We'd better leave in a minute.' Jordan moves to get his coat.

'Wait—' I grab the arm of his jacket to stop him from putting it on '—I need to tell you both something.'

'Sounds ominous.' Sarah looks nervously at Jordan, who sinks back into his seat.

'I know you both said you weren't referred to the group by your GP, so how did you find out about it?'

'Erm, some Facebook post, I think,' Sarah says.

'I saw a flyer at another group I went to.' Jordan frowns. 'Why?'

'So neither of you saw it advertised within the NHS? No hospitals, or health websites or anything?'

'No,' they say at the same time.

'Right.' I lean forward. 'Well, when I went to the doctor, I told him I was going to a support group, and he told me he'd never heard of it. I gave him the address, Fran's name, everything, and he said nobody he knows has ever referred to that group. He told me to be careful.' I raise an eyebrow.

'Well, is your GP local? Maybe it's a different catchment area or something,' Sarah tries.

'I thought about that,' I agree, 'but he seemed really weirded out by the fact that nobody had *referred* me. And then I remembered you guys saying you weren't referred either, and I thought – isn't that *strange*? How do you get into NHS group therapy without your GP's say-so?'

'Good point.' Sarah chews on her nails worriedly.

'So I did some research, and it's nowhere. All I could find was Fran's website, where she lists all the clubs she runs. There are *tonnes*. It's so weird, honestly. And isn't that funny, too? That she runs so many clubs in so many different specialties? Surely you have to be a professional to host a government-funded mental health group?'

'Bloody hell.' Jordan looks delighted. 'Do you think she's a *fraud*?'

'I don't know. But I think we should go and find out.'

The church hall is empty when we arrive, even though we're five minutes late.

'Where is everybody?' Jordan looks around. 'Reckon she's been arrested?'

'Let's not be dramatic.' I nudge him. 'Look, the back door's open.'

We walk across the hall and to the door, and as we get closer, voices start to filter through.

'No, Geoff. Be *gentle*. He doesn't mean you any harm.' It's Fran.

'He's looking at me funny!' Geoff retorts. 'He's got a wild look in his eyes. I don't trust him.'

'The fuck?' Jordan murmurs, and we walk through the door. I stop in my tracks.

The entire group is in the back car park, standing in a circle around Fran and Geoff, who is attempting to straddle a Shetland pony.

'Oh, you've decided to join us!' Fran smiles and pats the horse's neck. 'Come and meet Gordon.'

'What?' Sarah whispers, her mouth hanging open.

'Don't look so frightened, Sarah! Gordon is a therapy horse. He helps people to feel calm.'

As if on cue, Gordon whinnies loudly and Geoff screams.

'I don't like horses.' Stuart takes a step back from the circle.

'Everyone likes horses, Stuart! They can smell your fear; don't stand like that.' Fran smiles as Geoff finally settles on Gordon's back, his feet scraping against the floor like an adult on a child's bike. 'Now, give him a little hug. Feel that nice peaceful energy.'

'He smells.' Geoff wrinkles his nose.

'He smells of *nature*.' Fran tuts.

'He smells of horse shit.'

Jordan steps forward. 'Fran, where the hell did you get a therapy horse?'

'Language!' Fran wails, and Gordon neighs and takes a couple of steps forward. Geoff squeals. 'It doesn't matter where he's from. Come and have a pet.'

Jordan goes forward and strokes Gordon's neck. Geoff flaps. 'Don't freak him out! He'll leg it!'

I take a couple of steps back while Fran is distracted, and skirt back into the church hall. I walk the perimeter and scan the walls quickly, passing leaflets for judo and AA until I find Fran's. I rip it off the wall and study it; the wording is the same as the flyer I spotted outside, but the bright-blue NHS logo in the corner is pixelated up-close.

I step back outside. Gordon has Jordan's wig on his head.

'Take it *off* him, Jordan!' Fran is trying to battle through the circle, which has shrunk as people move closer to take a picture. 'He's not a show pony!'

'Where *did* you find him, Fran?' I call over the clamour and everyone hushes.

She sighs. 'For goodness sake, is it really that *important?* He was in the field behind the church so I borrowed him for an hour. There, happy now?' She finally reaches Gordon and pulls the wig off his head. 'Now. Everybody please *calm down,* and we'll get Geoff off so somebody else can have a go.'

'I think you should give the horse back now, Fran,' Sarah says confidently, and I stare at her. She nods to the leaflet in my hand.

'Nobody's going to *notice,* Sarah—'

'Fran,' I interrupt, and hold up the flyer, 'is this really an NHS-funded group?'

Fran colours. 'No, and I never said it was.' She pulls Gordon to one side as Geoff finally dismounts. 'Come on now, Gordon. Let's fix your saddle here.'

'You've got the logo right here.' I point.

'That's not the NHS logo,' she says defiantly. 'That's *my* logo. The National Holistic Society. It's a lighter shade of blue.'

'Wait, so you're not a doctor?' Jane looks traumatised. 'Are you even a therapist?'

'You told people you were a *doctor?*' Jordan gasps.

'No! I never said that!' Fran looks like she's about to explode. 'I'm a helper. I'm just trying to help!'

'But you don't know what you're doing, Fran,' I say kindly. 'You're not helping at all.'

'Excuse *me!*' She whirls towards me, wisps of her hair flying. 'Stuart told the postman his hat was nice yesterday! Do you think he did that by *himself?*'

'I bloody well hope not,' Jordan says drily.

'Why do you do it, Fran? Why are you running all of these groups?' Sarah asks gently. 'What's in it for you?'

'Nothing's in it for me!' Fran screeches, looking outraged. 'I want to give something back! I know how to help people, so that's what I'm doing.' She turns back to Gordon and runs her fingers through his mane. 'And it's nice, isn't it, to meet lots of people? Lots of other people with other problems? Is that *illegal?* Is wanting to offer support something to be ashamed of?'

'Couldn't you have gone to knitting club or something?' Jordan asks.

'*Knitting?*' Fran looks horrified. 'Why would I do that?'

'You've got to stop this,' Sarah says. 'You're giving everybody false hope.'

Fran looks at us all desperately. 'But don't you feel *better?* Don't you feel like you're improving every week?'

Nobody says anything.

'I think it's nice that you want to give something back, Fran,' I say carefully. 'I just think that if you're lonely, there are more responsible ways to fix it.'

'Like what?' she glowers. 'Go to bloody walking group or improv classes where everybody's oh-so-perfect?'

'I don't know.' I shrug. 'But you can't just hang out with damaged people because they make you feel better.'

'And you *definitely* can't give them therapy when you don't know your arse from your elbow,' Jordan mutters.

'What are we supposed to do now?' Jane looks around at us all desperately. 'Where do we go?'

'Go to your GP,' I say. 'Get some proper support.'

'I've been to my GP fifty-eight times this year,' Geoff snarls. 'He says I'm a hypochondriac.'

I have to remind myself that it isn't my place to pass judgment.

'Change doctors. Get a second opinion. I don't know, I'm not an expert,' I say, exasperatedly. 'I'm sorry. We can all support each other, but we can't treat ourselves. And we certainly can't get better by being forced to dance with ribbons and scream about how sexy we are.'

Fran picks at her nails, her head bowed.

'So what do we do?' Stuart asks quietly.

Jordan steps forward. 'Let's take this bloody horse back for a start.'

33

It took quite a while to manhandle Gordon back into his stable. His owner found us all lurking in the field, and Jordan had to pretend we were part of the RSPCA to stop her from calling the police. She showed us Gordon's bright-pink hairbrush and £120 shampoo as proof of his wellness, and let us get on our way.

At some point during the commotion, Fran slipped away.

I'm on my way into work for the first time in over a month. It feels strange to be back on my usual commute, after so long being a house hermit. I've got actual adult clothes on, too, instead of my usual jeans and crusty jumper.

My stomach is somersaulting, but in a manageable way. I imagine what Jason might say to me, in front of everybody, and a faint pain jabs my temple for a second before it disappears. By now, the whole office will know what I've done. Wiggy will have told them all that I absconded after messing up the meeting, and there have probably been round-robin, company-wide emails with memes about me. The thought makes me feel queasy, but I swallow it down. I don't have time for shame; it's not productive.

I get off the bus and walk through town. There are so many *people* here in the daytime, all running around and making important phone calls and worrying about their hair. It's mad.

I keep my head up, for once, and drink it in a bit. It's stressful, for a while, and I'm desperate to stare at my feet, but after a moment I feel less like I'm sticking out, and more like I'm blending in. Nobody takes any notice of me.

I get to my building and walk through the lobby, flashing a quick smile at the security guards. They smile back. I feel a sudden desperation to be back here, where everything is busy and warm and connected.

It's a pity I'm about to be fired.

When I reach my floor, the scene is the same as it always is apart from Wiggy, sitting in my chair and squinting at his screen. The team look up as I walk past.

'Oh, hi, Briony!' Carl calls. 'How are you feeling?'

'I'm OK, thanks.' I hurry towards Jason's office, but something tugs at me. I risk a look back at my section. Nobody is staring at me. They're all smiling, or getting on with their work. Wiggy gives me a nod. I stop. 'How are you guys getting on?'

Everyone looks up. 'Good!' Carl says, eventually. 'We're doing really well.'

'I'm glad.' I smile, and move away.

Jason is in his office, rummaging about in a drawer. He stands up when he sees me. 'Morning, Briony.' He skirts around me and shuts the door.

'Morning.' I sit down opposite him. My legs are shaking a little, but my mind feels clear.

'How are we doing?' He sits back down and clasps his hands over his stomach.

'I'm good, thanks. I'm . . . better. I feel better.' I nod.

'That's great to hear.'

'Yeah.'

There's a moment of silence, and I wonder who's supposed to speak next. Should I apologise, or is he going to bollock me first?

'So the project is going very well,' he says, before I can open my mouth. 'It's really picked up speed these past two weeks.'

I nod. 'That's good.'

Jason stares at me for a second. 'It's better than good, Briony. It's great.'

'Oh, yes. Of course. It's really great.' I shuffle in my seat, and glance through the glass wall. Wiggy is watching, and he whips his head back round when he sees me.

'It's a real credit to your team,' Jason continues. 'You should be very proud.'

'Oh, I am,' I say, confused. What does he think I have to be proud of? And *my* team? It's a credit to Wiggy's, surely?

Jason cocks his head to one side. 'Nothing to say for yourself?'

I go to speak but there's a knock at the door.

'Come in,' Jason calls, and Wiggy steps in.

'Oh, sorry, I didn't know you were in here.' Wiggy looks at me, and I frown. Yes he did, he just saw me.

Jason smiles. 'How can I help?'

'I just . . . well, I knew you were going to meet with Briony, and I just thought you might want to show her these reports of how the project has responded to testing.' He holds out a piece of paper and Jason takes it. 'I thought she'd want to see . . .'

'Great, thanks, Wiggy,' Jason says, and Wiggy nods.

'Right. Yep, OK. That was all. Sorry again.' He steps out.

'Even better news, Briony.' Jason scans the document as the door closes. 'Testing is almost done and it's all very positive. Looks like you're ahead of schedule.'

'Me?' I say, before I can help myself.

Jason puts the paper down and leans over the desk slightly. 'Wiggy told me you've been helping him. There's no way this would be so far forward without your input.'

'Wiggy told you?' I parrot. Wiggy gave me the credit? 'Why?'

'Well, isn't it true?'

'Yes! I mean, yeah, it is, but I didn't want to step on anybody's toes . . .'

'And neither did Wiggy, it seems.' Jason raises his eyebrows at me, smiling.

What is going on? Wiggy had an opportunity, right here, to take credit for a project that took two tech leads to complete. He'd have been a total hero for finishing it ahead of schedule. Why did he tell Jason the truth? What's his game?

I look through the glass again. Wiggy grins at me.

Oh, god. The answer slots into my brain, simple and pure: he was being fair. And kind. And a good colleague and friend. The thoughts in my head battle to reject the concept – no, there must be something in it for him, no, he's after your job – but the truth is too obvious to ignore.

Jason is still smiling at me. I suddenly realise something else. Wiggy didn't tell him about my fuck-up.

'It was beyond the call of duty, Briony,' Jason says. 'You were off on leave, and you shouldn't have been helping out. But, of course, we're very grateful that you did.'

He's looking at me across the desk, his eyes twinkling and his face kind.

I can't accept this.

'Jason—' I sit up in my seat '—I'm really glad it's all going well. It's great news. But it'd be going even better if I hadn't messed it all up in the first place.'

Jason frowns and my suspicions are confirmed. Wiggy hasn't said anything. 'What do you mean by that?'

'I had a panic attack in the ideas meeting. When Carl first presented. I didn't hear anything anyone was saying, and I agreed to the project without knowing anything about it. I was so embarrassed . . . I couldn't admit what had happened, so I ran away. I gave Wiggy the project and then ran away.'

There. It's done. Out in the open, my big, shameful secret. My body sags with relief. I welcome the punishment, now. Jason tried to help me at the start of all this, and I shrugged it off. Now I'm helping him in return by giving him the perfect excuse to fire me.

Jason studies me. 'That sounds like it was a really difficult time for you.'

246

I falter. 'What?' His face is warm and open, and he looks genuinely concerned. 'Aren't you angry?'

'Of course not. We all have our moments.' He shrugs. 'I wish you'd spoken up sooner, of course. We could have sorted something out and saved you all the worry.'

Saved *me* the worry? I almost ruined our entire team. 'But I should have been worried!' I say, frustrated now. 'It was completely unprofessional!'

'We can't always be our perfect selves in every situation, Briony. Sometimes life gets in the way. Everyone has stuff they're dealing with.'

I sit back in my chair. I can't process what he's telling me; it doesn't fit with anything I think or believe. What I did was bad. What I did was my fault. What I did was shameful and unforgivable.

But if it's so unforgivable, why do I feel like I'm being forgiven?

'Well, thank you,' I say, meaning it. 'I really appreciate everything you've done. You tried to reach out to me and I didn't deserve that. I'm sorry I've caused all this drama.' Jason opens his mouth to speak, but I carry on. 'I really enjoyed my time here. I just want to say . . . well, thank you for the experience, really. It's been such a great place to work.'

I feel good, suddenly. Like I've wrapped everything up in a tidy little bow. I've made peace with Jason, Wiggy can go forward and do a great job, and I can rest easy, knowing my secrets have been exposed and put to bed. I look through the glass wall once more, my heart swelling. I really loved working here. I'll miss it.

'Are you leaving?' Jason is frowning at me again.

'Well, if there's nothing else to discuss . . .' I go to stand up, taking my cue.

'That's a shame.' Jason shakes his head. 'Is there nothing we can do? We can look at extra support, or if you like, I can show you the re-shuffle? You can have some input into the plans?'

'What?' I pause with my hand on the armrest of my seat. What is he saying to me?

'I mentioned the restructuring in my email, didn't I?' Jason taps at his computer. 'Yes, here. Maybe you'd like to look at the plans and see where you think everyone would be best placed? You certainly know the personalities better than I do, so your opinion would be—'

'Hang on,' I interrupt, raising my hand. 'Are you firing me or not?'

Jason looks bewildered. '*Firing* you?'

My head is spinning. Does he think I'm handing my notice in? What is happening? What have I done?

'I don't want to leave!' I squeal, suddenly. 'I don't! I thought you wanted me gone, I thought you were trying to push me out and fob me off with excuses about kitchen refurbishments and restructures, and I wanted to make it easy for you because I've caused so much aggro—'

Jason stands up and I stop talking. He looks around the office and through the glass wall and then gestures with his hand. 'Come with me.'

I stumble to my feet and follow him out of his office, my heart pounding. I don't feel panicky; it's a new kind of energy, or one that I haven't felt in a long time.

He leads me towards the back of the open-plan area, to where the kitchen is.

Or, where the kitchen *was*.

All the cabinets and cupboard have been ripped out, and transparent plastic sheets are hanging from the ceilings. The desks that used to sit in the surrounding space are gone, and the carpet is bare.

'We've had to ask forty people to work from home,' Jason says, gazing at the empty floor. 'It should all be done in a couple of weeks, though.'

The truth slots into my brain again with a *clunk*. Transparency, honesty, genuine intentions. Alien concepts.

'Oh,' is all I can say.

'Yes.' Jason looks at me out of the corner of his eye.

'I've been working on something else, too,' I blurt, lifting my head and staring straight into his eyes.

'Oh?'

'A new user interface. Well, the beginnings of one. Cleaner, and softer. A step away from any of the other social meet-up apps. It's less complex, more . . . streamlined,' I babble, wanting to shove the words back in as soon as they're out. But then I force myself to remember that Jason wants me here, and my ideas are good. I roll my shoulders and take a deep breath, steadying my voice. 'I'd love to show you, if you have time?'

Jason is nodding, his eyes shining. 'Do you have your laptop?'

'Yes! Yeah, I do.' I stride off back towards his office, excitement flooding through me. Jason follows, and I open up my computer on his desk. 'So, you can see here, I've completely rearranged the layout of the match page. Where it used to be those clunky buttons, I've made softer, more fluid menu bars, and—'

Jason takes over the computer, navigating from page to page. My stomach swirls. I *know* it's good. But what if he sees this as a big 'fuck you' to our previous format?

There's a few moments of silence, broken only by the clicking of the mouse. Jason whistles between his teeth. 'This is incredible.'

Relief floods through me. 'Thank you.'

'Can you present this at the next project meeting?'

I stand still for a second, familiar feelings jolting through me. And then suddenly, unexpectedly, I throw my head back and laugh. I laugh so hard, tears start gathering in the corners of my eyes. For a second, I think I've gone mad. I think I've finally cracked and they're going to have to call security and wheel me out of here in a straightjacket and a mouth guard. But then I realise that I'm clearer than I've ever been. I feel *vivid*. I feel completely and utterly alive, because I am in control.

It's hilarious, because I've *always* been in control. I just didn't realise it until now, and the relief is like a drug. I'm as free as I want to be.

'No,' I say eventually, shaking my head, my breath heavy. 'No, Jason, I can't.'

Jason grins. 'Silly question?'

'Really silly question.' I smile back, sighing, and close the lid of my computer. 'But you know I'll work my arse off on it.'

'I know you will.' He nods.

'You know—' I slot my laptop back into my bag '—I think I'll take you up on your offer. I'd like some extra support, if it's practical.'

I don't know what makes me say it. I just suddenly feel like it's not the most stupid thing in the world to need a bit of back-up, and to shout when you're not coping as well as you could be.

'Of course.' Jason sits at his desk and taps quickly on his keyboard. 'I'll email HR and they'll send you a list of all the present options available to you, and we can sit down together and go through some of the more individual things we can put in place to make you more comfortable.'

My chin wobbles. 'Thank you.' I swallow. 'Really, thank you. Thanks for not giving up on me.'

'No one deserves to be given up on, Briony.' Jason smiles kindly. 'So, shall we go and have a look through those restructure plans? If you're planning on staying?'

'OK.' I nod, glancing through the glass window once more. 'But can Wiggy come, too?'

34

I'm officially starting work again on Monday.

I'll go straight back into my Tech Lead post, and Wiggy will return to being a senior on his own team. He suggested it himself, during our restructuring discussion, and sagged into his chair when Jason went to get some coffee, whispering 'thank fuck for that' under his breath.

I'm cleaning the house from top to bottom. I've opened all the windows, dusted every surface and I'm now using the hoover to suck up great balls of dirt that are floating across the floorboards like tumbleweeds. I've got the radio on in the background, and the sun is shining. I almost feel normal.

I'm wrestling with the hoover wire when my phone pings with a message.

Jordan: *Finally got hold of Fran . . .*

Me: *Omg. Tell, tell, tell!!!*

Jordan: *I'll fill you in when I see you – you free tonight?*

Sarah: *What did she say?! You can both come to mine for tea if you want? Six-ish?*

Me: *Yes, please* ☺

Jordan: *Plan.*

I check the address Sarah has given me on Google Maps. It's only a ten-minute walk away, but I'm sweaty and gross and need a time-consuming, industrial-level shower if I'm going out in public. I shove the hoover in the cupboard and take the stairs two at a time before throwing myself into the bathroom like a woman possessed.

I am *desperate* to know what's happened with Fran. After she disappeared the other day, Jordan agreed to try contacting her until she responded, and said he'd threaten to take her to court unless she took her website down and came clean about who she really was: a bored, lonely pensioner. I feel a really strange sadness when I think about Fran, despite all the weird stuff she forced me to do. I hope Jordan hasn't gone in too hard on her.

I wonder if she's left the country. Would she do that, for the sake of a dodgy support group? What could be the punishment for that kind of thing, anyway? Fran wouldn't last long in prison. Although, actually, maybe she would? There are all kinds of activities available in jail; she could even retrain as a genuine counsellor. If I was her, I'd probably turn myself in just for the career opportunities.

No, I wouldn't – I can't even bear going to the hairdressers.

I dry myself off and put on a fresh jumper and a pair of high-waisted jeans. I'm just pulling my boots on when there's a knock at the door.

I walk down the stairs tentatively, peering down through the frosted glass of the front door. There's a shadow there, but the light is behind them and I can't see who it is.

I push my ear against the wood. 'Who's there?'

There's a loud and familiar sigh. 'It's me. Open the door, we need to talk.'

I grip the door handle and check my watch. I'm due at Sarah's in twenty minutes. 'I don't have long,' I say.

'Oh my god, just open the door.'

I unlock the door and pull it open, and Sami tumbles in. Her hair is greasy and scraped back into a bun, and her eyes are dark and heavy.

'Right, come on. Let's hash this out.' She strides past me and into the living room, dumping herself on the sofa.

'Hash what out?' I say, standing in the doorway.

'Sit down.'

I sit.

'Look.' She sighs and rubs her hands on her thighs, and I notice her nails are chipped and broken. 'I said some bad things, and you got upset. I can only apologise for that. I've not been myself.'

'Go on, then,' I say.

'What?'

'Go on, then,' I repeat, surprising myself. 'Apologise.'

She blinks. 'I just did.'

'No, you said you *can only apologise*. You didn't actually say sorry.'

She looks at me, her eyes wide. I suddenly realise that she doesn't know how to take me; she had ideas of how this was going to go down, and it wasn't like this. 'I'm sorry, Bri.' Her eyes fill with tears. 'I don't know what's wrong with me recently. I've pushed you away, I know that. I've been awful.'

I feel my resolve waver, and the guilt creeps in at the corners. Why am I being so harsh with her? I see Sami in front of me as she was over a decade ago, holding me close in her bed while I cried about my mum, providing a safe space I didn't have at home. I remember her squeezing my hand as she walked me back to hers when I'd wandered the streets because I didn't want to go home. I remember her putting our favourite film on and making me soup. When was the last time I asked *her* how she was?

'I didn't know that,' I say softly. 'I'm sorry, I should have asked.'

'You should.' She sniffs. 'It's been very difficult.'

'What's been happening?'

'Lots of stuff.' She waves her hand. 'I got in some trouble over some MDMA. And Julia won't really talk to me any more.'

I feel a heaviness sink down into my stomach. She's here

because Julia doesn't want her any more. She doesn't want *me*, she just wants somebody. And I'm the easy target.

As soon as the thought enters my head, something fights back. *No, she's your best friend. You've known her forever; she's always looked out for you.* I remember the draughty cold of the church at my mum's funeral, and Sami's warm arm pressed against me, her head on my shoulder. I remember her finding a hidden room behind the bar at the wake and pulling me in there, wrapping her arms around me as I let myself collapse and cry for the first time since I watched them lower my mother into the ground. My only port in the storm with my dad's behaviour already slipping, the neglect already creeping in.

But has there been a *lifetime* of good memories? I think back to all my interactions with Sami over the past few years. What changed? She tells me I'm ridiculous, and then changes the subject. She gives up on me when I'm not at my best. She ditches me for more interesting people. She shares my secrets and doesn't support me. Perhaps she got sick of me being the victim, or maybe she just grew up and isn't the same person any more.

'I've realised something, recently,' I say.

'What's that?' She looks bored already.

'I've made a habit of assuming the worst of everybody.' I lean forward a little to make sure she's listening. 'I always think everyone's got it in for me. My boss, my colleagues, new people, everybody. I think they're all out to get me.'

'Yeah—' Sami nods '—you're paranoid. We know this.'

'But not you.' I shake my head. 'I've always thought the best of you. I've always thought you were on my team.'

'You're right.' She reaches for my hand. 'I am, Bri. I've always been there for you. That's why it's so *silly* for us to be having this argument—'

'But I was wrong, wasn't I?' I pull my hand out of hers. 'Nobody wanted to watch me fall. Nobody was waiting in the sidelines for me to embarrass myself. Most people had their own shit going on, or just wanted the best for me. Most people are kind.'

Sami nods. 'Yes, you're right. They are. You just overreact all the time and think everyone hates you. I've told you this; it's not healthy.'

'I only survived my teenage years because of you, Sami. You know that. But it doesn't work any more, does it?' I take a deep breath. 'You're the person who enjoys hurting me now. You and my dad. And for some twisted reason, I've been placing my loyalty at your feet for longer than I should have been.'

Sami looks at me like I'm insane. 'What are you *talking* about? I've been with you every single time you've fucked something up. Every time you ruined something for yourself, I've been right next to you. That's what friends *do*. And yes, maybe I am hard on you sometimes, but it's called tough love!'

'There's no love involved at all though, is there?' I shrug. 'Just because you look after someone in their worst moment, doesn't mean you can treat them however you want and rip the rug from under them once they stop dancing to your tune. You've been using me to make yourself feel better since you learned how to talk. And I'm bored of it now.'

'What?' Her face has gone pink.

'I did fuck things up—' I'm on a roll now '—but it wasn't intentional. It wasn't malicious and it wasn't the end of the world. I made mistakes. And you weren't there to help me take the impact.' I stand up. 'I've got to go now.'

'Go where?' She narrows her eyes at me. 'What are all these plans you suddenly seem to have?'

'That's not really any of your business any more.' My hands are shaking, but only slightly. What I'm saying feels right; I can sense it in my gut.

'You're being a *really* good friend right now.' She raises her eyebrows at me. 'But sure. Leave me. Leave me when I'm feeling like shit and go and have fun.'

'Stop trying to guilt trip me!' I shout. 'Your problems aren't my problems! Your moods aren't my *fault.*'

'Right, well, I can see all the care I gave *you* won't be reciprocated.' Sami stands up and pushes past me into the corridor. 'Maybe we can talk properly when you're not behaving like the most selfish twat on the planet.'

'Oh, fuck off gaslighting me, Sami,' I say. 'Go home.'

She stares at me, her mouth open. 'You can't – it's not—'

I reach behind her and pull the front door open. 'Delete my number, please. I'm done.'

35

Sarah's mum's house is a pebble-dashed, 1920s semi, set back from the road by an immaculately kept garden. The crazy-paving pathway to the front door is surrounded by signs declaring 'this house runs on laughter and Prosecco', 'home is where the heart is' and 'this way for love and cake'.

I knock on the door anxiously. Sarah answers wearing an old hoodie and leggings. I immediately feel overdressed.

'Hey!' She pulls me in for a hug. 'Congratulations! Don't panic about being overdressed, Jordan's worse. We're just far too casual.'

I texted Sarah and Jordan as soon as I left the office, and they were both ridiculously dramatic about how excited they were for me. I take my shoes off in the hallway, which is cluttered with photos, teddies and yet more signs, all stacked up on shelves either side of me. Everything is immaculately clean.

'Come on through, they're in the living room.' Sarah leads me through a door to her left.

Jordan is lying on his back on a vast cream leather sofa, his shiny blonde hair fanned out behind his head. He's wearing a velvet maxi dress and dramatic burgundy lips. His shoes are off, and a woman I assume is Sarah's mum is tickling his feet.

'Helen!' Jordan squeals. 'You'll make me wee.'

'Sorry, love. I'll increase the pressure a little.' She pushes into the sole of Jordan's foot with her thumb. 'I can see the life line is very long indeed. But here . . .' She pauses and takes her hands away. 'Have you ever had a run-in with a lobster?'

'No.' Jordan lifts his head, looking worried. 'Is there one on the horizon?'

'I'm afraid so.' She sighs. 'And it doesn't look good.'

'Oh, god.' Jordan lets his head fall back again and spots me. 'Briony! The woman of the hour! Come and have your feet read.'

Helen turns around and gives me a smile, getting to her feet. 'Hello, love. You must be Briony. I've heard so much about you.' She pulls me to her chest, and for a second I think I smell my mum; that soapy warmth of her, and my eyes start to fill. I squeeze her back and sniff, hard.

'It's lovely to meet you,' I say, when she lets go of me. 'Thank you so much for having us.'

'Helen is a genius.' Jordan has sat up on the sofa and is putting his heels back on. 'You know I'm going to meet an ethereal waif? An *ethereal waif*, Briony, can you imagine?'

'Wow.' I raise my eyebrows. I don't know what the significance of this is.

'I love these, Helen.' Jordan has begun walking around the room, running his fingers along a giant mosaic of photos above the fireplace. 'Did you take them all yourself?'

'I did.' She smiles. 'They're lovely, aren't they?'

Sarah sighs and shakes her head. 'Do you need a hand with tea, Mum?'

'No, no. You three catch up, I'll go and see to the lasagne.' Helen leaves the room and I walk across the carpet towards Jordan. It's warm and bright in here, and it feels so homely I just want to curl up and soak it all in.

'This one is my favourite,' Jordan says, jabbing his finger against one of the photos in the middle.

I look more closely, and blink. It's a fanny. It's a photo of someone's bits. I step back a little, and take in the full mosaic. They're *all* fannies. There are millions of them.

'Bloody hell!' I say.

'Oh, don't.' Sarah groans. 'It's so embarrassing.'

'Why, is one of them yours?' Jordan winks at her.

'No!'

I stare at the wall. All those vaginas. 'Where did she get these?'

Sarah shrugs. 'She's an artist. They do life drawings and she asks the models. She's been collecting them for years.'

'They're all really . . . different,' I muse.

'Yeah.' Sarah laughs. 'Does a lot for your self-confidence, doesn't it?'

It actually does. There was me, thinking my hoo-ha was strange at my smear test. I don't think I could even pick it out of this line-up.

'So, tell us what Fran said!' I say, tearing my eyes away from the wall and sitting on the sofa. Sarah joins me.

'Oh my god.' Jordan plonks himself on a pouffe opposite us. 'It was crazy. I called her about fifty times, and when she eventually picked up she was really upset. She told me to check her website, and everything had gone.'

'What, all of it?' I ask. 'All the different groups?'

'Yep. She's changed it all. The logo has gone as well. It's called *Handy Helpers* now.'

'Specialising in . . .?' Sarah says.

'Odd jobs. Anything anyone needs.' Jordan shrugs. 'It's not very specific.'

'We should keep an eye on her.' I load the website up on my phone and see that he's right; the blue NHS logo is now a pink HH. 'She might start doing it again.'

'Way ahead of you.' Jordan smiles mischievously. 'I've had Aiden and Priya call her and ask for psychological help. She said there's nothing she can do and told them to go to their GP.'

'Well, that's good,' I concede. 'I hope she's OK, though.'

'Never mind whether *she's* OK—' Sarah shakes her head '—what about the others?'

I shrug. 'What can we do? I'm not sure it's our responsibility, really.'

'It definitely isn't,' Jordan agrees. 'I think we've all got enough on our plates.'

Helen pops her head around the door. 'Tea time!'

We go through into the dining room, where a silver, glittery table is adorned with weird, twisted cutlery, goblets and a giant, steaming lasagne.

'Wow,' Jordan breathes.

'I know how to throw a dinner party.' Helen winks and we sit down, putting cherub-patterned napkins on our laps. It feels like every day is a special occasion in this house; if a few friends over for midweek dinner is a party, I can't imagine the kind of stops Helen pulls out at the weekend.

'This looks delicious, thank you.' I watch as Sarah puts a melting square of lasagne on my plate.

'You're welcome any time, love.' Helen carves crispy chunks of garlic bread, spraying crumbs all over the table. She hands some out, and then sits back. 'I believe congratulations are in order?'

'To Briony!' Jordan raises his goblet and I laugh, clinking mine against it.

'Thank you, but it's the same job. No big deal.'

'It's wonderful news, darling.' Helen smiles. 'Sarah's got an interview next week, too.'

'Really?' I look at Sarah, who is hiding behind her fringe again. 'Sarah! You didn't tell us that! That's amazing!'

'Don't, you'll jinx it.' She laughs. 'It's just a receptionist job at the vets.'

'Wow, that's really brave,' Jordan says sincerely. 'Exposure at its finest.'

'I know, my new therapist suggested it.' She shrugs.

'You're seeing a therapist?' I ask.

'Yeah. I started last week.'

'How's it going? I've got my first appointment soon.'

'It's good.' She nods. 'So far. I think it'll take time.'

Helen reaches over and squeezes Sarah's hand. 'So, who else has news to share?'

'Mum,' Sarah groans, but she's smiling. 'Are we really doing the daily bulletin?'

'Yes!' Helen pretends to look outraged.

'I've got some more news, actually,' I say, surprising myself. When was the last time I spoke first in a room of people? 'Sami just came over to mine out of the blue.'

Jordan gasps, but I give Helen a bit of background before elaborating. 'She's my best friend. Well, was. We had a bit of a falling out because she kept treating me badly. I think I've finally come to my senses.'

'What did she *say*?' Sarah mumbles through a mouthful of pasta.

'She apologised. Sort of. Then she tried gaslighting me again and I told her to leave.'

'Oh my god. Is that it, then?' Jordan asks.

'Yep. I'm done. It's been an hour now, and I still feel done, so I think I'm pretty certain it was the right thing to do.' I smile and start scooping the middle out of an end-piece of garlic bread. I *do* feel better, actually. For my entire life, losing Sami has felt like the worst thing that could ever happen. It would keep me up at night, the idea of her growing out of me. But now I've pushed her away myself, and I feel lighter.

'What's the situation with Ben?' Sarah turns to Helen. 'Ben is Briony's boyfriend. They've been spending a bit of time apart.'

'Still radio silence.' I shrug.

'Are you missing him?' Jordan looks at me carefully.

'I am.' I nod. 'It's strange. I'm missing him, but it doesn't feel as . . . frenzied as I expected.'

When Ben first left, it felt like the plug had been pulled on my entire life. I didn't know who I was without him; I didn't have an identity beyond our house with him in it. But now . . . now I feel calmer, like I want him, but I don't *need* him any more.

'Can you go and talk to him? I'm sure you can figure something out,' Sarah says.

'He says he doesn't know me any more.' Unexpected tears spring to my eyes and I swipe them away, horrified. He didn't know me when he left – what will he think of me now? 'I feel like I've changed even more since he's been gone.'

'Changed in what way, love?' Helen looks at me kindly.

'I don't know. I've just – I've spent our entire relationship trying to be the perfect person for him so he won't leave. And now that he's gone, I feel freer, because I'm not pretending any more. I'm a different person. But I still want him – I loved our life together.'

'Why did he want you to be someone else in the first place?' Helen asks.

'I – I don't know,' I say, thinking back. 'I don't think he ever necessarily said it, I just knew that he'd be happier if I was better.'

'What do you mean by better?'

'You know, more fun. More outgoing. More interested in stuff like politics and hiking.' I sigh. 'I don't think I can keep up that façade any more.'

'And you think he won't like you once you let the mask slip?' Helen asks.

'Exactly.'

'Have you ever thought—' she puts her knife and fork down '—that the façade might have been what pushed him away in the first place?'

'No.' I shake my head. 'No, definitely not. He'd have preferred me more like his ex-girlfriend. Or more like Sami; wild and bossy and owning every room she walks in to.'

'Didn't he hate Sami?' Jordan frowns at me.

'Well, yeah, he did, but that was just because of how she treated me.'

'So, if he hated her for treating you badly, why would he want to be with someone who does the same to other people?'

'No, it's not that—'

'Do you *want* to own a room, Briony?' Helen interrupts.

'I—' I falter, my head spinning. Do I? I thought I did. I'm not sure any more. 'I don't know. Maybe? But maybe I only want to because I feel like I should.'

'Maybe it's better to just own up to yourself, love. Nobody can live up to somebody else's idea of perfect.' She smiles at me, and I wonder what life would have been like if I'd had my own mum to smile at me like that. Would any of this have happened? Would I have had a grounding force to stop me going off the rails?

But I *had* a grounding force, didn't I? I had Ben. And now he's gone. The tears come back, and this time I don't try to stop them.

'Oh dear.' Helen reaches over and holds my hand. 'It's a really tricky situation, isn't it?'

I nod, my eyes streaming.

Jordan comes around the table and crouches next to me. 'What were you like when you first met Ben?'

'I can't remember.' I sniff. 'I don't know.'

'Maybe you were you.' Sarah smiles. 'Maybe you were yourself, and that's why he fell for you in the first place. Maybe you just got scared of losing something again.'

'You know what?' Jordan takes my hand and stands up, pulling me into a hug. 'We like you *exactly* how you are. Even when you're crying into your lasagne.'

'Thank you.' I laugh and pull away, wiping my eyes with my napkin. 'I just don't know what to do. I've told so many lies, I don't even know if it's worth trying with him any more.'

'Well, love—' Helen leans forward '—there's only one way to find out, isn't there?'

36

I open the front door, keeping my shoes on, and run upstairs. I spritz myself with some perfume and check my hair in the mirror. It'll have to do.

Ben should be home from work by now. His parents finish squash at eight, so if I can get over there within the next ten minutes I should have time to explain myself privately. I'm terrified that he'll ignore me, or that he won't open the door, but I won't leave until he's heard me out. I can't let this go without telling him the whole truth.

I run back downstairs and pick up my bag and my car keys from the hall table. I'm about to open the door, when I hear a rustling noise behind me.

I spin around, but there's nothing there. The rustling has stopped, and the house is quiet. I shake my head and turn to go back to the door, but something stops me. What if it's a burglar? What if there's a sex pest in the kitchen and he's wanking over my out-of-date brie? What will I do?

I could just leave. I could shut the door and pretend it isn't happening. It's probably nothing anyway. But it'll be dark by the time I get back, and I won't have the balls to come back in if I don't go and check.

I grab an umbrella from the stand by the door and walk

slowly towards the kitchen, holding it out in front of me. I push the door open with the tip, and move quietly until I'm in the doorway.

My heart stops.

It's Ben.

He's standing next to the fridge, some papers in his hands. He looks awful; his face is unshaven and his hair is dull and flat.

'What's this?' he says, without looking up.

'What are you doing here?' I put the umbrella down.

He holds up the papers and I move forward. It's my therapy questionnaires. 'Are you OK?' His eyes search my face. 'What's going on, Briony?'

'Why wouldn't you talk to me?' I try to stop my voice from wobbling.

'I can't – I needed time.'

He clips the papers back on the fridge, and we stand in silence.

'Will you come with me?' I ask. 'I want to explain everything.'

'Where?'

'Please? Will you just come, and then you can make up your mind? I promise, if you decide you never want to see me again, I'll respect that. I won't call you or text you if you ask me not to. Just let me explain. Please.'

He studies me quietly, his blue eyes steady. 'Where are we going?' he asks again.

'Will you get in the car? Then I can show you?'

He hesitates for a second, and then moves forward, walking past me up the corridor. He goes through the front door and I follow, locking up behind me.

I unlock the car and he gets in, clipping his seatbelt on quietly. I start the engine and pull out. It feels so surreal to be sat next to him now, after all this time. Just me and him, on our way somewhere in the car. If I screw my eyes up tight, I can probably convince myself that we're on our way to Costco to buy ice cream and a chicken for Sunday lunch. But if I screw my eyes up tight, we'll probably die, so I'd better not.

'Where are we going?' he asks for the third time, and the break in the silence makes me jump.

'You'll see. It's not far.'

The car goes quiet again, and Ben starts jiggling his leg up and down. I can feel the energy coming off him in waves. He doesn't want to be here.

After less than a minute, we arrive. I pull up on the side of the road.

'The church hall?' He looks at me, nonplussed.

I turn the engine off. 'I lied to you, Ben. The ceiling didn't fall in at work.'

He stares at me for a second, and then glances around him. 'Explain.'

'I had a panic attack. I went to work, and I had to speak during a meeting, and I had a panic attack. I completely messed up, and my boss signed me off on mental health leave.'

'What?' He shakes his head. 'Why didn't you—'

'I avoided the problem for ages before I got signed off. I stopped going to work and stayed at home. I hid all that from you, and then when it finally blew up in my face, I couldn't tell you. Because you'd know I'd been lying already.'

'But – what – why weren't you just honest with me in the first place? We could have talked it through.' I notice that he looks hurt, and the surprise hits me like a knife to the stomach. I hadn't thought that he'd be upset at me shutting him out. I imagined he'd be angry; I didn't think he'd take it personally.

I push on. 'I joined a social anxiety support group.' I nod to the church hall, and he turns to look. 'You and I both know that I'm not the most confident person. I think I need to admit that now, so that you know that I know the truth. I know you've seen behind the mask, and I can't pretend any more.'

'Pretend about what?' He looks dazed. 'I don't get—'

'I met some really nice people at the group. Jordan and Sarah. They've been an amazing support to me through all of this.' I gaze at the pathway up to the door of the hall. I feel a twinge of sadness that we'll never go there again. 'That's who I was texting; there's no affair.'

I look back at Ben. He's crying; big, silent tears rolling down his cheeks. 'Why couldn't *I* support you? Why wasn't I enough?'

The air leaves my body. I suck in a huge, wobbly breath. 'Oh my god, Ben, it wasn't that. It wasn't that at all.'

'It wasn't what? That I'm a shitty boyfriend you can't tell your problems to?'

'No!' I wail. It isn't true. He's incredible and would have supported me; I know that now. 'I just thought you'd think differently of me if I told you what had happened. I thought you'd think I was crazy, or weak or something.'

Ben wipes his eyes fiercely on the back of his sleeve. 'Don't you think I *knew* who you were, Briony?'

'I think you knew who you wanted me to be.' I shrug. 'I think I did a good job of pretending to be something you'd like.'

He snorts. 'You give yourself too much credit – you're not that good of an actress.'

'What do you mean?'

'I *know* you, Bri. I mean, I thought I did. You're quiet and thoughtful and nervous. You're sweet and kind and hard-working. You like olives and homemade brunches and shitty TV. You don't know anything about politics, and you don't want to, either. You care what people think about you, and that's your weakness. You put people on pedestals because you don't think you're good enough.' He leans forward. 'Don't insult my intelligence by saying I didn't know my own girlfriend. *That's* the Briony I fell in love with. *That's* who you are, who you *were*, before this big, secretive nightmare started. If you thought I liked something different, then maybe it's you that doesn't know me.'

I stare at him. I can't think for a second. All of the words he's using – sweet, kind, thoughtful – I've never even contemplated assigning to myself. I thought I'd done such a good job;

I tried so hard to hide myself, but he saw me anyway. And what would be the point otherwise, really? If he'd loved my façade, he'd have loved something that didn't exist. All those panicky nights, all that energy wasted, when I could have just let myself be.

'But how can you love that?' I whisper. 'How can you love something so . . . boring?'

He laughs. 'You're not boring, Bri. You don't need to be a public-speaking party animal to be fun.' He reaches forward and grabs my hand. 'You're passionate and excitable. You're all the crazy things, too. You're not just *one* thing.'

I sit back in my seat and stare straight ahead. Is he right? Am I multi-faceted? It feels like I've been trying to cram myself into two, tiny boxes. One I knew about: the one where I was 'perfect Briony', the ideal girlfriend and easy-going best friend. The other, if Ben is right, was the real problem: the boring box, the quiet box, the uninteresting box. The box of my own identity that I created in my head, the one I was convinced I belonged in and could never let anybody see.

Ben is still holding my hand. My head is swimming with thoughts, but I can't process now. He still doesn't know everything. What comes next could change it all.

'There's something else I have to show you.' I take my hand out of his, put the car in gear, and start driving.

37

My nerves are surprisingly steady, considering where we are.

I turn off the engine and Ben looks out of the window. 'Whose house is that?'

It looks even worse than I remember. The front garden is so overgrown with weeds you can't see the front path. The gate is hanging off its hinges, and one of the downstairs windows is smashed and covered over with newspaper. The street isn't the prettiest, and most places have upturned wheelie bins and soggy sofas out front, but this house is the worst by far. The ugliest house on the worst estate.

'Come on.' I get out of the car and stand on the pavement. 'There's someone you need to meet.'

I haven't stood on this street in over a decade; I've idled here, in the car, not frequently but more frequently than I'd have liked. I haven't stepped foot on the ground since the day I left.

I battle my way up the garden path, kicking beer cans out of the way. Ben follows behind. 'Briony, this place looks really sketchy. I think we should go.'

I knock on the door. I have keys still, and the locks almost certainly haven't been changed, but using them would feel like accepting that this place is a part of me, and I don't want to do that.

Dad answers the door in a stained white T-shirt and thread-bare pyjama pants.

'Briony!' he slurs, his eyes drooping. 'You've decided to pay your old man a visit. ''Bout bloody time.'

I turn around and grab Ben by the wrist. 'Ben, this is my dad, Steve. Dad, this is Ben, my boyfriend.'

'Poor sod.' Dad laughs but it catches and becomes a rattling cough. He takes a drag of his cigarette to halt it.

'Nice to meet you, Steve.' Ben reaches forward, offering his hand. He's trying to be polite, but I can see it in his face: this is the worst thing he's ever seen.

'Oooh, we've got ourselves a posh one.' Dad grabs Ben's hand unsteadily, pumping it up and down. 'How do you *do*, my good sir. What's she paying you then, eh?'

'I'm sorry?' Ben smiles, looking confused.

'What's she paying you to put up with her? Must be a bloody fortune.' He laughs again, his throat crackling.

'Can we come in, Dad?' I step forward, and he stumbles backwards, knocking an ashtray off the hallway table and sending plumes of grey dust into the air.

'Fucking hell!' he roars. 'Watch yourself, will you?'

He kicks the ashtray to one side and sways up the hallway, knocking his shoulder against the bannister.

'Briony . . .' Ben murmurs.

'Come on.' I follow Dad, trying not to look up, not to look down, not to look at anything. I don't want to see it. I know it's worse than it was when I left, and when I left it was worse than when we were happy. I don't want further memories clouding the shreds of what I remember from before she died.

'What we having? Fish fingers?' Dad has deposited himself on the sofa in the lounge, his stomach bulging out from under his top. The carpet is grey with dust and splodged with stains, and there are cartons of cigarettes and Pot Noodles all over the coffee table. Another ashtray smoulders on the arm of the settee. The curtains are drawn, but I can still see that everything is the same. The wallpaper, the furniture, the television. All shabbier, all more scuffed and uncared for, but nothing has changed.

'We won't stay for tea, actually, thanks.' I perch on the edge of the armchair. 'I just wanted to introduce you to Ben.'

Dad drains the last of his beer. 'Well, grab me another from the fridge, then, Let the men talk, eh?'

I leave the room, grateful for the respite but worried about Ben. I shouldn't leave them alone together. Dad is usually fine with other people, though – charming, even; it's me he can't stand.

The kitchen makes me stop in my tracks. The sunset has set the room ablaze in a way so familiar to me, I feel faint. I can see myself at the kitchen table, colouring, Mum's hair tickling my cheek as she leans down to inspect my work. Big bowls of mashed potato when I was poorly, sitting on her lap, her stroking my forehead as the sunlight glinted off her wedding ring.

You have to be yourself. Do you promise you'll remember?

Then, later: Dad punching the fridge, throwing a glass at the wall. The table leg falling off, and nobody replacing it. Scrubbing sticky rivulets of beer off the floor so they wouldn't dampen my socks and make me stink. The sunset reflecting off the greasy, smooth surface of Dad's forehead as he screamed, his face puce.

And now. Now, quiet and alone. The same scene, the same lighting, just the one character. Two cupboard doors hanging off their hinges; a broken light bulb; flies on the hob.

The fridge is empty. So is the freezer. No fish fingers. I go back into the living room.

Dad is laughing, and Ben is smiling politely.

'There's no beer, Dad,' I say.

'Shit.' He bangs his fist on the coffee table and checks the time on the TV box. 'Lend us a twenty, will you?'

I pull some cash out of my purse and he takes it from me. Ben watches. 'Ta. Been sniffing around?'

'No. I was just looking for beer, like you asked,' I say.

'God, you're a cheeky little madam, aren't you?' He's lolling to one side now, one meaty fist clutched around the banknote. 'Bane of my bloody life.'

I look around the room at the detritus of a life gone wrong. A loss so heavy, it couldn't be carried.

'I can't do it any more, Dad,' I say, my voice thick. 'I can't keep picking up after you.'

'Picking up after me?' He laughs manically, his head thrown back. 'Oh, that's rich. You hear that, Ben? She picks up after me. Funny, that, isn't it? When she hasn't stepped foot in this house in over ten years. What're you picking up, Briony? All the money and free dinners you scrounged off me all those years?'

'You're my father,' I whisper. 'I wasn't scrounging.'

'Pfft.' A string of saliva dangles from his lip and he wipes it with the back of his hand. I feel a fresh surge of sadness as I realise I can't remember what he used to look like, before he made himself this way. He digs down the seat of the sofa and pulls out a bottle of vodka, the dregs swilling around at the bottom. He necks it.

'I won't be coming to the police station, or the hospital, or anywhere else. Not any more,' I say, straightening my shoulders. 'I'm not doing it again.'

'Oh!' he hoots. 'She's not doing it, did you hear that? What a selfish brat you turned out to be. If I hadn't seen you come out myself, I'd wonder if you were related to your mother. How proud she'd be of what you've turned into.' He spits into the empty bottle.

'Mum is dead!' I shout. 'She's been dead for over fifteen years, so she can't see or comment or have an opinion on anything! I'm still here. I'm still fucking here, Dad!' I lean forward and jab myself in the chest, hard. 'Here I am. I've always been here, and you've made me fucking miserable, and I'm not doing it any more.'

Dad stares at me, his eyes red. 'Don't you *dare* talk about your mother like that.'

'Why not?' I cry, my voice shaking. 'She's not *here*. She's not coming back, and that's not my fault. It's *not*. I'm sorry you hate that it was her instead of me. I've spent my whole life being sorry. But it wasn't a me-or-her situation, Dad. It wasn't a *choice*. She died, and everything else died with her because of you.'

For a second, he just looks at me. And then he sways to his feet and lunges forward. Ben throws himself between us, putting his hands on Dad's shoulders. He's never hit me, and probably never would, but Ben doesn't know that. 'Let me go!' Dad yanks Ben's hands away and moves towards me. His face looms close to mine, but there's something unrecognisable behind his eyes, a sudden clouding. He freezes, his hand dropping the empty bottle, and scrabbles for his chest. He staggers backwards, once, and then drops to the floor.

'Dad!' I crouch down, my hands on his face, but he doesn't react. Panic blooms in my chest; did I make this happen? He's all I have left; all that ties me to her. 'Dad!' I shake his arm. I say a prayer to whoever is listening: please don't let this be it. Not now, not here. I'll do anything. I'll go to the hospital, the police station; I'll go to fucking Australia for him if you just give me a little bit more time.

Ben is already out in the hallway, his phone pressed to his ear. He asks me what the address is, and I reel it off automatically for the first time in over a decade. I squeeze my dad's hand. He's breathing, but he's pale.

'They're coming.' Ben comes back into the living room and crouches down, holding me steady. 'They're coming, Bri. It's OK.'

'They say he's responding well.' I join Ben on the wall outside the hospital. The sun is going down, and the cars stream past in a golden haze.

'That's good.' Ben squeezes my hand. 'I'm glad.'

This is the first time we've spoken properly in almost a week. It's been a blur, a rush of hospital visits and near-misses. Dad's heart gave out; the pressure of years of alcohol too much to cope with. He crashed twice in the ambulance, but they brought him back. They washed him and fed him and, in the first two days, while he was sleeping, I caught a glimpse of the man he used to be. Without a drink in him, he's been shaky, remorseful, filled with disgust at himself. I've sat with him every evening, and we have talked. We have talked about everything. The conversations weren't perfect; the dynamic between us is too fractured to be repaired this easily. He still brings out my self-loathing, and I still remind him too much of my mother. But there's nothing either of us can do about that now.

The doctors have told him that if he drinks again, he will die. He isn't leaving hospital any time soon and is enrolled in every alcohol-withdrawal and recovery programme the NHS has to offer. I gladly hold my hands up and leave the responsibility in their professional hands.

I pull a packet of cigarettes out of my pocket. One more thing my dad can't do in his current state, and I didn't want to leave the temptation on his bedside table. 'Want one?'

'You don't smoke.' Ben smiles.

'No.' I pull one out and roll it between my fingers. 'But it feels like a moment for a cigarette.'

Ben takes the lighter from my hand and holds it to the end of the cigarette as I take a drag and then stop, spluttering. 'Jesus.' My eyes are streaming.

'Give us a drag, then. If we're being cool.' Ben takes it from my fingers and smokes effortlessly, staring out into the road. I watch him for a moment, taking him in.

'You know I smoked weed with Sami the other week,' I say.

'Oh dear.' He taps the cigarette against the wall and a clump of ash drifts to the floor.

'Aren't you angry?'

He turns to look at me, his face incredulous. 'Why would I be angry?'

'I thought you hated it when I did that.'

'No, I hate when you do things that make you hate yourself. Like smoking weed and spending time with Sami. If that made you happy, I'd be happy. But it doesn't.' He sighs.

'I know. I'm not friends with Sami any more.' I nudge him, and he passes the cigarette back to me, his brow furrowed.

'What? What happened?'

'She treated me like shit, so I told her to do one.'

Ben whistles between his teeth. 'I bet that felt good.'

'It did.' I smile. 'Thank you for not saying *I told you so*.'

'What would be the point in that?' He turns to look at me and leans forward, so our foreheads are touching. 'I think you're brilliant, Briony. Just the way you are.'

'Fucked up families and decisions aside?' I whisper.

'Fucked up families and decisions *included*.' He rubs his nose against mine. 'You deserve so much better than how he's treated you.'

'I know.' I close my eyes. 'I know I do.'

'Promise me something?' he says and kisses me softly.

'Anything.'

'Promise me we'll do this together. All the bad times, all the past trauma, all the bollocks, we'll get through it as a team.'

My stomach twists and it feels beautiful. I open my eyes and look straight into his. They're steady and calm. Ready.

'I promise,' I say. 'Together.'

38

It's the most beautiful autumn day. The kind where the leaves haven't had chance to get mushy yet, and they're still all crunchy underfoot, making every step a dog poo minefield.

I leave my office at 3.30 p.m., as agreed with Jason, and walk out across St. Peter's Square. I'm tired, but in a good way; we've just launched the new user interface I designed, and it's already receiving brilliant feedback. Wiggy is going to present our project timeline at the next directors' meeting, and I'll be going along too. I'm not sure if I'll speak yet.

I'm just waving for the bus when my phone buzzes with a text. I settle into my seat and read it as we set off towards the outskirts of the city.

Jordan: *GUYS. We did it!!! We won the case. The baby will be coming home to us* ☺

Me: *Oh my god! Jordan! Congratulations. I'm so, so happy for you. What does this mean for your firm?*

Sarah: *YESSSS – I knew you could do it!*

Jordan: *Not great for them, obvs. Not really my problem* 😏 *Come and meet him when he comes home!*

Me: *Let's have a welcome-home party for him – Helen can do the decorations*

Sarah: *Not sure how appropriate vag napkins would be for a baby's party*

Jordan: *Potentially v appropriate? LET'S DO IT*

I sit back in my seat and smile. I can imagine how he's feeling right now. I've learned that when Jordan wants something, when he feels something is right, he won't stop until he's got it. That's why having him as an ally is the most incredible thing in the world.

Jordan, Sarah and I have been meeting at least twice a week, to work on Jordan's 'coming out plan'. Jordan being Jordan, he isn't happy with the idea of just sitting down with his parents and explaining that sometimes he dresses like a woman. He wants to put on a surprise show on Canal Street and lure them both there under the ruse of a dinner. Then he'll perform a 45-minute set, before asking them both to come on stage and publicly accept him. It's a lot.

Ben has popped along to a few rehearsals, and he loves it. He gets along so well with Sarah and Jordan, and it's a whole new experience for me, sharing and opening up every facet of my existence. We've even met up as one big group a couple of times: Ben's friends, me, Jordan and Sarah. It's been easy and unproblematic and fun, a far cry from the group ventures I used to organise with Sami. I'm slowly beginning to wonder whether I wasn't the problem all along.

Ben is so happy now; his work is taking him down to London less often, and we're starting to settle into a routine with his hours. I'm also trying my best with the whole 'transparency' thing – the other day I plucked up the courage to tell him that actually, I'd rather die than go on a hike in the rain. He just laughed, kissed my forehead, and went by himself. He brought croissants back for me and I ate them while I watched my soaps.

The bus stops and I get off right outside the building. I give my name at reception, like I do every week, and then sit and wait.

'Briony?' Diane pops her head through the door. 'Do you want to come through?'

I follow her into her office and sit in my usual chair, facing the door. The first time I came I sat in the wrong seat, and she

277

had to move me. Apparently, they can't let me block the exit in case I freak out and hold Diane hostage. The thought hadn't even crossed my mind, but now I worry I'll do it just because I know I shouldn't.

'How are you this week?' she asks, once she's sat down.

'I'm OK, yeah.' I nod. 'I'm having the further tests done.'

'That's good. You said you thought that'd make you feel better.'

'Yeah. I think it will. I mean, I'm certain the pain's directly related to my anxiety, but it'll be nice to put it to bed.'

She nods and smiles.

'I wasn't always like this, you know,' I say, because she's leaving a silence for me to fill like she always does. 'I've been doing a bit of soul-searching. I've always been quiet, I think. And nervous, probably. A bit of a wallflower. But I think I knew who I was. I think my mum made me believe that I was worth something, and I remember feeling like I knew that, once. But everything with my dad . . . I think it broke something in me. Almost like I was conditioned to believe that the whole world thought I was useless. And then the world became scary. Because if your own parent thinks you're such an awful human being . . .'

Diane nods again. 'What reason do you have to believe everyone else will think differently?'

'Yeah. Exactly that. And I think the promotion triggered something in me. I don't know, like everything was hiding under the surface, waiting for the switch to be flicked.'

'We can explore that. Have you spoken to your dad this week?'

'A few texts here and there. They let him out, so this is the worst time for him. He seems OK. I've not had any trouble, and I usually would have done by now. I just don't know if I'm ready to actually see him. Outside the hospital, I mean.'

'And I think that's fine,' Diane says. 'I was impressed when you came here; you'd already come to accept that this wasn't your responsibility. That's a big step.' She pauses, and looks at me carefully, reading my mind. 'Do you feel guilty?'

'Yes.'

'Why?'

'Because there isn't anyone else. It's just us.'

'Do you want to be a part of that "us"?'

'No. Well, yes, but not like it was.'

'You know, Briony, there's a chance your father will never be the man he was before your mum passed.' She puts her notebook down on her lap. 'But I think you already know that. I think we should explore those feelings a little bit.'

'I still can't get it out of my head. The idea that I'm bad, that I've done something shameful.' I sigh. 'But I can't identify what that thing *is.*'

'Sometimes, something happens to us when we're young, and it becomes the blueprint for how we view the world. If something awful takes place, and someone you trust directs their anger at you, it's easy to start believing that you had some kind of control, and that it was somehow your fault.'

'But I know it wasn't my fault. I know that now.' I twist my necklace around my finger. 'There's just still a part of me that thinks that everyone is going to find me out.'

'Find you out for what?' Diane asks.

'I don't know. I really don't know.'

'Nobody is looking for your flaws.'

'Everyone's much more interested in themselves.' I nod, knowing the speech well by now.

'Let's get our formulation out.' She pulls a piece of paper from the folder beside her and traces her finger around the circle we created together as she speaks. 'So, someone draws attention to you in front of people, you feel vulnerable and exposed, your heart starts hammering and your hands start shaking, you try to escape, which draws more attention to you, and the cycle continues.'

I nod again.

'We're going to start to try and break that cycle today. It's going to take a lot of work, and it isn't going to be easy, but we're going to do it together.'

'What if it isn't about that, though?' I ask. 'What if there's genuinely something broken inside me?'

'You believing that you're not worthy is exactly that, Briony: a belief. And it's a belief we can change if we work together.'

Can beliefs be changed? I'm different now. Better. My life is full and the people I love are near and happy. My world is still small but it's enough. Yet somewhere, right at the core of me, I still don't believe I'm good.

What I do believe, though, is that I deserve to give myself a chance.

'OK.' I sit up straight and look Diane in the eye. 'Yes, I'm ready.'

Acknowledgements

Since I stamped the last triumphant full-stop onto the final sentence of the first draft of this book, the world – my world, everyone's world – has changed. It would feel wrong to have worked on something during such an historic time and not mention it, so here is my hateful little nod to the virus, and here are some thank yous for the people who are getting me through it.

To everybody who helped to get this book into readers' hands – thanks a billion. Tanera, Rachel, teams Darley Anderson and Orion, you know I couldn't have done it without you (I am almost incapable of doing anything without an endless stream of support, actually) so thank you for your hard work and generosity.

Alex, Amie and Lauren: We have never seen each other so little, or messaged so much. Our WhatsApp group is like a helpline, and not a day goes by when one of us doesn't need emotional intervention at a borderline clinical level. I feel very lucky to be part of our community of unstable (but not unemployed) psychologists.

Zara: I wrote this story primarily to stop you asking about the next book, so it's all thanks to you, pal. Thank you for being my supportive, excitable, motherly partner in crime for the past decade. I couldn't ask for a better best friend and, let's be honest, neither could you. Thanks also for the 85kg of tarka dal I've eaten since we met.

Mum and Dad: Thanks for allowing your almost-thirty-year-old daughter and her labrador-esque partner to move back in while the world crumbled to shit. One day, I will take the money I saved on rent and buy you a hamper or something. Thank you for cosy fires, games on the grass, butter and laughter.

Patrick: Thank you for being my financial advisor and beer aficionado. George: Thank you for Starbucks and shopping and inappropriate jokes. Both of you: Thanks for the streams of Instagram memes and forwarded TikToks that make me gag and laugh in equal measure.

Paul and Linda: Thank you for heading up the Mary Hargreaves fan club by buying 83 copies of each edition of my first book. When the world is normal again, I will sign every single one with my fancy pen, whether you like it or not.

Nora: I am obsessed with you and have nothing more to add at this time.

Taylor Swift: As above.

Liv and Holly: Thank you for being the loveliest long-distance friends who write the most beautiful sentences. It is so nice to know that you're sharing a boat with some bloody brilliant human beings.

Finally, Stef. Thank you for being you, and for loving me, and for being the chalk to my cheese. With a glass of wine in hand and a blank piece of paper in front of us, anything is possible.